My L
Pakistan

By D M Byrne

My Life In Pakistan

A forward (of sorts).

I would like to say this book is a journey of discovery, where a young boy sees the world beyond his comfy middle (lower) class bedroom in the heart of England's commuter belt, and returns a young adult ready to be a tool used by society for the better.

However it is not, instead this book charts a period in England and Pakistan, where great change was happening in the both countries, not that Michael gave a stuff about the world around him, all he wanted was a Sony Walkman, and to take his green body warmer to one of the hottest countries on the globe.

This book is loosely based on true events, however some of the names and situations have changed to protect the innocent, and the stupid.

My Life In Pakistan

CONTENTS

My Life In Pakistan

For *Dad*,
Who put up with one *moody* teenager, for three whole months,

My hero.

"The case that had to be won"

Chapter Twelve

The final showdown!.

So it had come down to this, a man a woman and twelve good and true citizens, but of course life was never that simple. The man was a pervert; the woman was a killer, and at least four of the *Good and true* had been bribed or had hidden secrets that was been used against them. Jim knew he should tell the Judge, but why rock the boat, the trial was going his way, well in the most part and he could yet win the case.

It had all started twelve long weeks ago, until then Jim was a clerk in a law firm in the wrong part of town, that helped low life's get away with petty crimes and misdemeanours. Then *bang* like an angry middle aged drunk woman, looking for justice at the bottom of an empty gin bottle, and using her soon to be ex-husbands black ford piece of crap to bull doze her way through the streets of the city that had kept her trapped, contained, until she could take no more, Jim was handed a case, No, *the case*. Not only was he charged with saving his bosses very life, but Jim's girlfriends to. He knew the stakes, winner takes all, loser takes the fall, and people die.

The heat wasn't helping either; it must have been close to 30 degrees. The whole week had been sun drenched; you couldn't sleep, eat, or think. But now storm clouds could be seen on the horizon, it wouldn't be long until the rain started to hit the ground, at first just the odd spot, then it would start to pour out of the sky like the gods throwing out their dirty dish water.

But no one was looking outside, no one was going to miss a second of the drama unfolding before them, this was *the* event of the season. Sweat poured down Jim's face, He wasn't the only one suffering though, despite having fans all around them, the Jury were boiling, a couple were even using handmade fans to cool themselves. Jim knew he couldn't take more than two minutes to sum up the defence's case, mainly because any longer would bore the Jury. In this heat you don't want to think. You could tell the juries just wanted to get into the room that would decide his client's fate, and tear into them, bitch and laugh about them, then either condemn the pair or set them free. The other reason Jim didn't want to take too long was simple, they had no defence, they were guilty as hell, he could speak for a week and it would not change anyone's mind. But he still had to try.

There she was, Jessica Carmit, sitting there in all her finery, Jim had been through the whole, don't dress up! Wear sensible shoes talk with his client, also *acting* hurt and innocent wouldn't harm her defence, but of course that wasn't her style.

Those legs, Christ those legs and why those heels? No normal person could walk for more than a couple of steps without collapsing in agony, but of course Jessica was no ordinary woman, and believe Jim she was all woman. Her husband also knew this; Rick Baltimore (true name) plucked her from the justice system five years ago. She was a petty whore and pick pocket, normally she would get a fine or a smack on the wrist from the judge, after getting caught again with her sticky fingers in someone else's pockets, and maybe if the judge was lucky she would let him smack her somewhere else. But then she had to pick a senators pocket, bad move, she was looking at hard time.

She could have mentioned the affair she once had with another of the cities high ranking, *I'm one of the people and I love my wife and kids* Elected officials, but kept quiet. She felt his Italian friends may not be too happy if the truth came out about Mr Family man. But Rick helped her find a loop hole and bam, freedom, and so began the whirlwind romance that would lead directly to this very court room, Jim remembered telling her 'You can run but one day justice will find you' she had slapped him hard and he had enjoyed it.

So this was it, his moment, Jim's moment to shine, save the day and.. At first Jim hadn't felt the bullet that had torn through his side, it wasn't until he was on his knees that he understood what had happened, he smiled, a big stupid smile, and then he laughed, and then he died.

End chapter.

Michael stared at the pages, what was missing? *Something* he thought, but what? Nope I can do better than this and proceeded to tear the pages out of the note book on the bed. As he walked over to the waste paper bin he stopped short, he sat at the desk next to the window and thought again; maybe I can use this, well Some of it. Maybe if I stare out of the window, the world may give me inspiration! Michael looked out of the window, after five minutes it dawned on him. Staring at the Pakistani desert was not going to help with a court room drama set in New Orleans. *Time for a seven up I think.* Finish it later was the thought that was never to be realised, still when you're Fourteen, there's always another tomorrow.

So how did a teenager from Essex end up in a villa just outside of Karachi, well in the 80's anything seemed possible.

My Life In Pakistan.

Chapter One.

Life in a southern town.

What a year 1983 was turning out to be, In January Britain's first breakfast television programme, *Breakfast Time* was Broadcast on the BBC, a month later ITV would hit back with TV-am. All those bright fluffy Jumpers, all those happy smiley souls, trying to wake you up, trying to make you feel good about the world around you, getting you on your way with a hop and a skip, bastards to a man. It wasn't all bad though, without knowing it a musical revolution happened, in March. The first Compact Disc went on sale in the UK.

Morning's up to that point were, - wake up, fall back to sleep, get kicked out of bed, eat some cereal with a crust of sugar so dense mice could ice skate on top without fear of falling through! Then march of to school hoping for a snow day or some other small disaster that would mean no school. Yes mornings were great until the green goddess let us all know just unfit we all really were. Ah School, yes it is true, *they are the best days of your lives*, for several reasons, for starters a 3.30pm finish, three breaks in the day, six weeks of holidays in the summer, never mind Christmas and half term. Come to think of it was Michael ever really there? But of course at the time it didn't feel like that, oh no, it felt like a prison, without parole or time off for good behaviour, throw in homework teachers and the bullies, and well, it was no wonder teenagers always looked depressed. Of course it wasn't all bad; there were plenty of friends to hang with, the science and sports facilities were top notch, and there were teachers who tried to help you reach your full potential, although some just turned up for the pay packet.

School was Mayflower High, location Billericay Essex. Billericay was a commuter town that was, well rich, not the part Michael lived in of course, his home was a council house, however it was in no crime ridden *estate*, but a nice quiet cul-de- sac, with about twenty houses, all with big front and back gardens, the house was spilt over three levels, and had a huge oak tree in the front. Everyone in the street seemed nice and polite and got on with Michael's family. The rest of the town was full of or at least appeared at the time be to full of stock brokers and bank managers, all living thatcher's dream. In the town there were two main high schools, Billericay with the farm and huge wooden posts keeping parts of the school from falling over the other was Mayflower.

Michael didn't mind going to this school, in fact he quite enjoyed it, However he was slightly puzzled by the local education authorities decision to send him to mayflower, when they had sent all his friends and neighbours to Billericay high, which was clear on the other side of town, and by neighbours this was literal, he lived in a semi-detached but somehow the border for the schools went through the middle of the two houses, so Michael went to Mayflower, and Sean, his then best friend went to Billericay, for some reason Sean's mum argued because he had bad eye sight he *needed* to go to Billericay High School? Sounds silly but it worked. So Michael was on his own that first scary day at high school, thanks guys. *Sean*, Sean was every Girl's dream guy, they all liked him, no *loved* him, 6ft nothing slim and gormless, just what the girls liked, unlike Michael who was 5ft 7, also gormless but had slightly greasy brown hair and spots. Sean was a laugh, by day he and Michael would play football and action man, by night beat the snot out of each other, over who had the best Smurf figure. Michael had once witnessed him eat £10's worth of sweets in a day!? and £10's was a lot of money to blow on just sweets!! Michael was impressed until the obvious happened, he really shouldn't have gone on those swings after all that chocolate. This could also have been instant Karma as Sean had *borrowed* the £10, without asking his mum. Not only was Sean a nice lad, he was handy to have on your side; especially when it came to fights or disputes, he could also talk Michael into doing things he didn't really want to. He once convinced Michael to play rugby for a local side as they were short a man, after twenty minutes Michael had become bored of receiving the ball, only to get battered by the opposing forwards, because in part he hadn't the foggiest what to do with the ball once he received it, Michael was going to leave but Sean charmed him to stay the rest of game, after a few more tackles Michael started to enjoy himself, even getting involved in a few attacks up front. The second half was a lot better and even good fun, all was going well until ten minutes from the end, when Sean *tackled* a young lad by picking him up and throwing the kid on the floor, Michael later found out Sean had broken this lads arm and right leg, and announced his retirement from rugby that very same day. Michael also joined the Boys brigade, scouts and a local church youth group, all because of his *best friend,* they would join together, then after a couple of week's Sean would get bored and jack it in, leaving Michael to go on his own. Out of a sense of duty Michael would carry on going for a bit longer, not wanting to let anyone down, Scouts was fun though. Where else are you allowed to set fire to things as a teenager? So Michael carried on going for three more years.

The area itself was great for a kid to grow up in, a large woods to knock about in, a big park with a swimming pool, several lakes, 9 hole golf course, and a tennis court, add in the fields and streams all around the town, and well, you were never bored.

Billericay was also 30 minutes away by train to either London or Southend- on- sea, oh yes Michael was living the dream. The town also had a football club called funnily enough Billericay Town Fc, Michael used to enjoy watching game's at Roots hall on a windy weekday night with his dad. As his dad worked away from home so much it was a nice treat, and for a small town they had a decent team, in fact Billericay had won the FA Vase trophy at Wembley in 1976, 77 and 79. No Mean feat. And later Michael's PE teacher Mr Burton would leave the school to Manager the team; alas he did not leave before taking what seemed an insane amount of free kicks aimed at Michael's head. Every PE lesson would be football, Michael would always be in goal, and every game there would be a free kick, oh yes Mr Burton fancied himself as an 80's Beckham.

Billericay's highlights included a museum with a two headed Lamb, a Woolworths, and a few years later it would have a 7-eleven. It also had a few pubs, a few meaning *a lot of pubs*!, not that Michael know about of such things, that would be a further four whole years, but if you every wanted a decent pub crawl, Billericay's your town. it also had its seedier side, in 1986 The Conservative MP for the town was Harvey Procter, that year the people newspaper published claims that Proctor had taken part in spanking and cane beatings of male prostitutes, he resigned and was replaced in 87 by Teresa Gorman.

Like most kids Michaels Dad made a big impression on him, parents of course were meant to play a part in a child's life, but his dad was more than that, he was a character. When you hear that expression, *character* It's never normally in a positive way, everyone knows one, or maybe is one, but Michaels Dad just was that guy, it was no exaggeration, everyone knew him, no matter where you went, people would shout 'hi Michael', 'nice to see you Michael', 'thanks for the pint mate', yes he was popular, and yes he was also called Michael, Son and dad both had the exact same name, it was a nightmare. All Young Michaels post had to have Jnr on it; even his driving licence would have Jnr on it! Some years later Michael Snr wanted to name Jnr's son Michael as well, carry the name on. *Michael the third!* This was shot down by his wife, not by words but by a look, anyone in a long term relationship knows *the look*. Another reason his dad stood out was the type of work he did, Snr was a trained plumber, however by the mid 80's plumbers were known as heating engineers, and heating engineers were needed around the world, so he went where the work was, Holland, Germany, Saudi Arabia, he was even due to leave for Iraqi, just days before the Iran Iraqi war kicked off. And of course Pakistan. These trips made Snr appear a bit more exotic, *a man of the world*. And boy did he play up to it.

He would be gone for months, yet his son would miss him but not miss him, if that makes sense, Michael loved it when dad came home for short breaks, there was of course the presents and gifts he would bring back with him, they would have days out to London and such, Dad would also take Michael to Upton Park and watch the hammers, West Ham Utd, they both loved that, he would also send Michael letters, via air mail.

There was also the visit's to Heathrow or Gatwick airport, to see Dad off safely. What always amazed Michael about either airport, was the noise levels and the sheer amount off people using them, all colours races and religions, people from all other the world coming and going, laughing and crying. From above they must have looked like an ant colonies, all those people moving, moving in every direction possible, never standing in one place for more than a moment. One noise and distraction which caught Michaels eye every time was the video arcade machines, it was a cool place for any kid to be. One such visit would change Michael's life.

Diary entry -
Wednesday March 30th – Gatwick Airport.
'going to see my dad at Gatwick'

Hardly a stirring opening entry, but every journey has to start somewhere. Up to now the entries in the diary consisted of such gems as **March 5th 'Got pay from my paper round'** or **march 17th ' Had a crash on Dave's bike, arm cut'** not really life changing stuff, although the bike crash nearly did change Michaels life, to death. Picture the scene, a scout is late for a troop meeting, is in a hurry, so he borrows a friends bike, wraps his plastic carrier bag with uniform in it around the handle bars then sets off, minutes later going down a steep hill, a one in ten, or something like that. A bus is coming up the hill; plastic bag gets caught in wheels, scout is off the bike, before he knows it skids along the road towards the bus, just missing it. Funny enough Michael was late to the troop Meeting that night.

So off to Gatwick they went, a rare family day out, mum son, and five year old sister Sarah. First came the thirty minute train journey to London, then the tube ride to the airport. Anyone who used the tube system in the 80's will know what a fun journey must have been. There was always a *certain smell!* You couldn't put your finger on it, nor would you want to, but it really wasn't a nice odour. once at the airport there was the usual hassle of beating a path through the crowds and finding the gate for dad's flight, and even though the flight was on time and they knew Dad was on the plane, there was still that moment of dread, that for some reason he's not on the flight and something had gone wrong. So you scanned every face coming through customs, trying to make out a familiar piece of clothing or facial feature, then the elation of seeing them, maybe slightly older, maybe more whiskers on the beard, but it was still them. It was still Dad.

Soon everyone was hugging, Mum got a kiss, presents were given out, then it was the long journey home.

The next entry spoke for itself.

Thursday 31st March - Home.
'Babysitting for mum and dad'

Saturday 2nd April – Billericay
'Went to see Billericay town play, score 3:0 to Billericay'

Despite the cold of the evening, and the long bus journey facing them, Michael was looking forward to the match, and why not, Dad was home, and no matter where the two of them went, dad always treated his son right, be it food, clothes of toys, Michaels father wasn't rich, far from it, but he always seemed to have enough so they could enjoy themselves, and tonight that meant football tickets and a hot pie or two, it didn't even matter who Town was playing, no Michael was with his Dad. A boys day out, so after watching the home team win quite convincingly it was home, to mum and sis, after one more quick pie.

On the bus journey home Michael and dad chatted about the game, TV, films, Michaels love life, or lack of, Michael always *loved* that conversation, dad just did it to tease his son, a few minutes later they hit the town centre, they were halfway home. Michael always liked being out after dark, everything took on a slightly sinister appearance, Car's would light up passer-by's or wooden benches that in turn would throw odd and unusual shapes on to shop fronts, you would also get the older kids hanging round chip shops and pubs looking for trouble. It was whilst Michael was looking at a group of teenagers walking along that dad asked, 'so are you coming Back with me or not?', 'Huh' replied Michael, he turned to face dad. although they had discussed the subject about Michael going over to Pakistan with Dad on his return, including numerous letters on the subject over the past couple of months, it was suddenly on that cold night sitting there on the bus that it felt *real*, Michael still wasn't sure, leaving his mum, sister, his *friends* behind, not to mention where the hell was Pakistan!

Then there was school, Michael would be gone till July, school would not be happy. 'Well?' Michael could tell Dad wanted an answer, preferably before the end of the journey, 'well, I, it's not that I don't want to' Michael didn't want to disappoint his Dad, but was caught between words and emotions, 'look I won't be angry, but I need to know' that was the one thing Michael could rely on, the fact that Dad, who could get angry, never had a cross word for his son. Dad again probed in the hope of getting an answer, of any sort. 'Are you afraid, is it the plane journey?' God the journey! Michael had forgotten about that, it wasn't so much the hours as the days it was going to take, but that wasn't the thing holding Michael back. 'No, it's just, well what would I do over there' Dad Laughed, a little too *loud*, People looked their way, Michael shrank a little in his seat, 'Sorry Son, I didn't mean to laugh'. This one subject had played on Michael's mind more than any other issue, just what would he do over there, he was fourteen?

Too young to drive, to drink, travel out on his own. over the rest of the bus ride Dad explained life over in Pakistan, and what was on offer, as they got off Michael said thanks and thought for a second, 'Ok I'll go' and that was it, Dad patted his son on the back, smiled and no more was said.

Sunday 3rd April – Home.
'It snowed all night, got a cold but still went and played football up park'

A new game was born that day, Blizzard ball. Of course it had started out as a normal game of Football, the fact that there was at least 3 inches of snow on the playing field was nothing to Michael and his friends, even when it started to lightly snow this again was not a problem, in fact it made it more fun, unless you were making a run with the ball towards the oppositions goal, and felt the thump of a cold wet snow ball hit you on the head, at least you hoped it was a snowball! Snows yellow right?

About twenty minutes into the match, the snow fall got heavier, nothing to worry about there, it was only after bearing down on goal a few minutes later that Michael realised how bad the storm had become, there was no opposition goalkeeper! He had buggered of home, as did four of Michaels team mates, Michael had an open goal, or would have if he could make out where the goal was. So a draw was declared and the long, cold walk home started.

Monday 4ᵗʰ April – Billericay
'Cup - Liverpool played Man city, won 4:0'

Despite being in the headmaster's office, with his Dad of all
people, all Michael could think of was the new *Entry* system
outside the heads door, known as the traffic light system. A
green light would of course mean come in and the red would
mean go away or wait! But what was yellow, did it mean hang
on I won't be a minute?. Michael was vaguely away of the
usually pleasantries going on, 'hello' and 'how are you', opened
the head with Dad replying 'fine' and 'nice of you to see us so
quickly', all the usual adult stuff, after the offer of tea or coffee
was turned down, the head started to lay out his reason's as to
why Michael shouldn't go, 'your son will miss too much school
work and won't have time to catch up' followed up with 'this
is such an important time for your sons development', once
finished the head looked at Michael then Dad, there was
silence, one of those silences where the talker had said their bit
and there's no more to say, no more to discuss, the end, and
the people opposite would have to just lump it. Then the head
made a mistake, instead of saying 'Thank you for your time
and good day' he asked if Michael's dad had anything to say in
reply. The head of course thought, *like there's anything this man
can say to change my mind., but let's give the chap a chance.* So the fifty
something brown suited man leaned back slightly in his chair,
and started to clean his thick rimmed glasses.

Now Michael's Dad was a nice pleasant man, a joker and a
laugher, but still polite, and in the right light reminded Michael
of a young Oliver Reed, however been a Londoner he also
spoke his mind. He would threaten (over the phone mind) a
local travel agents about two years later, that if the plane tickets
to Spain were not ready on time, he would put their windows
through, Michael wouldn't see that day as the families proudest
moment, although the family would laugh about it, in time, and
it got the job done, the tickets were indeed ready on time. Plus

Michael didn't think his Dad would really go through with his threat, but that was the man he was, passionate. However even Michael was surprised by what came out of his dad's mouth that day, 'He'll learn more over the next three months with Me then he'll learn at this school over the next three years' 'plus he can surly take course work with him' Both Michael and the head looked at each other, dumb struck. The head sat forward and went to speak, but couldn't, sweat started to form on his thinning hair line. Dad then proceeded to explain his son was going with him, regardless and that was that, cool. Extended holiday!

What followed was a blur of activity; Michael would need a Passport, for which he went to the passport office in London, so to rush things along! He would of course need a photo. *Now what to wear* thought Michael, like it mattered? But really there was only one choice of clothing for the hip Fourteen year old, for the past year Michael had worn pretty much only one jacket, a green body warmer He loved it, and wore it everywhere, *everywhere*, be it spring summer autumn or winter, add his favourite blue wellies to the party and, well what a look. Michael and his dad nearly fell out, and Michael nearly didn't go because he insisted on packing it, 'a bloody body warmer in Pakistan!,' screamed Dad, Mum tried to calm things down and by the end of the day dad had calmed down enough to talk to Michael, to try and talk him out of taking the bloody thing, Michael finally agreed, as long as he was allowed to have his passport photo taken with him wearing it. So that was agreed and Michael had his passport, a firm black official document which showed Michael was British. And ready to travel.

Saturday 9th April – Billericay
'Played football'
Liverpool 0 – 3 Swansea
Position – Top

Four days left in England, Four! And what did Michael do with one of them, play Football. Then again what else was there to do? Well of course there was packing, *what does someone pack for a hot climate for three months?* He thought, *Hmm a pair of shorts and a t shirt?* No, that wouldn't do. He sat on the bed and looked in his draws; he simply didn't own enough underwear and socks for such a long trip! Packing was impossible, after a brief panic mum took over, Dad said he would also help, because he knew the type of clothes to wear over there, but Michael was sure this was just a ploy to check he didn't try and smuggle his beloved body warmer into the country. Dad also took charge of Michaels Passport and plane ticket, so what was left, football.

Later that evening Michael watched TV, Tales of the unexpected was on. The story was about a hit man being given the job of killing an old school friend, the episode was called "A passing opportunity" the usual fare, A nice idea, but with a budget of ?50 and theatre grade actors.

Then bed.

The next couple of days must have flown by, or were so boring they didn't warrant any mention in the diary.

Tuesday 12th April – Home
'Said goodbye to my friends'

Like a typical teenager Michael could have been going camping for the weekend, opposed to going to another continent for three months, 'alright, see ya' Called Steve, Sean's younger brother from his bedroom window, another shouted 'don't forget to bring a present back' even his best friend muttered barley a few words, 'see you in a couple of months', cheers people! To be fair a couple of weeks before this, a friend of Michael's called Scott had moved away, and all Michael had said was 'See you later mate' hardly heart felt.

Now Scott was an interesting kid, and Michael would take two real memories away from knowing him. The first involved Scott's so called "medical condition", the other a car. Scott was a nice lad, but a bit of a wuss, Michael was hardly Action man, but he liked playing out, climbing tree's, throwing rocks at friends, and playing football, however Scott wasn't like that, and anyway he couldn't play football, because, 'if I head the ball I might die' these were Scott's exact words, to which Michael replied 'say what!!, apparently Scott was born with a soft top head, so any bang on top of his noggin could kill him, but for some reason he never wore a helmet when he rode his bike? So no to the normal rough stuff, this lead to a different type of play date.

One such adventure was playing spy. Dressed in their combat clothing, ex-army gear bought at a local market, they would make their way through the field located next to Scott's house, the field was about 300 hundred yards long and 400 yards wide, then up a slope which lead to the main road, at this point they would lie on their stomachs and watch cars go by, making silly comments about the drivers. Normally there were no problems, why would there be? However one time, after the council had repaired part of the road, leaving small stones on the surface and put signs up warning "Chips on the road" and "Slow Down" which of course every driver ignored and drove at their normal speed, fast, something happened which was rather unexpected. One summer evening, whilst watching cars go by, one suddenly stopped, maybe a flat tyre, a cat in the road? Coffee on the crouch? Nope, none of these, instead a man in his late 30's flew out of his car and started to rant and rave at the boys about them throwing stones at his car! Sorry his piece of crap car. Apparently not spotting the signs about the road works, or stones left on the road, he barked on about damage to his car and *Talking to their parents about repairs to the body work,* perhaps the pair should of ran off or spoke up for themselves, instead they just sat there and watched on as the man continued to rage on, he then started to run out of steam, perhaps spotting the signs or just deciding this wasn't worth his time, so as quick as he had arrived he left. How bizarre. Funny enough the pair never played Spy again, a month later Scott moved.

So with all friends accounted for, it was next stop, the Middle East!

Wednesday 13th April – Home/Heathrow Airport.
'Went to the Middle East with my Dad, on an aeroplane'

On an aeroplane!! How else would Michael be getting there? Swim? Drive? He really didn't try with that entry, however there really wasn't time to get poetic at 6 in the morning, that day was just rush rush rush.

After getting kicked out of bed by Dad, Michael attempted to wash through some very blurred eyes, he really wasn't in the mood, but dad was pumped and in full travel mode, Dad even threatened to wash and dress his son unless he got his lazy arse in gear, so a newly motivated Michael had a quick wash then got dressed. After the third attempt at putting his socks on, he was ready, which gave him just enough time to panic, so he double checked his bags, then checked them again, with this done Michael finely calmed down just enough to sit with dad and wait for the taxi. After kissing a tearful mum/wife goodbye, they got into the waiting cab and fifteen minutes later arrived at the train station, Dad grabbed the tickets and with a few minutes spare they waited on the long platform for the 07.30, a commuter train heading to London.

Packed was an understatement, you just couldn't move let alone get a seat, and four short years later Michael would be a regular on that service, and hate it. People were crammed in like tuna, all heading to the big smoke, ready to fight for a place on the escalator, so they could be first out of the station, ready for more battles throughout the day, resting where they could, so they would have the energy to battle for a seat on return journey. No wonder so many had a *Swift half* in the pub or club before returning home to their loved ones.

This day however would be different, the crowds would not bother Michael, for the Tuna were going to work, and he and dad were not, no they were going on a trip, so the suited and booted umbrella carrying times reading middle management types could have their seats, the ones they had *every day*, for they would have to sit in a stuffy office somewhere in the city, whereas Michael would be in a comfy aeroplane seat being waited on hand and foot. London as usual was chaos, Dad of course know how to battle the crowds, straight through, no hassle, he wasn't knocking old ladies to the floor, but he wasn't taking prisoners either. They headed for the tube network and soon found the Piccadilly platform that would take them to Heathrow, and then boarded perhaps the loudest tube carriage ever made, despite being the financial capital of Europe, maybe the world, and every couple of years the centre of fashion culture and music. The rolling stock was, well tired, old, smelly and loud; some corners would make you wince at the sound of metal on metal, and like fingernails down a blackboard, would set your teeth on edge.

Around 2pm they arrived at Heathrow, with a slight ringing in their ears, it was three hours till lift off, three hours! *How would we kill the time* thought Michael? It was different when picking someone up, you would turn up half an hour before the persons flight was due, and hope their plane hadn't been delayed, *too* much, and wait. But flying wasn't the same of course, for starters you had to join the long queue to book in and get your boarding ticket, also you had to book your bags in, then came the excitement off finding the right gate, it really was all the fun a kid would want when flying long haul for the first time, however for a seasoned traveller like dad, it wasn't so much, especially when the kid in question keeps asking questions about *everything* every five minutes, but Michael was on holiday, so sue him.

Although Michael had been on plane's before, this trip was different, for a start it was bigger, the plane was a Lockheed Tri-Star L1011-100. Before this Michael had only been on small 737's, but the Lockheed was a much bigger beast, it was nice and airy, had comfy seats, with decent leg room, and the toilets, well the toilets were another story, he was to discover people's attitudes towards using the loo differed depending on what country they came from. After using the WC on the plane, it felt like the people who had used it before him had never seen a flush Toilet before, or indeed one with a seat. The stewardesses were all American, they wore a head dress with a partial veil, to observe Middle Eastern customs regarding woman, which they of course wore with style and made them look, for a better word mysterious and sexy. Although to Michael most woman were, *damn* hormones! Michael was used to BA stewardesses so these ladies were a welcome sight, not that Michael thought the former were ugly, it was just, well, BA seemed to employ prim and proper older ladies, instead of the athletic staff Gulf Air employed. Another plus Michael found was *the young falcon club*, really it was just a device to occupy kids on a long journey; you got a colouring book, a newsletter, and a pen. All a little lame for a teenager but you also got a Log Book, about six inches wide by 4 inches high covered in nice brown fake leather, it had all the flight details including the flight number 'GF 026'. And it was signed by the captain. How cool was that. But no amount of newsletters was going to fill the 3,100 miles to Karachi, so after the Meals and general excitement had died down, there were two options left, sleep or talk to Dad, and Michael was in no mood to sleep, So the questions began, '*do you like flying?* 'Dad could tell Michael wasn't going to sleep and had prepared himself for a short question and answer session, 'Not really" he replied Michael of course was ready for a follow up question, '*Oh. What don't you like about it then'* Dad seemed to think about this, 'The time, it takes, it's too long'. So the conversation tennis match continued, service Michael, '*So what do you do to pass the time?*' Forehand return by dad, 'Reading the paper or sleep' baseline return by Michael, '*What if you don't have a paper?*' This went on for about twenty minutes, finally after Michael ran out of sensible questions, he moved onto ones about the plane, at this point Dad politely asked if perhaps it was time for a nap.' *But I'm not tired!'* Michael protested, however as he said this he could sense by Dad's stare and body language that his father was not up for any more questions and just wanted some peace, Dad spoke softly yet firmly, 'look it's a long flight and when we land you don't want to be knackered do you?' Michael was going to protest further, however he managed to catch his words, they had three months ahead together, maybe best to keep any further enquires to a later date.

So to sleep, you close your eyes, and drift off to the constant background hum of the plane's engines.

There's something weird about waking up on a plane at night, Dad was asleep, as was most the plane, a few stewardesses were busying tidying and cleaning with all the stealth and quiet of a ninja, some passengers were looking out the windows others were stretching. For the first half an hour of waking it felt like Michael was watching a silent ballet going on around him, Slowly everyone started to wake up, Dad was one of the last, by now the day was awake and daylight was pouring through the planes windows.

Thursday 14th April – Plane.
'Still flying in the morning, got there in the afternoon'

Within the hour everyone was awake and breakfast was being served. Michael noticed people were getting up, stretching their legs, along with other body parts, and some needed the loo, which he to needed, but would wait, he had used the Loo's once, and that was enough for one life time. Soon the Arabian Sea gave way to land, and life, however below was not the lush green fields and busy towns and cities of England they had left behind, instead there was brown patches and dust, it looked like an alien world, and a new adventure, Then they landed, Jinnah International airport, Karachi, Pakistan. About lunch time.

Without doubt the overriding Memory Michael would take from the whole trip, was the moment he left the airplane and walked down the steps onto the tarmac, the second he walked out the plane Michael was hit with a humid dry heat the like he had never felt before, it was a truly a wonderful moment, which was only spoiled by the blinding sun that was boring into his eye sockets. Sunglasses were needed and stat but first they had to make it past customs. Maybe it was the fact they were British or maybe it was the fact that customs was two guys talking in the corner, whatever it was, all Michael and co had to do was vaguely wave their passport's in the air, walk over to the carousal, pick up their bags, walk to the exit and leave, that was it. They were hardly smuggling guns or drugs, ok dad was bringing 500 cigarettes a bag full of newspapers some perfume oh and some alcohol, but apart from that they were cool. However that wasn't the point; they could have been bringing in all sorts, but no one seemed to care.

Paul was already there; he had parked just outside the main terminal, and would be their driver for the day. Paul was one of four lads that Michael would be sharing a villa with for the next three months, he was Young, late 20's, tall skinny with a bit of muscle, and tanned, where as Michael was short (Still waiting for his teenage growth spurt), slightly overweight and whiter than photocopier paper. Although these things would change over the coming months, He was also polite, and asked how they're flight was and if Michael was looking forward to his stay in the country.

The ride back was an experience in its self, so many colours, smells, and people, the streets were simply overflowing with people, people on the move, always busy, everyone just doing something, never stopping, that was until a car with westerners stopped at traffic lights, then five pair of hands would appear out of thin air, all trying to clean the windscreen at the same time, all using dirty rags and even dirtier water, Paul had long since given up trying to tell these people to bugger off, so would let them finish then throw some money on the floor and let nature take its course, this action had been given a name by some of the Europeans who had been in country maybe a bit too long, *survival of the fittest.* It was at the second set of lights that Michael noticed a boy sitting on the floor, he must have been about six, maybe Seven, Sitting was probably the wrong word, he was more slumped and leaning at a very odd angle, surely no one's legs could bend that way thought Michael. The boy appeared to be begging, he had a sign in the local language and a box with coins in front of him, Michael was not normally one to give to money to beggars, but even then, aged 14, if he had any money on him he would have given it to the boy. As they drove away from the lights, Michael noticed more and more boys and girls begging, their arms and legs pointing at silly angles, Paul had clocked Michael looking at the kids and gave him some local knowledge, *'poor Bastards'* Michael looked at him and nodded, *'I know the parents are poor, but still, I couldn't do that to my kids'* at first it hadn't registered with Michael, the last part of the sentence, it took a few seconds to kick in. *'sorry, what did you say Paul'* Paul seemed to take an age in replying, perhaps trying find the right words for a kid Michael's age, but there wasn't really anyway around it, *'they break their arms and legs on purpose, so they can make more money begging'* Paul went on to explain that there are so many families living in the city, there was simply not enough work for everyone, meaning parents couldn't afford to feed or care for their kids, so the only way forward was to put the kids to "Work" this meant limbs were broken and bent, in the hope a passer-by would feel sorry for the kids and give money. Michael was quiet for the rest of the journey, deep in thought, so much so he didn't even notice the dead house lying in the middle of the road.

The best way to describe the road they would be living on was Dust and high walls. It was as if someone had picked up a row of thirty large Villas, all detached, about twenty yards apart from each other, and plonked them in the middle of a desert, with a bumpy road attached, they really were on the very edge of a vast sandy wilderness. The view out of Michael's bedroom would be miles and miles of desert, littered with stray dogs, most of whom had rabies. Oh and at the end of the dusty road was a corner shop, where you could buy everything and anything you wanted, expect Bacon. Another feature, which gave the whole area a warm friendly feeling, was all the Villa's and mansions had high imposing wall's surrounding them, at least ten feet tall, however dad explained this was an essential part of daily life in that part of Pakistan. As they pulled through the gates to their villa, Paul introduced Michael to the house *Boy* Ali, who was 65, if he was a Day, and couldn't speak a word of English, Paul explained *'This is Ali, he sleeps out here and guards the place with a knife'* Ali seemed to sense they were talking about him and showed them his Knife. A knife! That wasn't a knife thought Michael it was a machete or possible a small sword!

As they walked into the villa, Dad explained Ali was once attached to the British Army, a cook or something like that, whatever he was Ali had loved it, and he loved the English, apparently he saw them as his betters, he would kill and if need be die for them. Christ where had Michael moved to? Over the coming days Michael would learn this type of behaviour was more common than he first realised, and would find more of this mind set in the locals he encountered. The Inside of the villa was nice and cool, with marble floors, marble walls, and big celling fans. It had three reception areas and a large open plan kitchen; there was one bedroom downstairs with four upstairs. Michael would be sharing with Dad, this normally wouldn't be a problem, Michael had only just started dating and wasn't expecting to *hook up* with any of the locals, and Dad, well dad was married so no problems there, however there was one *tiny* problem with the room, there was only single beds, and Michael was used to having a double at home. This would take some getting used to. The room itself was quite sparse, apart from a wardrobe, a side cabinet and a desk with chair, there was nothing else; it felt like a basic bedsit set up. To make the place feel more like home Michael decided to put a wrangler jeans poster on the wall, where a young girl was showing off the jeans stitching!, there was also a choice of toilets, A European (or a toilet you could sit on and flush) or a local version, where you squatted over a six inch whole and well, afterwards flushed with a bucket of water, Michael chose European. Lastly there was the view; it may have been just desert but what a sight, so still, so calm, so hot, Dad pointed out if you trained your eye on one part of the horizon, you could just make out a palace some guy was building in the middle of all that sand, takes all sorts thought Michael.

Dinner was a quiet affair, Michael and dad were tired, Paul was there, along with Dave, a moustached brummie with an odd sense of humour, he must of being around 40, and Steve a young lad from York, Ali served a local fish dish, no one was quite sure what fish it was but it was huge, and tasty. As the talk developed a *Club* was Mentioned, they kept asking Dad 'Will it be ok taking him' everyone then looked at Michael, it was school all over again, then they carried on talking to each other, Dad said Michael would be alright and would be able to handle it, where were they going to take him? Thought number one son?

Around ten it was bed, and even though the sun had set, it must have been a hundred degrees! Thank god for the AC in the room thought a tired Michael, as he lay of top of the bedding Michael couldn't stop thinking about the morning events, was he was really here, in Pakistan, on another continent, as he drifted into the land of nod, Michael kept looking at the ICI malaria tablets he would have to take every day, they tasted like chalk, but were kind of essential. Then sleep.

Chapter Two.

A brave new world.

Friday 15th April – Villa in Pakistan
'Went to the beach, went swimming, got home, went to club'

Breakfast was series of fruit's, Mangos oranges and the like, the Kitchen was nice and cool with a big ceiling fan above the dining table, which could fit six easily, Michael and Dad were still tired and jet lagged, so instead of going to work, Dad thought the best move was a trip to the beach. So Michael, dad, Paul and Dave jumped in one of the two cars on offer, an off white 1980 slightly beaten Toyota Corolla., and hit the road, a very dusty bumpy road.

The drive was pleasant, but hot; yes they had the cars AC on, but it was useless and just circulated warm dry air, so you ended up just having all the windows open, which of course let in all the smells and sounds of the world outside. They passed row after row of houses, shacks, open sewers, markets and horses, lots of which were running free or been used by some local business man to transport goods of one sort of another. As they hit the coast road, all you could see was miles and miles of beach, yet strangely hardly anyone was on them? Very odd thought Michael, in Britain, the second there's any sun, everyone's on the beach eating chips and trying to lick an ice cream through chattering teeth. Yet here on a lovely clear day, there were two people and about thirty dogs enjoying the sunshine. Still they drove on. Past mountains which seem to have large rockets on them pointing towards India, past clumps of desert, along Hawke's bay, past French beach then paradise beach.

After several hours they reached their destination, a gorgeous isolated cove, about a quarter of a mile wide, just for them, they stayed for a couple of hours, dad played Frisbee with Paul, whilst Dave worked on his tan, he too hadn't been long in the country, and was almost as white as Michael.as for Michael, he went boogie boarding, the board in question was a three inch white polystyrene block, about two feet wide and five feet long, which after three waves broke, leaving Michael at the bottom of the Arabian sea, and in a foul mood. After a quick sulk Michael grabbed another board. Around 5pm they had had enough, and Dave was as red as a lobster, so they went home for a quick shower and change, then it was off to the club.

The *club*, which would become like a second home to Michael over the coming months, was a single storey building in the middle of nowhere, you walked into a small foyer, which then offered two options. To your left the toilets and to your right a door which lead to the main room and bar, where all the action happened. the main room was about fifty feet long and about forty feet wide, to your right was some tables and chairs with a full size snooker table in the corner, there was also a dart board, off to the left was some booths, and at the end of the room was a bar, which was a little odd for a country that didn't allow alcohol, however as the drinking was done in private, the local authorities turned a blind eye. There was also a door marked "film room", here you could watch any amount of VHS Videos, including all the latest Hollywood hits and misses, as well as some video nasty's, the *screen* was a top of the range forty inch TV. The room could fit about twenty people, and was normally half empty most nights, however there were some evenings it was standing room only, but these films were for adults only, so Michael wasn't allowed to watch them, he was pretty sure dad would have been ok with him watching them, but the other patrons may have been a little embarrassed.

That night they didn't stay long, a couple of hours, just enough time for Michael to drink his body weight in coke and 7 up, and to deliver the *supplies* they had brought with them from England, Newspapers, films etc., so after Meeting the regulars and a quick game of snooker, they were on their way home and to bed, it had been a long day.

Saturday 16th April – Villa/Hospital
'Went to where my dad works, got a job'
Liverpool 2:3 Southampton
Attendance high (?)
Position Top.

'Come on you lazy bugger it's time to go to work' as dad walked out the bedroom Michael opened one bloodshot eye and looked at his watch, 7am! 7am on a Saturday, *work*! What was Dad going on about? As he dragged his corpse out of his pit, Michael could tell the villa had been up for some time, fair play to the lads, they may go drinking almost every night, but in the morning it was all business. For some reason Dad wanted Michael up at 7am, *on a Saturday. But why?* Then Michael remembered, dad had made it clear before they left England, he wasn't going to let his son sit around the villa all day, doing fuck all. No, if Dad had to go to work, so did Michael, but on a Saturday? After taking His tablets and brushing his teeth with bottled water, Michael had a quick breakfast and hit the road, work was about half an hour away, this would give Michael time to wake up. The cool morning breeze coming through the back window felt nice, so far all he had seen since arriving in the country, apart from the villa and the club, was poverty and a simply way of life compared to back home, however as they approached the construction site where they would be working, you could just tell there was money been spent here. The buildings were all in light red stone, surrounded by lakes and lush green parks.

The site would become the Aga Khan University Hospital, a state of the art facility, a huge campus in the heart of Karachi, quite a bit of the work had been completed, in fact doctors and nurses were on site, however they were still a few months from completion. As you drove in you could hear the workers drilling and hammering, they parked up and walked into a port-a cabin, which doubled as the main site office, there Michael would meet a man called Dave, there was a lot of Dave's, This Dave was the foreman for Ellison, a company based in London who shipped all sorts of construction workers around the world.

Dad had worked for them for about three years, and from today Michael would to, 'So what have you got from him' enquired father, 'brickie, plumbers mate?' they both laughed, 'No, for the son Michael we've got something even better' the foreman's smirk worried young Michael a little, He was then handed a letter which stated Michael would be employed with Ellison at this site for the next three months, working in the stores. After a tour of the site and a very brief health and safety talk, basically don't do anything stupid and don't drop things from roofs, it was lunch, so dad took Michael to the canteen. as they walked in, Michael could have been forgiven for thinking he was back in the UK, He was surrounded by doctors and nurses from all around the world, and the majority of the construction workers were from the UK, it was only when it came to the food, that Michael realised he wasn't in London anymore, no instead of pie and mash, or some sort of cardboard sandwich, you had the choice of rice, fish, several types of curries, even *fresh salad!* The setting was also up on its UK counterpart, large windows, clean tables, marble walls and floors.

After lunch Michael let Dad go to his Job and went in search of his. Half an hour later, after trying, and failing to get directions from some labourers, who only spoke Urdu, he finally found the stores department, which was set in a series of port-a cabins. Michael was introduced to the manager, a local man called Matthew, who was around forty, 5 and half foot tall, with a well-trimmed beard. Matthew wasn't his birth name; he had changed his name from Akram, after finding Jesus and the Christian faith. What followed was the most bizarre first Meeting with anyone Michael would ever have, His new boss thanked Michael, *thanked* Michael for saving his young boys life, because, well, he was white and English, and because of this Michael was closer to god in Matthew's eyes, his boy a couple years of before had been sick, *really sick*, Matthew had prayed hard, the boy lived, so praise the lord and Michael. He was Michael's boss, he had earned this position, Michael was a 14 year old tourist who had been given a job to keep his Dad happy, yet in the mind of Matthew, this young white teenager was the bee's knees. Michael was shown his desk, and around the cabin, the loo's, and of course the kettle, Michael also met his new work colleagues, this took till around 2pm, which on a Saturday was home time, it had been a long first day and Michael was ready to go, looking forward to his first proper work day Monday, Matthew thanked Michael again, then Gods right hand man left. Nice man thought Michael, as he went in search of dad.

Once home Michael collapsed, he was exhausted, after all he had been up since 7am! So a light dinner was followed by bed, as he fell asleep he watched the stars from his bedroom window.

Sunday 17th April Villa/Club
'Went to Club'

Lazy day, got up late went to the club, played snooker.

The best way to describe the shop at the end of their road, was isolated, after walking a couple of hundred yards down the dusty road from the villa, you came to a junction. Which yielded the areas main highway, this again was a dusty road, you could go left which would take you into the desert, and right would take you to civilisation, eventually. 10 paces ahead took you to the entrance of the store, and it could have been any corner shop in the world, a couple of aisles of tins, bottles and cardboard boxes, a couple of fridges and a counter at one end, what was different of course was the language on the packages, just lines and squiggles, the pictures on them didn't help either, just people smiling or animals standing in a field, Michael couldn't ask the shop clerk for help either, mainly due to the fact neither he or the shop clerk, had bothered to learn each other's language. However the Man, an elderly gentleman around Ali's age, did seem polite and always tried to help Michael, and no matter what part of the world you're in, Coke and Pepsi cans always looked the same.

Monday 18th – Friday 22nd Villa/Work Club.
'Went to work/Club'

Michael had only been in the country a week, but had soon fallen into a routine; Just like England, he had to be kicked out of bed in the morning by dad, after which was breakfast, then to work, followed by home, then to finish the day of, a trip to the club, then home for eight hours sleep, then repeat. Michael thought this must be what it's going to be like when he was middle aged, not that he was ever going to be that old!. Thankfully he didn't have to go to work every day! That would have been stupid, some days he would just stay at home, you know how it is, after a hard day's slog at work you needed the next day off to recover, and dad couldn't *really* force Michael to go every day. Michael would hear his dad say 'Get up you little sod' or 'if you're going to stay home at least do some school work' but Michael would soon doze back to sleep and forget what was said, and Michael certainly didn't have to worry about his boss if he didn't want to go in, Matthew bless him didn't say a word, Michael was British and if he didn't want to come in, well that was good enough for him.

When Michael did go to work, all would be fine in the morning, he would get on with his work, filling in various forms and paperwork relating to the daily stores stock takes. Whilst writing, Michael would occasionally catch Matthew slyly looking in his direction, in awe. Not once did Michael feel creped out or in any danger, he (Matthew) like Ali really thought white Brits were it, better than them, closer to god, the British really did a number on that continent. After lunch though it was another story, slowly through the day Michael would fight off the urge to sleep, (looking back Michael would blame the heat, not the fact he was a lazy little bugger) lunch would save the day, for about an hour. it gave him fuel and got him up and moving around, most days he would eat with Dad, however this wasn't always possible, sometimes Michael would instead sit with his dad's friends, they were nice enough, and most of them managed to stop themselves when telling Michael stories about his dad, where any more information could have got Michael senior in a lot of trouble, with either his son or Michaels mum, one would say 'so there's Michael, blind drunk when he' there would be a pause then the group would look at each other and laugh like school kids, or 'Hey remember when Michael meet that blonde piece and..' he would then be stopped by Paul or Dave from the villa with either a look or kick on the shin. After lunch it was back to his desk, and back to the elephant in the room, being there was nothing for Michael to do in the afternoon, really it was a part time position. so by 2pm he would put his head on the desk and sleep, waking up about four, ready to go home, no one in the office seemed to mind or care, in fact it Meant they could get on with their work without worrying about finding Michael things to do, by Thursday Michael felt he was taking the mickey and resolved not to sleep at his desk anymore, instead he went into the toilets and slept sitting on the loo.

The evenings too had their own routine, home, get changed, go to the club, pop and crisps, a game of darts and or snooker, maybe a film, that week he saw, **Missing, Dirty harry, and mash**, there were other films, however he was not allowed to see them!! Still he was happy playing snooker, for Michael had to get ready for the upcoming tournament.

Saturday 23rd April – Villa
'Was invited to a wedding, did not go, jacked in my job'
Liverpool 0 : 2 Spurs
Position Top (don't know how when they kept losing watch week)

Today was going to be nice, thought Michael, a break from the Norm, if you can call working and living thousands of miles away from home, in a country where you can't understand anyone, and those you do interact with, see you as Gods right hand man, or are willing to die for you, *normal*. Still the day was going to nice, no great, because Michael was to going leave his job, he really couldn't take anymore sitting around doing bugger all. The one and only highlight at work happened about a week earlier, whilst sitting at his desk and still awake! Matthew appeared from the back office all excited, 'come with me Michael, we have a job for you!' now this didn't happen very often, in fact Michael was hard pushed to remember the last job he was given, if you discounted the tea and coffee runs. No this was different, this was *work*. Michael followed Matthew into the storeroom; it was full of plumbing supplies and various tools. 'We have been asked to conduct an audit' beamed Matthew. 'And I can't think of no better man then you to carry it out' Michael could, bloody anyone else! An audit, this wasn't work like filling, this meant doing something close to *real* work, it would take at least two hours to complete, this would mean no lunchtime nap, boy was he going to be tired later.

It took a full twenty minutes before Michael was truly bored, he had no radio, no one to speak to, just Michael and the plumbing supplies, and a bloody big snake! At first Michael didn't see it, he had moved the box the creature had been sleeping behind and he was writing the serial number on his list when out of the corner of his eye he saw movement, even looking directly at he didn't believe it was real, the snake was ten feet long, it wasn't a rattle snake that much for sure, but other than that he had no idea what it was. As Michael slowly backed away, he became aware of the commotion behind him, two of Michael's colleagues had walked in to see the son of an English man, face to face with a snake; god knows what was going through their minds, of course it was fear, fear and more fear. If Michael was bitten this would not look good on their personal records, so when they judged Michael was not within strike distance, and with no regard for their own safety, the two men launched a brutal attack on the snake, who had no intention on attacking the white lad and just wanted a kip. After that Michael was on desk duty, from 9am to four pm, expect for Lunch, dad could look after him then, other than that Michael was to stay a very worried Matthew's eyesight. So Michael had had enough and was going to tell Dad he wouldn't be going in anymore, Dad listened to the rational argument and told Michael, 'you're bloody going in' so that was that.

In other news, the villa had been invited to a wedding down the road, however no one could be bothered to attend, it wasn't really anyone's scene, another factor was the weather, it was a hot day, then again when wasn't it? Plus weddings in Pakistan were not quick affairs, so a trip to the beach was planned.

In other other news, Liverpool FC had lost again, how could they still be top of the league, when they kept losing?, Michael had supported them since 77, up until then he had followed West Ham Utd, not supported them mind you, just followed, then he heard about a player called Kenny Dalglish, a young Celtic midfielder. Michael used to love watching Kenny on Telly, then came the news the payer was moving to Liverpool, that was the day Michael started supporting them. Supporting Liverpool in the eighties was easy, maybe too easy; they seemed to win everything, with very little effort, oh how that would change by the end of the decade.

But somehow in 1983, despite losing what felt like every match, they were still top of the league? Go figure.

Monday 25th April – Villa
'Stayed home'

Although Michael had agreed to go back to the hospital, and
his job in the stores, he was still getting over the whole *snake*
incident. Add to that the soaring temps of recent days, and he
really couldn't be bothered with work, so he stayed home and
listened to Abba and queen. After a few hours he was bored
with disco tunes, so proceeded to read the weeks newspapers.
With no real contact with the outside world, they had no TV, a
radio that barely worked, and no phone, Michael like everyone
else in the villa, relied pretty much on people coming back
from England with newspapers and news of the London
season, but made you feel a million miles from home. Michael
read in one paper about Regan (Ronald) signing a bipartisan
compromise bill, that was supposed to save on Social Security,
Newspaper dated April 21st, Another newspaper Dated the
19th reported the bombing of the US Embassy in Beirut,
Hmm, thought Michael, *time to read the sports pages*. With the
sports pages covered, twice, it was onto the Comics, which of
course were timeless; you could read the beano from 20 years
ago and still find it both funny and relevant. After an hour or
so Michael had read them all, cover to cover, so he stood up
and stretched his legs. He had been in the Villa a couple of
weeks now, but never really had a good look around, of course
you couldn't look in other peoples bedrooms, but there was
still plenty to explore. he left the lounge, walked through the
entrance hallway, past the marble staircase, and into the
kitchen, he wasn't really hungry, just bored, after poking
around the fridge and cupboards, he took a large mango and
went upstairs, the first floor had three bedrooms and two
storage rooms, it really was a big place. The hallway was about
twenty feet long and ten feet wide, after licking his sticky
fingers, god he *loved* mango, Michael only hoped there had
them back in England, he proceeded to look in storage room
number one.

Michael really had no idea what he was expecting, but was a

little disappointed with the sight that greeted him, boxes, and more boxes, with the odd mattress. So he moved onto room number two. Michael already knew what was in this room, and knew he wasn't really allowed in there, but thought it was best to *Check* on the patients, this was what Dad had called them, Michael opened the door, half expecting the smell of booze to hit him, however the only smell was dust?, He counted them, *one, two, three…* 'yep' he said to himself, 'all forty two bottles accounted for, Dad had said the beer would take another two weeks, then they would have a party to celebrate, and Michael would even be allowed a bottle, maybe.

With the tour over, he headed for his room, Michael looked out of the balcony, and gazed into the never ending desert that stretched before him, occasionally he would see the odd person, who would just appear out of the sand, or another who would walk past the villa, wave, then take the long walk into the horizon, but that was it. After twenty minutes, he decided he had put *it* off for as long as he could, Dad had been quite clear on the subject 'if you don't do it' he had said in that whole Dad means business voice, 'there will be hell to pay' of course there were no real threats of violence , just the slightest *hint*. There was no way of getting around it; he would need to write a letter to his Mum.

"Dear Mum"

Ok, good start,

"Dear Mum
Arrived safely, so far not seen much of the country, apart from our villa and the hospital, dad has
Looked after me, and even got me a job where he works, in the stores, hope you and Sarah are well, write you again soon,

Love Michael"

34

Michael had really out done himself this time, three lines, *three whole lines* to the woman who had given birth to him, Michael thought about adding to it, or writing a whole new letter, but what was the point, there really wasn't a lot to put in it, that would make sense to his Mum. He would to better on the next letter.

Tuesday and Wednesday - was Home again Tuesday, On Wednesday bored with the Villa Michael went to work. Somehow Michael had become almost middle aged, he was starting to get into a rut. The again it wasn't like he could go out and play football with my mates, or go into town, and buy an LP from Woolworths anytime he wanted to. He was trapped, trapped by marble floors and tall walls.

The only real interesting point over the two days, happened on the Wednesday. On the way to work, they had to drive around a dead horse. It was the same horse from the day Michael and dad had landed, Michael had missed it the first time because of the begging kids, which still played on Michaels mind. What Michael didn't realise was, an even greater horror was only just around the corner.

Thursday 28th April – Club
'Went to party for the woman's Irish hockey Team'

The day started like most others, Dad having to wake Michael up, followed by a fruit breakfast, then Work, and for once Michael was looking forward to work, for he had a plan to mix things up. After the incident with the snake, Michael decided he would work outside for a bit, but there was no *Outside* work to do, then Matthew came to the rescue, his boss had not really slept since that day! So was more than happy for Michael to be out of the dark snake ridden cabin, so he gave Michael a very special task. 'So you want me to smash them up' asked Michael, slightly disappointed with the job in front of him, 'that's right' replied Matthew, 'Oh' was all Michael could

35

muster, Matthew walked away, maybe to have a well-earned cup of tea. Michael looked on at his latest project, in front of him stood three large wooden cargo boxes, they were five feet long and three feet high, they were some of biggest boxes Michael had ever seen, and his job was simple, smash them up and burn the pieces.

The job should have taken the afternoon, and no more, then Matthew would have to found a new job for the following day, but much to the delight of his Boss, Michael had come up with a plan, yes break up the boxes, then *build* something out of the pieces, both parties were happy with the outcome, even Michaels dad was happy when he heard his Son was finally off his arse and doing something positive, the only problem was, what to build? Michael pondered this. *What to build, what to build*, he measured the boxes again; happy with the figures he took a stepped back, put his hands on hips, and started to think the job through. Michael then started to draw some pictures, mainly of boats and fighter planes, he was stumped, in fact Michael had spent so long thinking about the build, he hadn't seen the crowd of locals and Europeans build up behind him, all watching this teenager muttering to himself, whilst walking around some boxes. Finally Michael hit upon an idea, he would build a table, yes the villa needed another one, he smiled, picked up the hammer, and walked over to one of the boxes, it was at this point he noticed the crowd behind him, Michael smiled and waved, thinking to himself weirdoes, then took to the box with full gusto, ten minutes later the job was done, well the first part, the box was in many pieces, and just in time, for it was home time, Michael surveyed the pile of wood on the floor, and said to himself. 'Good job son, good job'.

Michael couldn't put his finger on it, but there something different about the ride home, for a start the forty minute car journey only took thirty minutes, this included running a few *late ambers,* on some of traffic lights, normally this was wasn't done, or someone would make a sly comment like ' bad curry last night was it?' or something else in poor taste, but not today, no today everyone was quiet excited, what was going on? as soon as the men got back to the villa, they all ran into their bedrooms to change, even Michaels Dad seemed in on the charge, he informed Michael to get changed and wear something smart, oh and have a wash, a wash? Twenty minutes later it was back in the car, and to the club. The smell of old spice and brut was almost over powering, yet made a pleasant change from the usual pong of farts and BO, again the journey was quicker than normal, and with good reason, the car park for the Club was packed! What was going on? As soon as Michael walked into the Club, it became clear what was happening, after fighting through the packed dance floor, and through the acrid air filled with all the 80's aftershaves, Michael saw the big banner hanging above the bar "A warm welcome to the Woman's Irish hockey team"

It was a good fifteen minutes before the team was due to arrive, which gave the man an opportunity to add one more layer of aftershave and musk, to their faces, plus other parts, there was also time to get another round of drinks in, some of the lads needed Dutch courage, when it came to talking to the ladies. When the team finally arrived the noise and cheers were deafening, the team must of thought they had won a tournament or something. (even though they hadn't) they were over for the Woman's world cup, being held in Karachi, and were just looking for a quiet night out, instead they were met by a group of sweaty old perverts, polite and neat perverts, but still perverts.

There were seven in the group, including the manager, all were instantly offered five drinks each, a blur of hands thrusting glasses of god knows what in the ladies faces, however they were in training, so it was soft drinks only. As the *mob* moved from the door to the bar, Michael made his way to the snooker table, yes Michael *liked* Girls, and yes some were very pretty, but the facts were these, he was fourteen and these were woman, and most were married or been hit on by guys their

37

own age, so snooker and a pint of Coke was the order of the day, as time went on, the initial noise and euphoria died down, and the chat up lines began, one would say 'well I'm not management but the place would fall apart without me' another 'yeah I work out, I do about fifty sit ups a day', yeah if by sit ups, you mean getting out of your chair to change the channel on the TV, thought a bitchy Michael. Michael was so pleased with his witty comment, he had failed to notice the women were making their way over to the snooker table. By now, four of the group had had enough of the pawing and comments, had spotted Michael on his own, and thought, *he's no threat,* so made a bee line towards him. What followed would mostly be a blur to Michael, but what he would remember was the three games of snooker he played against the woman, and the fact that one or two had to bend over the table to make some shots, which allowed a now glowing Michael, to catch a quick peek of a bra, The woman didn't seem to mind, and Michael swore one winked at him when she caught him looking down her top, there was also the moment Michael had his picture taken with the group, this did not help the red glow on his face, nor did the kisses good night from the team, Michael didn't have to look at the group of man behind him, to feel the Jealousy. Over all a good night was had. Well by Michael anyway.

Friday 29th April – Club/Hotel.
'Went to club, also went to intercontinental'

'So where are we going again' enquired Michael, dad didn't even try to lift his head from the cars head rest when he weakly replied through his sun glasses, 'I told you a Hotel, now please let me close my eyes for five minutes, your old mans knackered', it was the day after the night before, and everyone had sore heads, expect Michael, being too young to drink he slept fine, and was bright eyed and bushy tailed, which annoyed the men in the car even more than their headaches. So After the fun and exploits of the night before, it was decided a day off was in order, and just to take it easy. They were heading to the intercontinental hotel, a tall white long building, dwarfing all around it, it had a large pool, with deck chairs and pool side attendants, who would cater to your every whim, and this was the gang's destination. This was also the hotel, Michael senior allegedly met a few months before the touring English cricket team, which included Ian Botham, a few beers were shared. Again allegedly. England had played Pakistan in Lahore, at the Gaddafi stadium, between March 19th to the 24th, by all reports it was a great fluctuating match, which ended in a draw, mainly down to some inept battering from the home side's middle order.

The day was spent plonked on a deck chair, eating all sorts of iced deserts, with the occasional soft drink; all brought by young men, who were waiting in the wings, sweating in their hotel issued suits with bow ties?, well this was how Michael spent his day; the rest of the group had some hair of the dog beverages, and baked in the midday sun, sleeping off the night before excess. It was a couple of hours in, when Michael really started to feel the difference between him and the waiters, here he was, with 50 or so other white man and woman from around the globe, all lazing around, doing sod all, surrounded by locals earning minimum wage, and you only had to walk out of the hotel, and go in any direction for a few minutes, to see the poverty and despair in the country. Michael managed to shake of the growing feeling of guilt building up from within, but these feelings were becoming more frequent, and this was troubling the teenager from Essex. Another coke should do the trick; Michael put his hand up and pointed to his empty glass, a man with a trimmed moustache run into the hotel to fill the guests order.

Life was tough.

By five everyone was baked and burnt, so it was home to relax.

Chapter Three

Homesick.

Saturday 30th April – Villa.
'Sean's birthday, Paul went back'
Liverpool 0 : 2 Norwich How are they still top?
Position top.

It was a big day at the villa, Paul was going home, being the youngest guy in the villa, (not including Michael of course) Michael had grown closer to Him, than any of the others, Paul was a great guy, he always found time to chat and offer advice, so Michael was feeling a bit down at the thought of not seeing Paul for a while, if again. This would of course happen again and again, people would come and go until the job at the hospital was done.

'You take care of yourself now, you hear me? And don't take any of your olds man's bull' Paul smiled at Snr as he patted Jnr on the back, Michael tried to think of a witty response but was empty, so he managed 'Ok I won't' Paul smiled and threw his bags on the back seat of the waiting taxi, and was gone in a cloud of dust. Dad came over to his son and Put his arm around him, 'come on it's time for work' as Dad walked towards the villa, Michael knew this was dad's way of trying to take his mind of Paul leaving, but it really didn't help, nor did the idea of going to the building site on the weekend, to compound matters, it was his best friend's birthday. Sean was fifteen now, somewhere in the world, far from the dust pit Michael was in, a Teenager would be waking up, eating crap, getting presents and watching cartoons, Michael needed cheering up. There was however one item at work that could help Michaels troubled mind, Wood, specifically a wooden crate, some days before, Michael had decided on building a table for the Villa, simple! A table had four legs and a top, again simple; however Michael had to overcome several

40

problems. First he had no tools, just a hammer, not even a sprit level, secondly a design, what did he want the table's style to be? Early Georgian? Maybe something suitable for a country cottage. Hmm, did Michael have enough Nails for those ideas.

Michael arrived at the stores Port-a cabin around 9am, clocked in, said morning to his boss Matthew, picked up the hammer on his desk, and headed to the wooden boxes, full of good intentions, ready to build something. Around 2 o'clock Michael was bored, hungry, and hot, the mid-day sun and done its job on the frail teenager, who had forgotten to bring a hat, so there was only one thing to do, fire as many nails into the thing as possible, and see what happened. Around twenty minutes later the "job" was done, Michael stared at his masterpiece, *Hmm something's not right* he thought. *Maybe if I stand back a bit*. He looked on and came to a conclusion, *nope that's pissed*. Pissed wasn't the word! The best way to describe the abomination was ski slope; there must have been a clear four inches height difference from one end to the other. Michael looked at his watch 3 o'clock, *I'll finish it off next week*.

Sunday 1st May – Karachi
'Went down to the markets, it ponged'

A day off, hurrah thought Michael, however there was no time to relax, for today Michael was to visit the local markets, followed by a trip into town, and to his joy and surprise, it was just him and Dad, which meant they could have a boys day out, Michael called shot gun. There was one other passenger, Ali, Ali the 60 year old house boy, Ali was a fixture at the villa, Michael had got so used to him being there, that when Ali went to visit his Family (Well Dad and Michael think it was his Family?) it felt *empty*, which was odd, when you think Michael couldn't speak Urdu, and Ali couldn't really speak English, well if he could he never let on to Michael..

One time Michael had tried to speak to Ali in his native

tongue, he had asked the lads in the Villa for a few words, and practised before trying them out on a live audience. Michael braced himself, and slowly asked the big question, in Urdu, it wasn't pretty, Michael awaited a response, after a minute, Michaels smug grin started to fade, as a Blank faced Ali then burst into laughter, Ali patted the young Brit on the back, and walked off, Michael had only asked 'Hello Ali, are you having a nice day?' where did he go wrong? A few days later, Michael found out he had actually asked, 'Hello Ali, are you having a nice dinner' so close, but so far. Today Ali was using Dad and Michael as a taxi service, as soon as the lads got to the Market, he was off, looking for fresh fish for the night's dinner, Dad said they didn't have to worry about him, as Ali would find his own way back. As they approached the market, well there was no other way of putting it, the place *stank*, Badly!, Michael could not believe a place of earth could produce such a smell, but when you have Fish, meat and spice sellers, with little or no refrigeration and a baking sun, well it was never going to end well. Despite this Michael loved the experience, the colours, the noises, and the people. The market was a series of tents in the middle of the desert, and by midday only a few were left, soon the only trace the market was ever there, would be the piles of rubbish awaiting collection.

Next stop was town, a huge place full, FULL of people, with an abundance of Smells and noises. Michael tried to take in all the sights, sounds, people, but there was simple too much to process, to his left people were rushing past, some on bikes fully loaded with goods and food, other on foot again carrying as much as they could, some carrying more than they should, it was the first time Michael had seen anyone carrying things on their head? To his right were rows and rows of shops, all brightly coloured, with cuts of cloths draped like hoardings on the buildings, smells were everywhere, the air was thick with the stench of commerce. But the over ridding sensual attack was noise, it was just all around you, like surround sound, even when you went into a shop or store, *noise* was just all around you, from the shop keepers, who used half the English they knew to say, with a board smile 'You English, come in come in, many goods for you here' to the cars and bikes rushing past outside, yet oddly the biggest noise was music, western music, every store had a cassette playing boom box thing in their store. As with everything else in the 80's, bigger was better, and the shop owners loved blasting out tunes on them. In most stores you could buy the tapes they were playing, these included local bands and tunes, for that truly ethic present experience, the type of present you get and give to a loved one, who on a rainy day in London, doesn't quite get the same experience as the buyer did, all those thousands of miles away in another land. Michael decided not to go the local route, and instead opted for western, he couldn't believe his luck, Abba, Queen, survivor, so many cool bands, but which to buy? Not that it mattered, they were so cheap he could have bought them all. In the End Michael went for Abba, oh and Queens Hot space album, Michael was introduced to the band by his Dad, He had never thought of his Dad being into music or pop culture at all, to be honest, Michael like most kids, thought his parents shut down like robots when he went to school, waiting for him to return, waiting to serve him once again, after all it was their jobs, But on this trip Michael was seeing another side to his Dad, a human side, with feelings and interests. And one of Dads passions was Queen, he *loved* them, many a night Tie your mother down or don't stop me now would be heard blasting out of the villa; god knows what the locals must of thought.

So with the music sorted it, was on to the real shopping, Dad wanted clothes, Michael thought this was odd at first, until Dad explained 'the clothes here are made out of silks, and the best cotton, at dirt cheap prices' Whilst looking around with Dad, Michael came to a decision, 'Dad' 'Yes son' 'can I have a shirt' Dad smiled 'You know what son, not only can you have a shirt, I'll ask them to put your initials on it' 'thanks dad' his own initials, how cool would that be. Within the hour a man with a cloth tape measure, took Michaels sizes and advised Dad the shirt would be ready tomorrow. Next stop a present for mum and Sis.

By the tenth shop Michael was full, full of coke, Pepsi and Seven up, at the first shop they went in, Michael was surprised to be offered a cold can of pop, for free!! How could he turn it down, by the fifth shop he realised *every* shop would offer them a can, the moment a shop keeper saw a white person enter their store, bang, a can of coke was shoved in their face. And in the tenth shop Michaels stomach was saying no more, but it was rude to refuse, wasn't it? So Michael started to store the cans his shopping bag, for the ride home. After another hour of shopping, four more cans, and a dodgy looking kebab for lunch, it was time to go home. The car journey was long and soggy, the air was hot and humid, Michael tried to cool himself down with one of the four cans he had left over, however the bumpy roads had taken their toll, and the second Michael opened one of them, its contents was spread across his face, Dad tried not to laugh, but couldn't help himself, great thought Michael, I'm hot, wet and now sticky, what a day.

Tuesday 3rd May - Villa
'Notts forest 1:0 Liverpool'
Liverpool still top of league.

How Can Liverpool still be top? They haven't won in *so many* games!!

Wednesday 4th May – Club
'Went to club, played snooker'

This was it, thought Michael, *the big day*, He had gone to work, but his heart just wasn't into hammering, for today was the big snooker final.

Silently, Michael had been working his way through the tournament stages at the club, and was now in the final, best of five frames, winner gets, well Michael didn't know or even care what the winner would receive, he was in a final. Michael's challenger was a guy, called Guy, a forty something Plasterer from Bristol, a nice enough man, but this was business; Michael had to get his game face on. Michael really wanted to win this.

Michaels sporting achievements were spotty, to say the least, it wasn't that Michael wasn't sporty, the complete opposite was in fact the case, he played, tennis, football, rugby, golf, he even went swimming, it was just Michael wasn't that bothered about winning medals or awards, it was about taking part. Or at least that was true of the past, now he wanted to win something, anything. Maybe it his age, maybe pride, but this final was his chance to prove himself a winner, be it to a bunch of drunken old farts, but you have to start somewhere. The summer before, Billericay town FC had held open trials in a local park, up for grabs was a chance to play for the youth team, Michael went down to try out for the wing or midfield, it quickly became obvious that although Michael could play decent football, there were better players trying out, so he tried Goal keeper, Michael hated the position, the only problem was the position loved him, he really quite good, Michael *really* didn't want to try out for Goalie, but if he wanted in the team, this was the only way to get a foot in the door. Much to Michael's surprise/horror he made it through the park trial, then came the second stage, which he past, now came the final test. The last trial was at the clubs ground, four Goal keepers were trying out for two positions, Michael would give his all, and in doing so impress the coaches and staff, but would come third, a good try but no lolly, so tonight was going to make up for all that had passed.

So after work, it was a brief dinner then to the club. Michael bound in full of confidence, to be met by a near empty room, even though it was final night, there was hardly a crowd, but that didn't matter to Michael, he just wanted to play, and win. Due to a problem with the Toyota, they arrived on time, but this didn't leave enough time for a practice frame. So within twenty minutes of arriving, Michael had a cue in his hand, and was calling heads on the coin that would decide who broke. Michael won and chose to brake, completely fluffing the shot, yes it hit the reds, and no the white ball didn't go down a pocket for four foul points, but really it was a nothing shot, and left his opponent with more than a few options, which he took, however much to Michaels relief, Guy only made 12, not that Michael took his next chance or indeed any of the opportunity's he had in that frame, he lost it 65 – 25, Hardly a big score, but then again they were hardly Steve Davie's or hurricane Higgins. So 1 – 0 down, all to play for.

The second frame started for Michael much as the first did, poorly, Dad tried his best to help with 'Its ok son, plenty of time to go' and 'I'm off to the bar do you want a coke and crisps' but Michael was in no mood to talk, although he said yes to a coke and cheese and onion crisps, Luckily his opponent was having some issues as well, and from nowhere Michael made a fifty Break, which meant he squared the match to one all.

The third Frame was a lot closer, real edge of your seat stuff, or so it felt to the two competitors, in reality nether could score more than 7 per visit to the table, bored by the unfolding events before them, some of the onlookers started to drift away and towards the bar, Michael too wanted to leave the area, but for a very different reason, by this point the coke had worked its magic, and he called for a loo break, Michael could tell Guy wasn't happy stopping, for the first time in the frame he was actually doing well and was on a break of 25, however when Michael politely yet *firmly* asked for a trip to the WC, his wish was granted and the teenager dashed to the bogs, Michael was only gone five minutes, but it most of seemed like twenty to his opponent, now back, Michael apologised, again, and Guy carried on with his break. It was at this point Michael noticed the crowd had grown, half the club must have been watching now, Michael clocked the crowd coming out of the cinema room, that night's film must have just finished. The third although close, ended like the second, with Michael winning, 80 – 75, he had managed to score a few fouls off Guy, through some very lucky safety shoots, much to the frustration of his opponent. Now 2-1 up, Michael could relax a bit, even if he lost, he would have made Guy play the full five frames, the crowd and dad couldn't have asked for more than that. It was also at this point Michael noticed Guy was mumbling to himself, and staring at him. *What was his problem?*

So to the forth, as his opponent broke, Michael suddenly realised if he won this frame, he would win the match. He was awoken from this moment, by the clatter of the white ball smashing into the reds, he looked around the room, everyone was now watching the game, *oh crap* he thought. No longer feeling relaxed anxiety kicked in. The forth was a complete blood bath of a frame, both playing as bad as each other, both potting a red then missing a colour, both getting low breaks of fives and tens, then came the moment that decided the frame, and tournament. Guy was leading 35 – 17, with three reds to go, then Michael fluked a shot, he had gone for a red, bottom left pocket, he hit the red, but didn't go in, instead somehow the white went behind the brown at the other end of the table, Guy was snookered, he gave Michael a stare, one of those, *you lucky sod, I wish I had done that* stares. Guy walked up to the Brown, had a look at the shot, then walked to where the reds were, he seemed to mumble to himself whilst doing this, he them walked back the brown, where the cue ball was, took a deep breath and made his shot, He missed, by a clear foot. Now the rules at the club were simple, if your opponent fails to hit a red, you can choose for the cue ball to be placed at the same spot and they try again, also they lose four points, or you take the four points and play from where the cue ball ends up, if it's in a favourable position, the cue ball was not, so back behind the brown, it took five attempts, five shots before Guy hit a red. Michael was now in the lead, 37 -35, only two in it, however Guys head had gone, Michael was not playing a happy camper, after another scrappy exchange, all the reds

were potted but with no colours, so it was 38 – 36 to Michael, .
and he was on strike. The yellow was tricky but on, down it
went, as did the green, so onto the brown, it was a clear five
foot shot, and would take some skill, or luck to down it, luck it
was, Michael again fluked it, he was going for middle left, but
somehow completely missed that hole, the brown then
bounced around the table, until it hit the blue and went in,
middle right, leaving the blue to win the match. Guy could not
understand or believe what had just happened; suddenly he
was staring at defeat to fourteen year old. Michael couldn't
miss, the blue was all but in the top left pocket, but it still
didn't stop the sudden attack of nerves hitting him from
nowhere, could he really win something, Bang! he hit the cue
ball, hitting the blue ball true, and it was in, Michael had won,
he hugged Dad and shook a few hands from the crowd, he
then turned to his opponent, just in time to see him smash his
own cue over his thigh, he then stormed out of the club, 'Sore
loser' said one of the crowd, so to the prize, a two piece
snooker cue, nice. Michael was also treated to half a pint of
beer by dad 'well done son, you deserved it'

Chapter Four.

Helen.

Thursday 5th May – party
'Went to a party around Terry's went home around 2'

Michael had had enough, the heat was just unbearable, he had been *in country* for a month now, and thought he was used to the weather, but today was different, and waking up bathed in sweat was not Michael's idea of having a good time, 'Come on dad can't I stay home?' it must have been a hundred in the shade! But dad was having none of it 'No you're going in!' he snapped, dad was just as hot, and not in the mood for his son's whining.

The car journey into work was hot and tiring, as they approached the hospital complex, Michael had already made his mind up, *middle stall* he said to himself that would be the coolest place to have a kip, sod work, the stores was up to date, Matthew was away, and his art project was going nowhere, so sleep it was.

Michael said later to dad, and headed to his *office*, deciding to use a cut through, a half-finished corridor, in the lower east wing of the main teaching and research building, Michael used this when it was raining, or too damned hot to be outside. As per usual, he was in a world of his own as he walked along, however halfway down the corridor, he caught sight of something *odd* happening on the celling, at first he couldn't figure out what was going on, then it dawned on him, 'hang on' he muttered 'that's not right?' Michael could see a sign on the celling flapping to a breeze, yet all the windows in the section were closed, then the light bulb moment, the air con was working! 'Yes' he shouted to himself, maybe a little too loudly, just as two male doctors went past, they went silent as they walked by, then carried on talking in their native tongue, looking back at him every few seconds, the boy from Essex didn't care though, he was cool, well not cool, but he was *comfortable*, and that was a start. Michael carried on along the corridor, he checked his watch for the time, he was early, so decided to have a look around, Michael had no real desire to look at any particular part of the complex, he just felt in a nosey mood, also he was due to leave before the Hospital was schedule for completion, so a quick snoop it was. After half an hour he had seen five wards, three staff rooms, a canteen, oh and two toilet blocks, all were clean, kited out, and ready to go, but all silently empty. He would meet the odd member of staff, but they would be too busy to pay any attention to the young kid lurking in the shadows, and when anyone did ask him what he was up to, Michael would show them his pass and say 'I'm looking for my dad, he's a plumber, have you seen him?' the Nurse or doctor would stare blankly at him, point somewhere, anyway, then walk away. Michael was going to call it a day, when he saw the words RESEARCH, Well he couldn't turn back now, so after a quick look around, headed for the big metal door which lead to the research department, as he grabbed the door handle, he froze, just like any smell or noise could trigger some long forgotten memory from the past, the touching of the handle brought back some memoires, and not very pleasant one's at that.

The summer before, Michael Senior had taken his son to Bart's, or for anyone outside of London "St Bartholomew's Hospital" a world renowned teaching hospital, Snr was drafted in to work on some re fit or extension, and halfway through the job, some earth workers had found roman remains, so a big dig was now in place. Dad wanting to show Michael what he did for a living, took an excited Son to the site, they spent the day looking around the dig, then dad showed Michael around the non-patient parts of the hospital, including the research labs, and that trip would stay with him for his remaining days. The lab was full of huge test tubes and jars, each had part of a human head or arm or leg, some even had deformed babies in them, it was like a scene from some video nasty, but it was the silence that really sealed the mood, complete silence, Just Michael Dad and the Jars. Later that day at home, whilst Michael was walking up to his bedroom, in the dark, Dad thought it would be funny to jump out on his son, 'Boo' Jnr Jumped a Mile 'Thanks Dad, I really needed that' Michael did not sleep well that night. Now it was the present, and Michael still had his hand on the door handle, not sure what to do, *'it can't be as bad as Bart's'* he said to himself, *'can it?'* He took a deep breath, then entered the room, a big white long empty room, 'oh'

After the events of the day, Michael was ready for dinner then bed, however this was not to be, 'But I don't even know Terry' Dad wasn't really paying attention, he was having a shave, dad never shaved, not even when the Woman's Irish hockey team was in town? 'Can't I just stay home?' a younger man was now staring back at Michael. 'Terry is a friend, and no you can't stay home, Ali is out, and no one will be at home' 'that's not fair' started Michael, but it was useless, he was going and that was the end of it.

You could tell, before even walking through the big brown wooden door, here was money, up till now Michael had felt superior to the locals, and workers at the hospital, he didn't mean to feel this way, it was just they were living in a villa, with a house boy, and two cars. And they were living in shacks, or worse, but compared to Terry, Michael and co were Living in a hole in the ground. Terry had it all, a top of the range CRT TV, top class bar, with at least ten optics, all the top sprit brands, a kick ass stereo system. A knock out wife, and a teenage daughter called Helen, who was fast catching her mum in the looks department. Michael couldn't stop looking at Helen, and it didn't help that Dad had clocked his lustful son's Gaze, 'go on, say hello' said dad trying to be helpful, *oh god, no way* thought Michael, she was way out of his league, Michael turned to say this to dad, or words to that affect, but was stopped in his tracks by the stupid grin on his father's faces, *Oh god he's proud of me,* Thought Michael, but why?, then it dawned on the young man, for the past couple of years, Dad had gone on and on about courting and if any girls had caught his son's eye's at school, Senior would go on about the girls he dated as a young man, and truth be told, Michael got the sense Dad was getting a little worried his boy didn't like Girls, and maybe liked playing Rugby a little more than he should have. So maybe it was more relief than any other emotion, but dad was now slightly happier with life, his son liked girls, however Michael wasn't happy, he didn't know what to say, he never really spoke to Girls, expect his sister, and she didn't count, Dad gently pushed his sweaty mess of a child in the young girl's direction, then fate stepped in and saved the day. 'Ah Andrew you must meet the family' Terry had spotted a business possibility and carted his wife and daughter in this direction, So that was the end of that, however after the relief did come a sense of, *Damn I wish I had at least spoken to her*, but Michael soon shrugged this feeling off, No, no good would of come from it he thought. And she was at *least* a year older than him.

By 10 pm the party was in full flow, meaning the adults were pretty merry and the music was getting louder and cheesier, all the hits of the 70's were booming out, Leo Sayer was earning his royalties that night. Michael noticed Dad was now putting the worlds to rights, by telling a couple of managers from the Site where they could stick their plan for a longer working week, for no extra pay, it was only a rumour for now, but rumours soon turn into facts before you know it. The managers were trapped in a corner, nowhere to run, so they had to listen, and they did, by 10.10 pm the working week was agreed to stay the same. Michael was amazed by his Dad sometimes, his Pa may of drank a little bit too much, and smoked 40 fags a day, also only had only a small amount of schooling by 1980's standards, But he had a trade, and a head fully screwed on, you really didn't want to mess with him, not when it came to family or money. Michael was still looking at his Dad, and his new found friends when he felt a tap on his shoulder, he turned thinking he was in some ones way, to be confronted by a girl, not any girl, but a teenage girl, called Helen, she had a wicked grin on her face, 'Would you like to see my room?' it took a second for this request to hit Michaels brain and register, here was a Girl, *a Girl* asking him to look at her room, and all he could say was 'Ok'. The pair slipped away from the party with ease; the adults were now in their own little world.

So this was what a Girls bedroom looked like, apart from the vanity mirror and desk, the room was lot like Michaels in Essex, yes she had stuffed toys and dolls on her bed, but Michael still played with his star wars figures and action men stuff, so really there wasn't a lot of difference there, Helen even had the same wrangler jeans poster as him, although his poster would soon disappear once he got home. 'So, do you have a name?' she asked, oh god, he had forgotten to talk to her, how smooth was this, oh crap what was his bloody name? 'Hi I'm er Michael' well at least he had remembered that much, on a roll he continued, 'Your Helen aren't you?' Helen put on her mock shocked face, 'Oh I see, my names been mentioned before has it, nothing to rude I hope' without even thinking Michael replied 'yes my Dad pointed you, sorry it out' Helen laughed, Michael realised she was having fun with him, god what a putz he was, she laughed again and smiled, he liked this, 'Don't worry I'm just messing with you, I saw you with your dad, he seemed nice' maybe it was the fact that she had said more than two words to him, without then walking away, which most girls seemed to do whenever he spoke to the fairer sex, or the fact she had kind eyes, but Michael was now more at ease then he had been with any other girl. They spoke for the next twenty minutes about where each other had come from, their back grounds, and other stuff that didn't really matter. Helen was 15 and three quarters, the family home was back in Chester, Cheshire, they had been in Pakistan for over two years, and she had an older brother, called Tony, who was back in the UK studying Chemistry at Manchester Uni, she liked horses and had a pony, called Charles, like the prince. The conversation then moved onto hair, She didn't mind been blonde, but hated long hair, due to the heat, however Mum wouldn't let her cut it, so she was stuck with the length, It was at this point, that Michael noticed just how close the pair was sitting, alone, on her bed, and he couldn't help but look into her eyes, were they green? Blue? Helen sensed this staring as a sign Michael liked her, so she kissed him, firmly on the lips. It wasn't like the movies, no love songs appeared from nowhere. No this was better, her lips were firm, yet tender, and then there was the heat, no one ever told him a Girl's lips were so warm. The kiss felt like it had gone on for Minutes, but in reality it lasted no more than 30 seconds, Michael also found his hand had independently moved to Helens back, so he could pull her closer, the kiss would have gone on longer, if it wasn't for the approaching footsteps. Like a jack rabbit Helen jumped up, Michael was still in a daze. 'You need to leave!' Helen was scared and in a panic. 'What' Michael really wasn't keeping up? 'Please I can't be caught with a boy in my room, again' Michael stood up and was ready to run across the hall, into a toilet when it hit home, 'What do you mean again?' the owner of the footsteps was now moments from Helens door, 'Please' Michael noted this wasn't the time for this conversation, so he kissed her on the cheek, then run into the room opposite. As Michael closed the toilet door, he heard Helens mum ask if she had seen a boy called Michael, as his Dad was looking for him, Helen said 'no', and put her best, *why would I know anyway* act on. There was a silence, then Michael heard Helens mum leave, he waited a moment, took a deep breath, then went downstairs. At first he couldn't see Helen, or his dad, then he caught sight of the girl with the red hot lips, Helen was in a corner, talking to her mum and Dad, Michael was just about to wave bye to her, when his own Dad appeared, slightly drunk 'Where the bloody hell have you been?' Michael couldn't work out if his Dad was angry, or just playing around, 'no way, I was Just talking to some other kids' Dad seemed to ponder Michaels reply for an age, then he smiled, 'Good, you need to knock around with more kids your own age'.

As Michael helped Dad into the taxi, he looked back at the large house, still full of life, he then got in, as the car drove away, Dad perked up, 'Do you think you'll see them again?' 'Hmm' said Michael, staring out the window, 'your friends, do you think you'll see them again?' 'Oh them, no I think it was just a one off' 'Shame ' slurred dad, 'it seemed to put colour in your cheeks' as Dad fell asleep up front, Michael could only think on that he never got a chance to say good bye, and he would never see her again.

How wrong he was.

Friday 6th May
'Went to the beach, went in the water for two hours'

The morning after, the day before.

Michael was still in a daze from the night before; he ate his bowl of Mango and banana, with carnation milk of course, without taking any notice of the events going on in the background. He was playing the night before events over again in his mind, dad however was a buzz of activity, despite the fact it was early and the night before he had drunk most of Terry's booze cabinet. It was 8am, yet dad was fully awake and full of energy, currently he was busy putting food and drinks into a picnic basket, he then walked over to a cupboard and stared into it, whatever he was looking for he could not find, so he called over to his son, 'Michael' nothing 'Michael!' again nothing, 'Oi, boy!' half shouted dad, Michael Jnr seemed to wake up, as if from a coma or trance. 'Huh?' He looked towards his dad, who was kneeling on the kitchen floor, with the contents of two cupboards next to him. 'Son have you seen the beach towels? They were in here last week' for some reason Michael's brain couldn't process the word blanket; it was working on full capacity, running through the events from several hours before, so his response was again 'Huh?' Dad had long suspected the heat would eventually get to his son, that and the fact that he was a lanky piece of teenage piss, who's brain hadn't arrived in the post yet, Dad had no time for this this morning, Steve and Dave, walked into the kitchen, and immediately wished they hadn't, all were given orders and ten minutes to follow them, today was beach day, all was going and that was that.

Slowly, as the car journey unfolded, Michael started to wake up from his pleasant waking dream; He certainly wasn't over Helen, or what happened, but the teenage mind can only concentrate one any one thing for so long, before it starts to wander. That was that, he had had a good time, but that was now in the past, time to move on, time to learn how to surf. They drove on, passing the large rockets sat on the mountain range far in the distance, they passed villages and small towns, soon they were on the outskirts of the city, where a huge white marble Library was located. For some reason the building had caught Michaels attention, and after staring at the mammoth marble structure for a couple of minutes, a question popped into Michaels head 'Where are all the people?' he asked out load, at first no one seemed to care what the young lad had said, eventually Steve clocked the young lads confused expression, 'What's up son' without looking at Steve Michael continued 'The Library we just passed, they were no people, no cars, nothing, is it a national holiday?' 'I don't think so' replied Steve. Dave jumped in, sensing his chance to climb on his high horse, 'You see lad' boomed Dave in his deep Birmingham accent, Steve rolled his eyes to the heavens and put on his Walkman. 'You see' continued Dave, 'the people at the top don't want the masses learning to read or write, to have a better life' *Oh god, not this speech again, thanks son,* thought dad, who too rolled his eyes, and wished he also had a Walkman, Sensing what Michael Senior was thinking, Dave looked at Dad 'Now Michael, you know I'm right, look at the poverty, the way the ordinary man lives and works, if he's lucky!' Dave was really on a roll, Michael Jnr had really hit a sore spot. 'If they tried that shit in west Bromwich, the powers that be would soon feel the wrath of the common man' both Dad and

Steve mouthed together that last part, they had heard it so many times before. 'You don't half talk shite Dave' interrupted Steve. 'Ah Then why build all these wonderful buildings, but not let anyone use them?' countered an eager Dave, for this no one had an answer, Dave happy with the fact no one could dismiss his reasoning, smiled smugly and sat back in his chair, Michael Jnr was not so happy though, why would someone build a library, then keep people from going in it? This thought kept with him for the rest of the journey.

When they arrived at the beach, the surf was already battering the coast line, so Michael thought this was the perfect time to break out the foam boards, and run head long into the sea. The foam boards were just that, Foam, each board was two feet wide by five feet long, and four inches thick, mainly used for insulating walls, and *not* surfing, none of this bothered Michael, not even the fact that he had never been surfing before fazed him, how hard could it be?. By the fifth dunking, Michael was beginning to get a little tired of the game, Where's my board?, It's lightweight structure was not helping, after each wipe out, the light foam board would fly off, leaving Michael to surface from the depths of the ocean, to begin the hurt for it all over again. Dad and the others had long become bored of watching the boy falling into the water, and got on with the serious business of eating and drinking, followed by a snooze, they had worked hard all week, so deserved a rest.

Michael's seventh attempt was the best, and would remain his best for the next thirty years; he must have travelled at last *a hundred yards* before a **huge** wave took him out. The following two tries were nowhere near as good, time for a rest thought a tired Michael, also Dad seemed to waving a burger in his direction, but why swim to shore when he could surf, surf right onto the beach, that would look cool thought Michael, with that he caught sight of a ten foot wave coming towards him, and took his chance, as the wave hit, Michael jumped on to the board, *yes*, his best mount so far, then two seconds later he hit the water, Hard! Dad saw this from the corner of his eye, and having seen his son fall from his broad many *many* times over, paid no real attention, however what followed did make him wonder about his child's sanity, from his point of view, several seconds after Jnr had goon under, he had reappeared, starting to look for his *board*, clocked that it was now in at least three bits, and in all honesty lost his shit, for whatever reason Michael Jnr was not happy, not happy at all, by the time he walked past Dad, the shouting and screaming had all but stopped, but his face was still of thunder, Michael stomped past and sat heavily on a deck chair, dad couldn't help himself and burst out laughing, this did not help his Son's mood.

After an hour, his son had calmed down, and was finally eating, 'Better now son' enquired Dad, trying not to smile too much, 'Yeah fine' well at least he was talking now, best leave it there thought Dad.

By 6 it was time to go, it had been a long tiring day, well for some anyway.

Saturday 7th May – Wedding.
'Went to a wedding down the road'
Liverpool 1:1 Aston Villa
Liverpool win the English league.

The day started like most others, hot and sunny, and despite the fact Michael didn't drink, and was a teenager, so technical in his prime, he still took exception to been woken after only ten hours sleep, dad explained what was happening, and reminded Michael they were going to a wedding. Normally they didn't go to them, but this was different, this was the big one.

They lived on an up and coming middle class area, and the weddings pretty well matched the ideals of this. The ceremony was going to be huge, and the after party of the hook, well that was the promise. Michael sat down to his fresh fruit breakfast, he was getting so bored of eating the same thing every morning, and longed for shreddies, or even god forbid porridge. After breakfast Michael put on his best jeans and monogrammed shirt, then headed for the house 2 minutes down the road, you could tell by the number of Mercs and BMW's this was not going to be a cheap do. Michael would take four memoires away from the day, firstly the Heat in the big outdoor tent the ceremony was taking place in, then there was the smell, both could have been helped by air con, Michael was also struck by the fact the bride and groom didn't not see each other until the end, and were separated by a huge cloth wall, and last but not least the ceremony *meal*, There was no other way of putting it; it was a bag of nuts, nuts dates and some red goo. At first Michael had no real intention of opening the bag, let alone eating the contents, but after the 2nd hour of sitting in the tent, Michael needed something, anything to eat. A few minutes later he had finished half the bag, and immediately wished he hadn't, if he had smiled at that point, it would have looked like he had been eating razor blades instead of nuts, his teeth were blood red. Half an hour later it seemed to be all but over, not knowing the local language, the group of Englishman could only guess at this, by the fact the bride and groom could at least now see each other, there was some hand holding, then clapping, followed by waving, ten minutes later everyone started to leave the tent. As they left, Michael caught the end of Dad's slightly un pc comment to Dave, about the brides nose piecing's, as they walked towards the after party venue, Dave was still laughing, Michael just thought it was rude.

The party was pretty much as Michael expected, all the locals kept to themselves, they were polite and nodded or shook his hand, but that was it, and the kids were either too young to hang around with, or the ones his age didn't speak English, so after an hour, with the diplomatic mission over, the group left the party, in part due to the fact there was no drink, but mainly because it had been a long day. On the walk home, Michael saw movement in the big crop of bushes across the road from their villa, but thought it was a dog, or some kids playing. Once home the grownups headed for the *bar*, grabbed a beer and sat in the lounge, Michael headed for the loo, he was bursting now, there was simply no way he was going to use the ones at the party, they had been port a loos, and the heat of the day had made the unusable. The relief was instant, he vowed not do that again to himself, if he needed the loo, no matter where he was he would.. *What the hell?* Thought a startled Michael, he had caught sight of his face in the bathroom mirror, his teeth were red, bright red, that bloody party bag of nuts and berries. God could this day get any worse.

At 10.30pm it did, the AC unit in their bedroom stopped working, the second it broke down Michael woke, the AC unit had served two purposes, one to keep things cool, namely Dad and Michael, secondly acting as a soothing noise to help get Michael to sleep. So when it stopped, things started to heat up, fast, and the noises of the insects got louder and louder. Dad gave his son two choices, one sleep in the lounge, with a small ceiling fan to keep them cool, option two, sleep on the balcony, Michael chose the latter. Thinking about it, it was a no brainer, yes the noises of the insects would be tough to deal with, but after a while you would get used to them, the main plus though was the breeze, that would really help him sleep, also the balcony was huge, so he could pick and choose his view, with that he dragged his bed with mosquito netting onto the balcony, got comfy and enjoyed one of the best sleeps of his life.

Michael was a Scout, veteran of at least three tours of some of the worst campsites Britain had to offer. So this was bliss compared.

Sunday 8th May – Club/Villa.
'Went to the Club, saw Benny Hill,
Then home to do Homework'

Like most teenage boys, it took Michael a good fifteen minutes to fully wake up. He gradual sat up, rubbed his eyes, ready for the new day ahead, it was at this point he noticed his briefs had come off during the night, so was completely naked, yet he wasn't cold, in fact he was boiling, he might not of completely woken up yet, but the sun waits for no man, or boy. Of course Michael wasn't completely *bare*. He had a hat on, a baseball cap to be exact, or to be 100% correct, it was a dark blue navy cap from a visiting New Zealand navy vessel. The amount of beach football matches Michael had played against visiting armed forces personal was amazing, they all loved Michael, and he could of started a hat store with the amount of caps he was given. So bare but happy Michael went back to sleep.

About 8am, Michael heard Dad shouting for his lazy arse son to get up, Michael put on his Briefs, got up and looked out over his part of Pakistan, it didn't matter he had been naked, no one overlooked the villa, they overlooked the neighbourhood. Ah what a morning thought Michael, it was at this point he idly scratched his arm, damn those mosquito's, he felt a couple more spots, 'what the?' was the only words he spoke until he found Dad.

It took Dad two whole minutes to stop laughing, what else could he do, his son was completely covered on the right side of his body, arm leg and torso in mosquito bites, his left was fine, not a bite in sight. It was like a before and after photo, finally dad caught his breath and could speak again, 'you dozy sod, did you even have the netting up?' Michael was still in a state of panic when he replied 'of course I did, my arm must of fallen out during the night and let them in' it was at this point Steve walked into the kitchen and carried on where Dad had just finished, however unlike Dad, steve couldn't stop laughing and left the room just as quickly as he had arrived. Dad felt it was his duty to make sure his son would be ok, partly because he was Michaels dad, and partly because Mum had threatened to leave him if her son came home with so much as a scratch let alone malaria. 'You have been taking your tablets haven't you?' enquired a slightly worried father now remembering his wife's threat, Luckily for dad, despite the fact the Tablets were huge things with ICI stamped on them, and they tasted of dust, yes, Michael had been taking his Malaria tablets. Dad sighed with relief, 'thank fuck for that'. A quick call later to the company Doctor, using the nearby corner stores phone, it was confirmed Michael would be alright, but his was not to scratch the spots, and was to make sure the bloody netting was put up properly next time, so what to do now, it was Sunday, so no work, no newspapers or comics till at least until tomorrow, so it was either homework or the looking out of a balcony.

Michael loved looking out of his bedroom balcony, the view was just desert, there was something so cold and lonely about that, it was just sand and more sand, with the odd snake, but today he would spice things up, and look out the front balcony, which at least had a road and some houses to look at. Ten minutes past, with barely a soul breaking the silence, bar the odd local making their way to the local shop, Michael was about to go in, when he noticed movement coming from the same bush he had passed the night before, on the way home from the wedding, something wasn't right, but he couldn't put his finger on it, for the next hour he was fixated by the bush, then all fell silent and still, He was about to go in when the brushes parted, and for a brief second he saw at least three, no four people, two kids and two adults, sitting around what appeared to be some sort of make shift camp site, Michael also spotted smoke coming from the vicinity, *were people living there*, no, they couldn't be!. In his short time in the country, Michael had seen plenty of poverty and crippled kids, but never thought about where they went at night, where they lived. But here right in front of him, opposite his house, a family was living in a bush, it was too much for a young boy to take in, and he was thankful when Dad asked if he wanted to go to the club. Michael didn't even mind the piss taking he got from the regulars about his bites, he just hoped that nights video or film would help take his mind to a happier place, it did not.

Benny hill, *Benny bloody hill!*. You can only say the phrase, it *was a different era,* so many times before it losses all Meaning, but when your thousands of miles from home, and there's no TV in the house, and if someone sticks a VHS tape in the machine, you're going to watch it, it could have been the mating ritual of the aardvark, and people would have still watched it. But Benny hill?, even then, in 1983, it felt cheesy, still in a Muslim country the sight of a half-naked woman running around was nice treat, no matter how sexist the program was. An hour later they were on their way home, and although Michael had become an expert at putting it off, it was time, time to do his Homework.

Back at the villa, Michael grabbed a coke and a sandwich, then headed to his room, full of good intentions, he sat at his desk, got his books out and waited, not quite sure what he was waiting for, but he waited none the less. The problem with been left to your own devices was thus, if there's easy homework, or hard homework, your goner leave the maths and science until your back in England, then pull an all night-er the night before your due back at school. So it was no to Maths and Physics, a maybe for biology, it was just "write names of organs next to the picture" type work, Arm, Leg, Eye, that sort of thing, then Michael looked at the English *punishment*, a couple of spelling tests, some grammar rubbish, and write a story, well how hard can that be? Two hours later he had moved beyond writing a simple short story, this was going to be a book, no a *novel*, he liked writing stories, so why do a short one, instead write a long one and see what happens. But what to what to write about, hmm Love maybe, nope, Helen had broken his heart, comedy, that could work, crime, now that sells, so began, - 'The case that had to be won'

It had to be sexy, dark, and set in a foreign country. A quick think later and it was decided, the location would be the United States, the Deep South, 1950's maybe 60's, people loved retro shit, centred around a court room drama. Michael would go on to write twelve chapters, but never finish it, things always seemed to crop up.

Tuesday 10th May – Villa.
'Stayed at home and played with the Gun'

Now really that should read Air Gun, NOT *Shot gun*, or *machine* gun, just Air Gun!

Michael had stayed home since the whole mosquito incident, and was bored, he was that bored, half the maths home work had been completed, well attempted at any rate, he had also written three chapters of his book, needing a break from school work, he went for a walk around the villa. Everyone was either at work or asleep, even Ali was out, visiting family, possibly, no one quite knew what Ali got up to half the time, in part due to the language barrier , also Ali smiled all the time, whenever anyone spoke to him, Ali would just smile and go and do his own thing, class act. Michael would often day dream that Ali was a spy of some sort, and the house boy would disappear during the day and report back to his handlers, well it was more exciting than Thinking Ali was going Fishing for the tenth time that week. Although quite what Ali could report back to the Pakistan secret service puzzled Michael, maybe how much Mango and fish the Villa went through in a month, because it was a lot.

Michael found himself on the bedroom balcony, with the Villa's air gun, he had about 30 rounds and a desert to aim at. The first five pellets were wasted on rocks and the ground, with the shooter trying to learn the arch of the barrel. Michael had become quite a marksman along South-end's Shooting galleries, he knew it would take a round or two to get to know the guns and how far the barrel's and sight's had been, well for no better word, because it was true, *bent* by the people running the stalls, once you knew, bang the top prizes were yours. So

now Michael knew the gun, it was time to shoot something, the trouble is in the dessert you have birds and lizards, and birds flew to high and lizards were hard to spot, so it became a waiting game, and five minutes later the big game hunter was rewarded, with some big game indeed, a dog, no ordinary Dog, no it was the Villa's guard dog, Rabies. It of course got the name because it *had* rabies, and foamed nicely at the mouth; however through some sense of loyalty to the Villa it patrolled the area, and never seemed interested
In attacking Michael, or the rest.

Michael wasn't a cruel kid, far from it, he really did feel sorry for the creature, and he had thought to himself many a time, no animal should live this way, and now it was up to him to help good old Rabies out. The first shot was a joke, a clear foot wide to the right, *damn wind* thought Michael, the second was better, then again how could it not be, the third actually made the dog stop licking itself, but was still a clear three inches off, Rabies thought the fly of whatever it was that had landed on the rock in front of it had now gone, so went back to licking. 'Ok, this was it' mumbled the great white hunter, Michael had a good feeling about the next shot, he carefully lifted the weapon, gently nestled the gun's butt into his shoulder, then waited, waited for the wind and sun to be just right, as he waited sweat started to form on his brow, then *bang,* Michael fired, well it was more pop then bang, but who cared, he *hit* the dog, he actually hit the damn thing. Michael had never felt such an achievement, was this the start of bigger things, he felt he could do anything, including a little jig, as the boy from Essex danced around the balcony, Rabies got up started to slowly walk away, Michael saw this and stooped his merry dance, 'no' he whispered, 'it can't be', he had hit the dog square on the head, yet it lived, how could this be? Michael then panicked what would Dad say? this was the first time he had thought about this, what if Rabies was missing an eye? Or half its head? he couldn't clearly see all the dogs skull, well there was no choice now, he had to finish the job, so Michael grabbed another pellet, cocked the gun, placed the pellet in the rifles chamber, then closed the gun, '*Shit*'

As Michael walked along the dusty road to the shops, he couldn't believe what had just happened, closing the gun on his index finger, what a tit. How was he going to explain the gaping wound and pouring blood to dad, but that was a problem for later, now he needed help, with no one at home, and no 999 service, he had but one hope, the shop at the end of the road, he wasn't expecting medical help, just the help of an adult. Michael burst into the store, a quick scan revealed there were no other customers, this was good news as he could feel himself getting weaker, was he going to pass out!, no, he needed to be strong, so with all the effort he could muster, Michael walked up to the counter, said no thank you to the free 7 up he was offered, and showed the shop clerk his finger, a single drop of blood fell onto the old wooden counter, Michael apologised. For a brief moment both parties stared at each other, the old man then walked into the back, and returned shortly with a box, he carefully opened it, took out some cotton wool, poured some of the 7 up onto to it, cleaned the wound then found a small plaster and wrapped it round the finger, Michael smiled and left, not even for a second thinking about paying the man or even a handshake.

Michael walked out the store and started the brief journey back to the villa, about halfway he realised that this was the first time he had been *in the store on his own,* perhaps he didn't need adult supervision any more, then again he did just lose half a finger in a botched hunting accident, as he pondered this thought Michael saw Rabies playing with a tin, it looked up and woofed, then went back to its game, damn dog cursed Michael, although he wasn't completely unhappy the dog would live to see another day.

Thursday 12th May – Work/Club.
'Went to work, later went to club, saw return of the pink panther'

Michael had taken the Wednesday off, to get over the whole "firearm ordeal" and was looking to take the Thursday off as well, dad however had a different take on the situation, and between the fits of laughter, had managed to compose himself *just* long enough to make it quite clear his Son was going into work, as dad walked to the car, he burst out laughing again, how could *anyone* hurt themselves with a gun, that at close range wouldn't peel the skin of a grape, let alone the skin of a dog?, nope dad couldn't get his head around it.

Michael's boss Matthew of course was a different story, 'Are you sure you're ok?' his English was really coming along nicely, 'if you still feel unwell I take you to the nurse station, then home', the offer of a nurse then home was tempting, but Michael needed to prove to himself, and Dad, that he was a big boy, no, not a boy, but an adult, and he could handle life's big problems. So he thanked Matthew for his concern, than sat down at his desk, ready for the day ahead. By 11am Michaels head was dropping, by Lunch he was all but a sleep, thankfully Dad appeared and took him to lunch, maybe dad had felt bad about laughing at his Son's misfortune, or maybe he was just worried what the boy would do next to his body. The rest of the afternoon just seemed to fly by, and before Michael could get a decent sleep in the loos, it was home time, once home it was shower, change, dinner then the club.

Maybe it was the fact it had been a *long* week, or it was down to the heat, it had been especially hot that day, whatever it was no one was interested in staying for more than a couple of hours, so whilst dad did some business with the barman, Michael sat down to watch that nights film, Return of the pink panther. Although not a huge fan of Peter Sellers, it was still silly enough for Michael to enjoy, and he loved the fight scenes, if you could call them that between Cato and Clouseau. After the film Michael went to find dad, who was just concluding his business deal. So Michael had time for a quick coke.

They arrived back at the villa around 9pm, although a little tired, Michael had missed his mid-afternoon power nap, he wasn't tired enough to go to bed, so he sat down in the villa's lounge, and picked up a random newspaper from the coffee table and started to read it. Michael couldn't believe his luck, the paper he had picked up was a Times newspaper, from only four days ago! And being the Sunday edition had loads of sports news and cartoons, he would enjoy this, but where to start, with the football pages of course. By 10 his eye lids started to feel heavy, so he decided to call it a night and sloped off to bed, although he was now tired it

still took a clear hour for Michael to drift off. At first it was a just a dream. A dream of a hundred frogs all saying 'pop', however the popping would not stop, and started to get louder, slowly Michael opened his eyes and swore no more cheese before bed time, he then saw the time, 1am? Bloody 1 in the morning, it was still dark? What the hell was he doing up at 1 am? The next pop made him sit bolt upright, was he still dreaming? He half expected a frog to hop in the bedroom and say 'pop', instead a flustered steve run in and shouted 'It's the beer' then run to the spare bedroom opposite, on hearing the word beer, dad jumped out of bed, stark naked, and run to help. By the time Michael arrived, complete with a robe for dad, half the beer bottles had already blown their capped tops; it was an incredible sight, bottle after bottle blowing their tops like some Volcano or Geyser, shooting clear 3 % liquid refreshment into the air. By now the whole house hold was up, all trying to stem the warm brown tide, an hour later they had done all they could and went downstairs, everyone was shattered and sticky. Ali made some Tea, the group sat around the kitchen table, long faced and pissed off, 'over half lost' mumbled Steve, '6 weeks down the fucking drain' said dad, being fourteen, Michael couldn't understand the problem, it wasn't like beer was hard to get in the country, so he had his tea and went to bed, he left the moping Minnie's to their sad tea party.

Chapter Five.

Larry the lobster.

Saturday 14th May - Villa.
'Stayed at home, did not go to club'
Liverpool 1:0 Watford
Position – Top.
Last game of the season.

So that was that, the English league division one was over for
another season, yet again Michael's team had won the title,
Liverpool, *the mighty reds*. He had supported them Since 77, so
with over ten trophies won from then to now, it was a great
time to support them. but with the final whistle came elation,
then sadness, yes they had won, but now the last real tie with
England had gone, it was his one real reason to read the
papers, yes he loved his cartoons and sometimes the news
could be funny or interesting, but from that point onwards the
whole experience of getting news from home would seem
empty. Now if Michael had been a cricket man, well, for
starters the season was just starting in the UK, so the papers
would be full of cricketing stories, and being in Pakistan, one
of the big cricketing power houses, we'll all one had to do was
step outside, even into the desert and you could find a match,
kids with no shoes playing in the dirt, and loving it, But
Michael just wasn't interested, so went to stare out onto the
world

Sunday 15th May – Villa.
'Went to work, got home, stayed in all night,
And did nothing. Oh and Larry the lobster turned up'

Bored and a little depressed, Michael sat on his bed looking
out at the desert, yet again it was another friends Birthday, this
time it was one of Michaels closest school friends, Trevor was
having his birthday today, and Michael wouldn't be there to

wish him all the best. It seemed every week Michael was missing someone's birthday or celebration, to cap the perfect day off he also going to work, on a Sunday! Michael turned to look at the clock, he sighed, it was 7am, 7am and he was fully awake. With no chance of going back to sleep Michael went down to the kitchen, Ali was there working on that night's dinner, it would involve crab and lobster, some of which were still alive and in the sink. Steve walked in fully awake and chipper, god Michael couldn't stand people like that in the morning. 'You pissed the bed again, not often you're up before you're old fella' Michael laughed in a sarcastic manner. 'Ha ha' Steve got some juice out of the fridge 'But seriously where is he?, if he doesn't get a shake on we'll be late' Steve tried to get a glass, but they were located next to the wildlife that currently occupied the sink, every time he went for one a pincer would snap at a finger, Ali quietly laughed at the daft white man, 'Well he was still fast asleep when I came down' replied Michael. Steve gave up on the Glass hunt, 'We'll go and shake him or something' Michael knew better than to wake dad, if he was asleep there was a reason for it, 'I'm sure he'll be up in a minute' Lied Michael, Steve also knew better than to wake the old man so it was stalemate. 'We could ask Ali?' ventured Michael, Steve paced as he spoke 'no, we have to be clever, we need to use stealth and cunning' 'we could throw a class of water over him' joked Michael, Steve stared at the Sink. 'Hmm, maybe not, come on think'.

By the time the pair had reached the top of the stairs they had dropped Larry three times, yes he would be cooked later, but Michael still felt for the creature every time it hit the floor. As they opened the bedroom door they gave Dad one last chance to wake up, they gently knocked on the bedside cabinet next to him, but he was out, out cold, so they put Larry to work, making sure he wasn't put to close to anything *too* sensitive, so they gently put Larry on the bed and walked out the room. As they walked down the stairs they heard dad get up, screaming for someone's blood, he just didn't know who's? 'What the fuck? Who bloody!' dad couldn't get his words out fast enough, he had woken from a dream into a nightmare, or was he still dreaming? No, he was awake, so he went to find the idiots who had put a live lobster in his bed. He didn't have to go far and spotted his prey from the top of the staircase 'You bastards' pointed dad at the pair who hadn't quite made the bottom of the stairs. '*You* I understand' dad pointed at Steve 'but YOU' he pointed at Michael, who should have been scared but couldn't stop laughing, Finally Michael could speak, 'Morning dad' Steve then burst out laughing. Dad walked back into the bedroom muttering 'bastards' as he went. It would take dad most of the day to speak to either of them, and a lot longer to forgive them.

Monday 16th May – Work/beach.
'Went to work, got home, went to club,
Saw an officer and a gentleman.

As Michael woke to yet another sunny day, he made a vow, a vow to stop being so down on life, letting things like birthdays and other missed events make him feel left out, and alone, so from today he would try and enjoy himself. This would start with work.

Michael stood tall in the early morning heat, he knew what to do, it was time to finally finish his masterpiece, if he could finish the table, it would more than make up for all the failed wood work projects he had fluffed or screwed up over the years at school. No scratch that, there was one project he had completed at Mayflower, a few months back he had actually made something in shop, despite not being the most skilled of carpenters; he had made a piano, it was about 6 inches wide and long and about three inches deep, it had five keys, strapped to on end, and when you played it went *plink*. Despite all this Michael could not have been happier, as far as he was concerned it might as well been a Steinway. But today he would top that achievement, if only in size.

After an hour of staring at the wooden pieces, a plan was formed. 'Of course' said a surprised Michael, 'It's that easy', so armed only with a tub load of nails, two hammers and a can do attitude; a table was born, then destroyed, the tin can he had placed on the table top to find out if it was level or not, had committed suicide, *hmm* thought Michael, maybe I could make it a little straighter. models two and three were no better, Four though was awesome, and level, it totally passed the tin can test, everything was fine until Michael did a mad thing, he put **three** cans on the table top, for ten whole seconds all was well, then a leg gave way. 'Ok, make the legs fatter' Michael mumbled to himself.

By three o'clock Michael had produced a table he was happy with, well at least the top of one, yet again there was a problem with the legs, and was working on a plan to make them more stable when dad arrived. Dad was more than happy to see his son trying to be creative with his hands, even though it was taking him forever to produce an end item, which made the following comment even harder to say, 'What do you mean we can't get it home?' Michael Jnr couldn't believe what he was hearing, 'Sorry son, but it won't fit in the boot of the car' dad really was sorry, but he couldn't change the laws of physics, 'maybe next time measure before building?' Dad was only trying to help, but Michael was not in the mood. After a short argument/discussion, a deal was reached, once finished it would go in Dads office. At least it would be safe there and Michael could see it each morning, this seemed to pacify the boy somewhat, but Michael still wasn't 100% happy, so dad decided the club was the way to go. So off they went.

It had been a few days since dad and son had been to the club, yet Despite this nothing had changed, then again nothing had changed at the club for the last five years, well that wasn't strictly true, for tonight there was a new movie, Richard Gere's latest, an officer and a gentleman. Michael enjoyed it, but was expecting more action from a film which had a back drop of the armed forces, but of course this wasn't another war film, no this was a bromantic drama, in which a distraught Gere decides Debra Winger's arms will be warmer than his dead buddies. The film also had the uplifting love song "lift us up where we belong", a timeless classic, sung by Joe Cocker and Jennifer Warnes, which Michael kept humming to himself for the rest of the evening, and got right on Dad's nerves.

Wednesday 18th May – Work/Club.
'Went to work, got home, played my new cassette player, Went to the club'

Pay day was still a week away! How did people manage to live on monthly pay cheques? Michael just couldn't get his head around it. He sulked his way into the kitchen and sat down to his healthy breakfast, still lost in thought over money, or lack of it, god he was sick of bananas and mangos, what he would do for a bowel of frosties. Dad of course had picked up on the *subtle* vibes coming from his teenage, this had been going on for two days now, and it was starting to get on his nerves. Part of the problem of course was his stick insect of a son was spoilt, if the boy wanted stuff he got it, maybe not the same day or week, but he got it in the end, an Atari wooden Computer game system, done, Action man tank and truck done, Star wars action figures and Death Star done, however the reality of the situation was simply, it was all Dad's fault, after all he was the one that bloody bought all the stuff over the years.

As Michael dragged himself to the front door, he noticed Dave and Steve pulling out of the drive way in the spare car, he then spotted dad next to the Toyota, 'Where are they off to' enquired Michael staring at the dust cloud left by lads, 'they need to be in early, and we have something to do before we go in' replied dad. As they drove away from the villa, Michael stared blankly at the surroundings and its natives, he was so engrossed looking out the window, It took him full five minutes to notice something was different, his first clue was instead of turning right then left at the end of their road, they went right and stayed on the main highway. 'Is this a quicker way or something?' Dad didn't take his eyes of the tarmac. 'As I said, we have something to do first' Michael went back to his sulk, *Great* thought Michael, another mindless trip or meeting with some dodgy guy who was selling a weird or wonderful item no one wanted, expect dad. Dad had form in this area, the rubbish he would come home with after bumping into *some guy* in a pub, that's where the family's monkey came from, a monkey? A Marmoset no less! What was the guy doing with it in the pub to start with? Then Dad bought home an ATM, well the guts of one anyway, because Michael liked computers?? So god knows what they would end up with today. Half an hour later they hit a small amount of shops houses and cows, lots of cows, a market must have been on. Soon dad found the shop he was looking for, so parked up, got out the car and walked in the shop, Michael tried to make out what sort of business it was, the store had crude hand painted symbols on the walls, one appeared to be a TV. Five minutes later dad left the store holding a box, *no* thought Michael, *no he hasn't*, dad got back in the car and handed his son a box, Michael could tell straight away what it was, 'thanks dad, but I don't get paid until next week' dad smiled 'just pay me back then, and no more sulking, ok' Michael found himself hugging his Dad, a rare event indeed, with the group hug out of the way dad started the car and looked in the rear view mirror, 'Come on then, let's get going, some of us have work to do' Dad drove of a happy man, yes he had given in to a pouting teenager, and yes he did it for a quiet life. But in the end it came to doing what you do as a parent, trying to bring your kids up right and make them happy when you can. The rest of the journey was a blur, Michael had a Walkman, ok it wasn't a Sony Walkman, but it did the same job at the end of the day, he took it out the box and looked on in wonder at the big grey brick of an item, did it have batteries, *yes*, thank god, then it hit him, he didn't have any tapes! *Bugger*, but it did have a radio, ok it would be local music and chat, but so what, Michael put the headphones on and tuned into a local station, whilst listening to some people yak on in Urdu, Michael thought on about what tape he would listen to first, Queen? Abba? Survivor? Hmm this was a big choice.

The rest of the day Michael sat clock watching, he could of course go at any time, Matthew would have said yes to anything Michael asked of him, but there was no way he could have got home on foot, as for public transport, that was not an option, so he had to wait. Bang on 4pm Michael rushed to Dads car, and waited, eventually dad appeared, he was holding a letter, *Ah dads been to the local post office* thought Michael. There was in fact no post office on site, just a made up postal system, and it work surprising well. Next to the main site cabin was another slightly smaller cabin, which had pigeon holes put in it, and anyone who worked at the hospital could have a pigeon hole, and it wasn't just for local post, sometimes loved ones from abroad didn't have the local address for husbands or wives, so would send post to the hospital instead. Maybe the letter was from mum thought Michael, because dad was smiling, a very big smile indeed.

Once back at the villa, Michael rushed straight to his room, all the way home he had thought about opening the letter, but there was no way he was going to do that with dad nearby, no this was to be done in private. He stared at the envelope for a good five minutes, then tore into it, why would she be writing to him, what did she want? After reading it a second time, Michael lay back on his bed and put a tape on. Of course Queen would be the first band he would listen to on his new cassette player, but what album?, in the end the greatest hits was chosen, so whilst Freddie and the gang crashed on about some fat bottomed girls, and bicycle races, Michael dreamt of the 23rd, and his next meeting with Helen.

Friday 20th May – Pool/Club,
Day Off, went to the midway swimming pool, went to the club, And played snooker.

After the excitement of the Walkman and getting a letter from Helen, Michael was emotionally spent, he didn't really want to go to work, and thankfully the rest of the villa agreed, although for different reasons. The home brew, well what was left of it after the night of a thousand exploding bottles, was now ready, and had been drunk the night before, so it was hang overs all round. To get over this, the villa headed for a local hotel, the midway, it was nice clean and above all *quiet*. The occupants of the hotel were mainly Europeans, and the odd rich local. Basically it was a nice escape for people that didn't want to deal with the real Pakistan first thing on a Friday morning. After a dip, then a quick snooze, it was off to the club, for a couple of games of snooker and some coke, however despite all the activities and fun, Michael was really just treading water until the 23rd. what did she want?

Saturday 21st May – Villa.
'Stayed home, did some homework'
FA CUP FINAL
Manchester United 2:2 Brighton – Reply needed.

There was one distraction in Michaels life, one event that could temporary divert Michaels thoughts about his upcoming meeting with Helen, the FA cup. It didn't even matter his beloved Liverpool weren't involved, at 14, football was football, and Liverpool had won so much that year, that one less trophy wouldn't really matter, also listening to the FA cup made England feel that little bit *closer*. The only problem was the time difference, Kick off was 3pm GMT, which would be 8pm local time, so Michael needed something to do for the next coup[le of hours. .

Like all students who know they have to do *some* school work but really didn't want to, Michael decided to waste an hour setting his stall out, making sure he had enough pens and pencils, his desk and chair were aligned in such away he would get a cool breeze, yet not be distracted by the view, *ah yes* he thought, snacks and drinks, I'll need them. 4pm he was ready, ready to choose want subject to hit first, would it be maths, English, science or RE, well straight away it was a no to maths, it was too damn hot for that type of thinking, and would be done in time honoured tradition, rushed the night before going back to school, plus Michael did some of his better work under pressure. English was a possibility, it was mainly an exercise to help with joined up writing, a skill he lacked, *hmm maybe*. Science would go the way of Maths, then there was RE, religious education, still compulsory at this point, but thank god he would loss it next year, it wasn't that Michael didn't believe, it was that he had much better things to do with his time then go to church every Sunday, and pray to an invisible being. Still it was easy enough, read five pages of a school text book, and write a three page story based on the events he had read about, the story was of Noah, so Michael read the pages then wrote a story, he liked writing stories, it allowed him to be creative.

By 6pm he had nailed both RE and English, and with two hours to kick-off, Michael headed to the kitchen for a snack, but this would only kill fifteen minutes, half an hour tops, Michael would have to find something else to do until the match started. There was of course his book, he could work on that, however the court room drama story line was starting to loss its appeal, bored he went on to the balcony, and looked out on the dusty hot surroundings. Whilst eating a mango he looked down on to the villas lawn, there as always was Ali's bed, complete with mosquito netting. It amazed Michael that a man in his 60's, would sleep every night, outside to protect them, with just his wits and a big machete. Still it worked, no one ever bothered them, although it did bother Michael that Ali never seemed to see his wife or kids, then again the money Ali made most of helped the family have a better life, that or he didn't like them much. At 7.45pm Michael was next to the villas radio, a huge thing with dials and knobs, frequency's from all around the world written on it. After ten minutes he found it, the world service, the build-up was all but over, this didn't bother Michael too much, he was more about the game itself and couldn't understand why people tuned in to listen to ex pros bang on for two hours about something that hadn't happened yet?, anyway the game was five minutes away, Just enough time for the lads to get the final batch of home brew down from upstairs, and Michael to get some snacks.

Bang on 8pm the match began. Manchester united were and should have been clear favourites, with the likes of Robson, Wilkins, Stapleton and Whiteside in their side, but Brighton proved their worth by taking the lead on 14 minutes through Gordon smith, and that's how the first half finished, at half time everyone went on a beer/coke/sandwich run, then sat down to discuss the first half. Around 8.45pm the 2nd half kicked off. by the 50th minute Michael was bored, not with the game, good end to end stuff, but re dialling the radio to find the game, every five minutes a crackle would start then slowly they would lose the signal and Michael would have to find it again. Then on the 55th Minute united hit back, through Irish international Frank Stapleton, this was followed by Englishman Ray Wilkins who scored on the 72nd minute, untied would surely go onto win now, but brave Brighton hit back, on the 87th Minute, whilst Michael was again on dial duty, Brighton scored, he was next to the speaker so the crowds row nearly put in on his arse, Brighton had scored through defender Gary Stevens, with the game finishing a draw it was down to extra time, Gordon smith had an easy chance to win it for Brighton, but in the end it was a draw, they would play again five days from now, same place, but this time at night.

Sunday 22nd May – Work/Villa/Club.
'Went to work, read some of my book, went to club, got there early, Saw film, convoy'

As soon as Michael walked in the office, he could tell it was going to be a busy day, however this was not the reason why Akram wore a worried expression on his face, no this was down to Michael, well Michael and Matthew. For Akram was Matthew's right hand man, and Akram loved this, normally, he had some power with little responsibility. But today Matthew was off, a rare holiday, today was also stock take day, and after the last one, where Michael had an all too close run in with a certain snake, Akram was now cursing Matthew for leaving him in charge. But the temporary boss had a plan.

Michael felt a bit of a fool as he adjusted his goggles, partly because they were slightly too big for him, also no one else was wearing any, but he know this would calm Akram down, but the gloves were a step to far thought Michael, so was the body guards, two of the day workers were tasked with following Michael and checking the racks and rooms for anything that slithered or had teeth, the two lads of course were in shorts and t-shirts, and had no goggles or gloves, however by now this sort of double standards no longer surprised him. By 2, it was all over, and Michael could take of his PPE (Personal protective equipment) and Akram could finally relax and go back to cursing Matthew. By 4pm Michael had completed his Audit paper work and was done for the day, so he went to the canteen and had a very late lunch, whilst waiting for dad to finish.

Once home it was a quick change then the club, everyone was excited, for tonight's film was *Convoy*. The timeless classic, made in 1978, everyone had seen it several times over the years, but still loved it, what wasn't to love? It had Truckers forming a mile long convoy in support of one their own, who was having problems with a sheriff, who was out to get him, and of course there was plenty on CB chatter. Michael, like most kids in the earlier 80's, had at some point used a CB radio, it was the first time you could talk to people from around the world, from your bedroom, although in reality it was mainly people from the local area, or at best someone from the next town over, but it was still good fun. The film had attracted a large crowd, dad had anticipated this, and had got their seats early. Third row centre, he had always said to Michael they were the best seats, 'first and second rows are just too close to the screen, fourth onwards to far back' dad also factored in the pillars, and the AC unit in the room, for a plumber he sure know he stuff when it came to the best seat in the house, so father and son seat together and watched the classic road movie.

Monday 23rd – work/Holiday Inn.
'Went to work today, found out when I will get paid.
Went to holiday Inn'

'Wednesday?' exclaimed Michael 'yes son Wednesday', Michael tried to take it in, 'But I thought pay day was today' dad was a little bored with the conversation but tried to reason with his son 'It's only two more days, look I'll see you at lunch time' as dad strolled of towards the building site, Michael was left to work out what he was going to do, he still hadn't told dad he was meeting someone later at the holiday inn.

Work was a blur, Matthew was also back, and was trying to engage Michael in conversation about his family, Matthew explained he had taken time off so he could witness his son pass out from school, his son was now a man, Matthew was very proud; Michael tried to sound happy about Matthews news, but had things on his mind. Eventually it was lunch time, Michael said bye to Matthew, who was a little puzzled at first 'Sorry I do not understand, you are leaving early?' 'Yes we've got that thing on today, all the engineers are having that meeting' a light bulb flashed in Matthew's eyes. 'of course that's today, sorry a thousand apologises' as Michael walked off to find dad, a tinge of guilt kicked in, he felt sorry for the local workers, the so called meeting was just an excuse to meet at a hotel, talk shop for twenty minutes, then sit by the pool for the rest of the day. Terry would also be there, so that meant Helen would be to. As the group arrived at the Holiday Inn, Michael suddenly felt a lot better, Terry wasn't due for hours, he had time to get a swim in and work on his tan, whilst listening to Abbas greatest hits. Dad and the rest of the engineers walked into conference room A and quarter past one, by 2 they were stripped to their costumes and walking to their sun loungers with cocktails in their hands, life was a bitch sometimes.

Michael had a problem, and it was quite a big one, his Walkman it didn't auto switch, so just as he would start to doze off to the beat of dancing queen, the tape would stop, and he would have to eject the cassette and start all over again, although how could anyone sleep with desert after desert being delivered pool side by waiters, with the odd Coke or Pepsi, was anyone's guess. By 3pm though he was a sleep, however twenty minutes later a shadow woke him up, another banana spilt maybe?, dad must of ordered it, when he opened his eyes he soon realised it was no spilt, just a girl, aged 15, wearing a bikini, 'Oh hi Helen'. As soon as he sat up, even without looking around, he could tell three pairs of eyes were staring at him and Helen, not sure what to do, Michael got up and started to walk Helen to the inside bar, 'Fancy a coke?' asked a nervous Michael 'sure' Replied Helen, she then smiled, the smile didn't help his hormones, *oh god* he thought, not a good time to be wearing swimming trunks, then he remembered, he had no money! thinking fast he hatched a plan, 'Helen you find us a seat, I'll meet you in there, I just need to grab my wallet' 'ok, just don't be too *long*' as she replied she stared straight into his eyes, and that dammed smile was back, of course she was just teasing and having a bit of fun with him, but Michael found himself next to Dad within two seconds of leaving Helens side, Dad had already put two and two together and now realised why his son had been asking when he was going to be paid, so he knew what was coming next, but decided to have some fun with his son. '*Dad*' 'Yes son' 'could I have a word' Dad sat up, 'Of course son' Michael for a second didn't know what to say, this was embarrassing. 'I don't suppose you have any spare change I could borrow' Michael put on his best smile, Dad seemed to take an age replying, Michael looked in the direction on the bar, 'Let me get this right, first I buy you that tape thing, buy you cokes and ice creams here' Michael was in a hurry and interrupted 'Dad!' by now Dave and Steve could not contain themselves and started to giggle. '*Dad*, dad please' Dad had had his fun and pulled some money out of his wallet 'Ok, but be home by 5, and don't spend it all in the same place' Michael was in too much of a hurry to reply or hear the laughing hyena's, and hopped and skipped his way into the bar.

After a quick search of the bar area, he spotted her sitting next to a window, on a wicker settee, he asked what drink she wanted, and two 7 up's latter she was explaining why she had asked to meet him again. Helen confessed she was embarrassed by the way it had ended at her parents' house party, where they had kissed, also she liked Michael, as a friend of course, and as she didn't have many friends, thought it would be nice to meet again and chat. 'So again sorry, my parents can be a real pain some times' 'hey don't worry about it, I had a good time' lied Michael, after that the conversation became a little awaked, apart from his mum and sister, he rarely spoke to Females, and he could tell Helen was starting to get bored. All Michael could talk about was sport, Music and the scouts? She didn't look like she was into Football, what girl was? And scouts was for boys, so all that was left was music, but what if she laughed at the type of music he liked!, then a plan formed, his Walkman had a belt clip attachment, and was currently hanging on his trunks, he careful un clipped it and put it on the table, just matter of fact, 'Sorry carrying on Helen, this was digging into my hip' 'Oh you've got one as well' exclaimed Helen, 'they're the best aren't they' this opened the flood gates, she couldn't stop talking after that, about the bands she liked and bands she didn't, Michael had heard of some of them, and even liked a couple, she was really into Culture club, Adam and the ants, and Paul young. She then moved on to Hair and makeup, via Adam and his ants, after an hour she started to lose steam, Michael was just going to order some more drinks when Terry appeared, a little worse for wear, and although Helen had seen it all before, she still sank into her chair, deeply embarrassed, she weekly smiled at Michael, he shot her a knowing glance, they both had been through this before, so many times. '*Helen love*, have you seen your mother?' Terry was barely able to stand yet alone understand his surroundings, 'Dad mum's at home' 'what, oh that's right, silly me' Terry then staggered to the left, he managed to stop himself before falling over, but he was now pointing away from the group, 'So where am I, oh that's right, Helen its..' realising he was pointing the wrong way, he turned to the wicker sofa 'Come on Helen its time to go, and I need your help to find the car' he fumbled with his car keys then dropped them, after several attempts he found them on the floor, he then stood up and took a second to compose himself, gently swaying in the wind, he then remembered he had a daughter and what he was doing before he dropped his keys, 'Come on let's go,' it was at this point Terry realised he was talking to himself.

Helen had fled, dragging Michael with her, eventually they stopped, finding themselves alone in a corridor linking the bar to the underground car park, ''Don't you think we should look after your..' Michael had no time to finish his sentence as he found his mouth busy kissing Helen, maybe high on the moment, or down to the sheer amount of sugar she had consumed, Helen had launched herself at Michael. At first taken a back, he soon found himself enjoying his first real kiss, yet as soon as it started it stopped, Helen pulled away and gave him the dirtiest grin he had ever seen, she giggled then ran in to a cupboard, it took his brain a few seconds to catch up and ask, *why aren't you following her?*. As he entered the small broom cupboard Helen put her arms around him, 'I almost gave up on you there for a moment' he smiled and tried to come up with a witty reply, only to find again his lips were busy, this time the experience lasted a lot longer. After a minute of heavy petting Michael's mind started to wander, he was thinking back to his close friends, and their experiences with the opposite sex, was there a move he should make now, some of the stories were obviously made up, one friend had been given a blow job by a 25 year old model, someone else said they had gone all the way with a teacher, however there was one that sounded realistic, and this would be Michael's move, without thinking Michael's sweaty right hand moved towards Helens breasts. As soon as he touched her she recoiled, 'Sorry I didn't meant to, I just assumed' she took a second to compose herself, then she kissed him, putting his hand back on her bosom, 'it's all right, you just took me by surprise' she panted, his move seemed to have excited her, they were now *very* heavy petting, this went on for a further two minutes before Terry could be heard shouting, sometimes swearing for Helen. After another twenty seconds Helen pulled her lips from Michael's, straightened her outfit and left the cupboard, Michael stood there still not sure what had just happened, Helen then peered back around the door 'To be continued' she then left to find her dad. Michael decided to wait a few minutes for things to calm down his end, before looking for his dad. And what the hell did she mean by *to be continued.?*

Wednesday 25th May – Work/Club.
'Got paid 500Rupees,
Dave the site super handed them out. got home, went to club.

Pay day at last, Michael could barely eat his breakfast for the excitement and was first in the car, 'I don't know what you're so excited about, most of your pay is mine' said dad, Michael didn't care, yes dad was right, but there would still be a small amount left over, and even that wasn't the real reason Michael was so looking forward to getting paid, no Michael had worked for a month, and wanted recognition for that fact.

As soon as they arrived at the hospital, Michael hurried Dad to the now gathering crowd, pay day was the one day you could expect 100% attendance, and the following day around 85%. Pay day worked thus, you would all gather outside Dave the supervisor's hut, and wait for your name to be called, you would then go up, sign a sheet of paper and get your envelope. Slowly but surely the crowd started to shrink, the people who had been paid wandering off, maybe to send money home, or more likely spend at the club, not much work was going to be done that day, that was for sure. With about ten people left, Michael heard his name called, well he didn't know of any other Michael's so he started to move forward, only for Dad to move in front of him, he smiled at his over eager off spring 'Remember son you've got Jnr after you're name' Dad was right, all of Michael's post had Jnr on it, in years to come even his driving licence would state this. The crowd continued to decrease until it was just Michael and dad, 'And now' proclaimed Dave 'we come to the main event, the one worker we couldn't do without' Dad managed to catch the laugh before it left his mouth, 'Michael Jnr, please come up' despite the build-up and embarrassment of Dave's speech, Michael finally got his golden envelope. And with dad paid there was still enough to get some sweets and other rubbish kids buy.

The rest of the day was a bit of an anti-climax, he had his Walkman, been paid, and he had no idea if or when Helen would show up again, so he wasted the rest of the day Looking at the pieces of wood that would make the table he had in his mind, he was now half finished, but without the right tools or skills he found the job hard going. Hitting bits of wood didn't seem to work, glue wasn't much help either, still he had a few weeks before he was due to leave, so there was still time to produce his masterpiece.

Thursday 26th – Villa.
'Dave flew back to England'
FA CUP Reply
Manchester 4:0 Brighton.
Close then?

It was another crap day at the villa, Dave the Brummie was

going home. When Michael first arrived, he and Dave only really nodded or said morning to each other, this was mainly down to the age difference, Paul was another story, because there was only 7 years between him and Paul, he was more like an older brother whereas Dave was Dad's age. But when Paul flew back to England, Dave and Michael started to talk more and soon became friends, then just like he was going as well. So Dave Dad and Michael drove to the airport and said their goodbyes, Steve would have come, but due to a stomach upset could not be more than 20 yards away from a toilet. After the good byes Dad and Michael went to the Club, had a drink and a game of snooker, then went home for a nap, for later that night the FA cup reply was on, unlike the first match which was shown 8pm local time, the reply was played during the week and started later, kick off was now 7.30 pm GMT 00.30 Local time.

Around 9pm both were up, so with Steve still in his room, afraid to leave sight of his loo, Dad and Michael sat down, along with the 91,534 men woman and children who made the trip to Wembley, and listened to a very one sided match. Brighton had made Untied play and sweat in the first game, but they were no match for them this time, the chances they had were all long range, and although the united keeper had to make some important saves, there was really only one team in it, on the 25th minute Captain Bryan Robson scored, a lovely left footed drive, then on the half hour mark Whiteside made it two, with a lovely header. With nothing to lose Brighton pressed forward, yet were caught out again on the 44th minute, Gordon McQueen headed on from a free kick and found Robson who scored his second, really it was all over, so at half time it was 3.0 to Manchester. It was now after 1 in the morning and dad went to bed, after all he was an old man, he was in his 40's!, this left Michael alone, with nothing better to do for fifteen minutes, he went into the kitchen got a drink and snack, sat back down, and listened to the 2nd half. Unlike the 1st, the 2nd half was a little sluggish, then untied hit a fourth on the 62nd Minute, Dutch Midfielder Arnold Muhren stepped up and scored a penalty, after Robson had been brought down inside the penalty area. 20 minutes later it was all over and Michael went up to his room. As Michael lay in bed he dreamt of scoring for Liverpool in some future cup final, maybe even a European final.

Friday 27th May – Beach/Desert.
Went to the beach, went surfing, had a lesson on driving, then
Went to club'

Despite a slightly later than normal start to the day, because of the previous night's massacre of a football match, the morning started off pretty much like any other, a fruit breakfast, then a spot off sitting around, reading a week old paper or comic, followed by bugger all, around 8, dad appeared, and decided to change the routine, 'it's about time you learnt to drive'.

Within the hour, Michael was in the driver's seat of the White Toyota corolla, engine off of course, dad was halfway through his speech about what button did what. Michael had seen it all before, although he had never driven, he had watched the other's many times before, driving was basically turn it on, rev the engine, throw it in gear and go, how hard could it be?. After ten minutes dad had finished the tutorial. 'So you understood all that?' Michel nodded, dad didn't look convinced, Michael seemed to have paid no attention to him, but with the villa behind them, and the whole of the desert in front of them, dad felt the worse that could happen was his son would hit a dune or something.

Dad was very clear on his first instruction, 'Ok so *all* I want you to do is start the car, *nothing* else' Michael turned the engine over and the three year old rust bucket chocked into life, Michael had felt the engine turn over many a time, but this was different, sitting in the driver's seat made it feel alive, more real. Feeling ok with the first part dad moved on, 'ok next I want you to put your left foot down on the clutch' Michael careful put his left foot down, 'now' Dad paused, 'Now I want you to put the gear stick into first. Michael started to feel beads of sweat starting to form on his brow, for some reason it wouldn't go, in the end it took two hands. Although ready for the last part, dad seemed to be taking his time, finally he was ready, 'now slowly, and I mean *slowly*, put your right foot on the accelerator and at the same time slowly bring up your left foot' for a second Michael had to think what dad had just asked him to do, it sounded like quantum physics. The moment Michael put his right foot down on the go pedal, the 1.6 engine roared, as his left foot come up, the car slowly lurched forward, Michael was driving, he couldn't believe it, *he* was driving, then he stalled it. Dad reassured him this was natural and they tried again, within five minutes Michael was driving again, be it very slowly, and in first, but it was driving, after a couple of hundred yards Dad asked over the screaming engine 'Shall we try 2nd gear?' 2nd thought Michael, *crap where's that*? After a keep glance he located it and after some interesting foot work they were in 2nd, instantly the engine thanked him and became quieter, they were also moving faster, they were now traveling at 15 mph, and despite dads initial reservations and nerves, the kid was doing well, dare they try 3rd. Michael was just having a ball, this driving lark was easy, then dad grabbed the wheel and they veered to the left, just missing a stray white dog, at first no one said a word, then Dad burst out laughing, 'Only you could nearly hit an animal with a hundred miles of desert to drive in' Michael didn't feel like laughing and found his eyes fixed on the horizon, his hands glued to the steering wheel. 'ok lets try 3rd' dad could tell Michael was scared by what just happened, but knew he would get over it. A reluctant Michael tried 3rd, the Toyota lurched up to 35 mph, to Michael it felt like 50, 'Ok son, up till now you've done the easy part' Easy thought Michael, *Easy*?, 'Now we need to turn the car around and head back to the villa' Michael had seen this done hundreds of times before, but his mind was now blank, dad sensed his son may need a hand, 'ok so we turn the wheel slightly to the left' he gently helped his son with the steering wheel, it was the biggest turn in history, oil tankers turned quicker in the north sea then the white Toyota did that day. After thirty seconds they were more or less pointing the right way, dad had decided third was the limit for the lesson, so he and Michael carried on at 35, enjoying the surroundings and waving at the locals they past, who were now quite bemused by the antics of the young white boy, who couldn't shot a dog, but came so close to running one over. The villa slowly started to fill the windscreen and dad had one more thing to teach his son, braking, 'Ok now we need to start braking, but not to *hard*' Michael nodded, he was ready, slowly he put his foot of the brake, the car started to make a weird noise and shake, 'ok you need to take your foot of the accelerator when you brake' as soon as Michael did this the car started to slow down, but again the car started to shake and wobble, 'remember what I said before, when you go faster you go up a gear, and when you slow?' Michael thought back to the lecture dad had given and he had ignored, 'You change down a gear' Michael ventured 'That's right' smiled dad, his son had paid attention, after a brief fight with the gear stick, Michael got the car down to 2nd then 1st gear, they were now traveling around 5 mph, and were 90 feet from the villa. Thinking he should stop the car before going through the back wall, Michael stepped a little to heavy on the brakes, throwing both man forward, dad then sat back in his seat, and calmly took the keys out of the now stalled car. As they walked towards the front gate dad put his arm around Michael 'not bad for your first attempt son, not bad at all' still on a high from the whole experience Michael asked 'can we do that again, soon?' dad tried to sound optimistic as he replied 'Maybe, we'll see' .

It would be three years before Michael drove any car again.

Saturday 28ᵗʰ May – Home.
'Had the runs, *did not go* to work,
Stayed home!'

Michael was dreaming about driving, and all that had happened the day before, this was something to tell his friends about when he got back home, as none had driven before, this was something he could brag about. He dreamt of having a Toyota back in Billericay, picking his mates up and cursing down to Southend-on-sea. Driving along the sea front, with the sun going down in the distance, the cool warm air of a summers evening, his friends would.. Michael woke with an urgency he hadn't experienced for over a year, but he know straight away what it was, he needed a toilet, any toilet, stat. He ran to the bathroom and sat on the loo, he had made it just in time, it was at this point he felt the fever and stomach cramp, *oh god the runs* he thought. He left the bathroom twenty minutes later, feeling like rubbish, dad had heard the commotion and left for work without him, Michael was staying home, alone, to die. He got back into bed and lay there in agony, half an hour later the dash was on again. By 10am he was cleared out and tried to sleep.

Michael had fallen to the *runs* the summer before, he had been away with the scouts, two weeks away from the family, no washing no bedtime, wearing the same outfit day after day, luxury. They also learnt how to cook, and maybe this and the hygiene regime, or lack off, had opened up the chance of getting a bug or two. It could also have been down the fact they were camping in a field in the middle of Somerset, where cows and goats wandered around, leaving their droppings, where ever they felt like, whatever it was, with three days to go before the troop was due to go home, diarrhoea struck, and how. Out of the thirty scouts and leaders, only five were spared, Michael being one of the five, the rest were moved to a nearby barn, and left to sleep on bales of straw. By the time the group were due to go home, Michael was still was unaffected, somehow he had escaped the terror, friends were wiped out, they had lost weight, could barely walk, most white as a sheet. However within five hours of getting home it had struck, Michael was just glad it happened when he was home, mum and dad weren't. So now he was in a foreign country, with bad gut ache, alone, well almost, he would wake from time to time and find a glass of water next to his bed, god bless Ali. By Five dad was home, he made a joke about Michael getting out of work by any means, Michael noticed despite dad's jokey manner, he was keeping his distance, dad had also brought up soup, which Michael managed to eat, but regretted an hour later, He was in for a rough night.

Sunday 29th May – Home.
'Still got the runs, but Michael Will be going to work tomorrow'

Michael awoke around 10am, his fever was gone but he still felt like crap, thankfully the rushing to the loo had stopped, yes he still had to go, but didn't feel like he was in the 100 meters sprint every time he went. On one of his trips to the bathroom, he pondered the pros and cons of the Local and Euro style toilets they had in the villa. The European was of course the best, you could sit on it, flush it and well it wasn't a hole in the floor, but the local did have its pluses, and Michael didn't want to dwell on it *too* much, but it was times like this when a hole in the ground, and a shower hose could prove useful.

About lunchtime Michael was hungry, a good sign, so he ventured to the kitchen for the first time in days, Michael thought best to stay away from fruit and went to make a sandwich, Ali appeared from nowhere and shouted at him, Michael was taken aback, Ali loved the kid, almost as much as his own kids, but he was not going to let the boy touch anything with *those* hands, this disease was not to spread. Michael sensing Ali was going to make the meal for him, left the kitchen and went to the lounge, a few minutes later Ali appeared, he then mumbled something in his native tongue, which Michael took as an apology for shouting at him, gave the boy his sandwich and left to go fishing. Michael was again alone. Around three Dad appeared, he had come home early to check on his son, yes he was concerned, but he also knew

mum would not be impressed if anything happened to her only boy, so dad was relieved to see Michael up and eating, but tried not to let on his feelings too much, after all the boy might take advantage and take the rest of the week off, no he was going back in tomorrow, it wasn't about the money, he had a work ethic, and it was get a job and pay your way in life.
So it was an early night for both of them.

Monday 30th May – Work/Club.
'Went to work, got home, went to club,
Beat Dad at snooker by 40'

Michael hadn't felt this refreshed and alive in months, yes he was going to work, but so what, it was a sunny day and he wasn't rushing for the loo. After getting dressed, jeans and a t-shirt for a change, he went down stairs for breakfast, Steve bumped into him in the hallway and in a theatrical manner jumped back and made a cross sign with two figures' Unclean' he hissed, Michael smiled as Steve carried on the insults 'another day and I was going to paint a plague symbol on your door' Michael ignored the silly grown up and carried on to the kitchen. As he entered he noticed Ali, and slowed down, they exchanged glances and the fact Michael had made it through another night was proof to Ali Michael could again touch things in his Kitchen. After a brief breakfast it was off to work.

'I'm fine, honest' Matthew was not convinced, as a manager He had to be sure all his workers were fit and healthy, but of course Michael was different, he had to be *really* sure 'Ok Michael, but the moment you feel unwell you tell me, ok' Michael smiled and sat at his desk, he liked the way Matthew cared for him and looked after his wellbeing, he wondered if all his future bosses would be so caring. Around 3pm Michael started to feel the strain of staying awake after such a brutal illness, he hadn't wanted to sleep at work that day, in case you know what struck again, and was thinking of calling it a day, when at last some excitement broke out. A part time worker called Johnny came rushing in, talking in a very excited manner to a colleague, (his name of course was not Johnny but Michael could not pronounce Ajmal) Michael couldn't tell what they were talking about, but Johnny was concerned about something, then Johnny and the guy he was speaking too got up, had a short conversation with Matthew and left. More than a little curious at this point, Michael asked Matthew what was up 'They are worried about the storm' Michael looked outside, at the sun and the clear blue sky, 'no no no, not today, tomorrow, weather is bringing much wind and rain, and most workers live in huts and tents, so they need to go home and get ready' Michael couldn't grasp the fact people had to prepare 24 hours in advance for rain? 'Can't they stay with relatives or friends?' Matthew seemed a little taken aback by this question. 'You do not understand, everyone lives with each other, mums and dads and sons and grandparents, all in same hut or tent' for the rest of the afternoon and ride home, all Michael could think about was what size tent the workers at the site were living in? They must of been huge, almost Tardis like to get all those people in them.

Dad and Michael hit the club around 7, the place was empty, dad had a pint Michael a coke, they had a game of Snooker, which Michael won by 40 points, he really was improving with every game he played. Dad asked the barman where everyone was, it turned out most people had stayed home to get ready for the next day's storm. Christ what was coming a tornado?

Tuesday 31ˢᵗ May – Work/Club
'Sarah's birthday, went to work, did a lot, went to the club, Played snooker, I won'

Michael woke up to yet another hot sunny day, ok there was one darkish cloud in the sky, but that was it, what was everyone worried about?. So because the world hadn't ended, it was business as usual, a quick breakfast then off to work. The drive in was not a pleasant one, *god its warm* thought Michael, the heat levels were raising, fast. They were about a mile from the hospital, when dad noticed a large crowd had gathered at the junction of the main road they needed to use, 'Fuck it' he mumbled under his breath, he wasn't happy, like Michael he too was hot, and this type of problem could take hours to clear, Steve wasn't bothered though, he had one of those battery powered hand held fans, so he was fine, until a cattle drive of cows stopped behind the car, then things started really to heat up, and smell, it was rank, Michael hadn't smelt the like since, well never. Five minutes later dad had had enough, and was just about to get out and find out what the bloody problem was, when the Pakistani army turned up, In a 1950's British army truck, wearing their 1950's uniforms, waving their 1950's ex British rifles around. Soon the crowd was moved out of the way, and the Brits were mobile again, as they drove past where the problem had been, Michael noticed a nice new white hatchback car in the middle of the road, with its bonnet bent and windscreen smashed, 'Nasty' said steve, again happy with life and his fan.

Once at the hospital they went their separate ways, Steve and Dad were going to be busy today, Steve had to oversee the plumbing for the research block, Dad needed to get some big pipes from one side of the main building to the other, and Michael, well Michael had his own job to get on with. Being the end of the month, the stores needed to fill in a butt load of forms, and then enter the data onto to the sites one and only computer, and with Michael's computer studies experience from school, he had been looking forward to this day for some time. So after talking to Matthew and discussing the reports, one very excited boy went over to the admin building, and sat down next to the creamy beige plastic lump that was the sites pc, once he had located the on button he was away. Michael couldn't get over it, he was using a computer, without a teacher present!, The big green letters of IBM appeared on the monitor, he stared in awe of them, how cool was this. Ten minutes later he was a third of the way though his work load, but then he started to develop a head ache, his head hurt from all the concentrating and staring at the monitor, so he took a small break and used the employee kitchen to make tea, life was good, maybe computers would be a good job for him, working in an office typing numbers on a keyboard, making cups on tea when he wanted, it was something to think about, after all he had no real ideas what he wanted to do when he left school. After the cuppa he hit the computer again, and by noon was finished, Matthew was so grateful he gave the lad the rest of the day off. So Michael went to find Dad.

Michael heard Dad long before he laid eyes on him, 'NO I SAID THERE! NOT FUCKING THERE!' Michael wasn't sure Dad wanted visitors, but Matthew said he could go and he didn't know where Steve was. So after a few twist and turns along a half-finished hallway, he found Dad, in a large bare room, not that you could see it was bare, it was dark, really dark, the only real light coming from a lamp on the floor, and a five foot square hole at the top of the far end wall, dad was on a step ladder pointing at the hole in the wall, and was not happy. From what Michael could understand, which was more than the Non English speaking work force, Dad had asked for a small hole, around 5 inches wide, for a water pipe, two of the locals had then picked up a sledge hammer, and had at it, with the wall taking the brunt, 'AND NOW, now I have to get this bricked up whilst getting the rest of the pipes in', Dad turned to the one worker who could speak a little English, and told him to find a brick layer, it was at this point Dad spotted Michael, this seemed to calm him down a little, he smiled, 'let's get some lunch'

'I'm not a racist' started Dad, 'but they're as much use as a chocolate fire guard this lot' Michael laughed, not so much at the fact dad thought his workers were thick, but at the comment. It wasn't really the workers, or even the black hole they had created that was getting to dad that day, he was just venting, no it was Sarah's birthday, and both Dad and Michael were both missing her, God Michael must have been homesick, or ill, missing his sister, what was that about!. It was little things like this that made them both think of home, still there was the telephone call later to look forward to, dad had asked his bosses if he could ring home about 12.30 local time, 7.30am GMT, so he could wish his daughter a happy birthday, how could they say no. With lunch done they headed back the *hole*, Jeff the brickie was there, and he was having a heated debate with two of the labourers, apparently Jeff had been a busy man over the last month or so, covering up peoples mistakes, and was getting a little pissed off by it all, dad decided to leave Jeff and the gang to it, they all seemed to be getting along, and headed to the site office to call home.

With the call home done, dad was in a better mood, he even hugged some of his man on his return, and even the fact that the hole had now been bricked up, without the water pipe been feed through it before hand, couldn't spoil the mood, it gave Dad a chance to show his lads the proper way to make a hole for a 5in pipe. Michael stayed to watch, he hadn't really seen dad in action, god he had energy, he wasn't still for a second, he may of smoked and drank and been in his forties, but he had more energy than Michael, that was for sure. By 4pm Dad was feed up and told the lads to piss off, it was time for the club, so it was home, quick change and out.

As they left the villa for the club, Michael spotted a few clouds in the sky, but that was it, really what was all the fuss about? there was no storm coming. At the club they found out there was again no movie, so it was snooker or darts, and been club champion Michael was not short of challengers. An hour later he had dispatched his next three victims, with ease, with no one left to play he and dad left. The drive home was uneventful, a couple of specks of rain hit the windscreen, but that was it 'Oh, this was the storm everyone was worried about?' Michael said in a slightly sarcastic manner, 'Yeah some blokes at work was talking about it raining tonight' replied Dad, as they drove on the rain started to get a little heavier, but again nothing special. By the time they got home, the rain, or lack off, had slowed right down, thinking that was the end of the *storm,* Michael started to walk into the Villa with only happy thoughts, then spotted something that troubled him a little, Ali's bed had moved to under the balcony and he was nowhere in sight, once inside they spotted him, in the Kitchen, just sitting there with a cup of tea.

Michael wasn't tired, not one bit, it was only 10 pm, so he made his way to the lounge and started to read comics, first the Dandy, then he moved on to the Beano. He was halfway through Denis the menace when it happened, he couldn't see outside very well, but he could hear the rain, it was getting louder, and louder, within ten minutes it was a full on Monsoon, which carried on throughout the night. As Michael tried to sleep, his thoughts were with the guys at work and their families trying to make it through the storm.

Thursday 2nd June – villa/Club.
'did not go to work, but went to club, beat Steve and Jeff'

By Thursday the weather have calmed down, and would remain nice for the foreseeable future, in other words hot. Michael guessed all was ok, because Ali had put his bed back in the front garden. Whilst drinking his morning juice on the front balcony, Michael surveyed his surroundings, everyone and everything seemed to have made it through the wind and rain, even the family across the street who lived in the bushes had made it through, by some miracle or other, so what to do after a storm like that, take the day off, and head to the club.

Chapter Six.

After the storm.

Friday 3rd June – Work/Beach.
'Went to work till 1pm, went to the beach'

'But we never go to work on a Friday?' it had just been that way since Michael had been in country, 'well we do today son' replied dad, Steve chipped in, 'And its only till 1' Michael wasn't happy but had little choice in the matter, he knew the guys were leaving work early and wouldn't be returning to the villa until late, so it was stay home alone, or do a half days work, after a brief think Michael got in the car.

It was the first time Michael had been back to work since the Storm, everyone seemed ok, but listening to some of the stories made him wonder how half of the workers had lived through the night, one man didn't make it back home, so he had to spend the night sheltering in some disused shed, another man's tent was blown over, and it took the whole family most of the night to get it up right again, the worst by far was Johnny's story, his niece got lost after going to the outside loo, she was found three hours later after a frantic search by the family and neighbours, all Michael had to worry about was the noise of the wind. Matthew again thanked Michael and God, for everyone making it through the storm safely, and saw the whole experience as another test by the almighty, which he and his family had passed. By 12 it was lunch.

Around 1pm Dad Michael and steve were on their way, they had been invited to the un official international beach football tournament. Basically several navies were all in port at the same time, and the some of the sailors from the New Zealand and Australia navy wanted to meet up, play football, then have a beer and BBQ. Dad had bumped into some of the sailors at the club a few days before, and after a couple of beers it was agreed the villa would represent the UK. Michael *loved* football, playing it, going to Upton park to watch the hammers, but he especially liked watching the game on TV, oh yes Saturday nights the TV was tuned to the BBC, what a show match of the day was, although Michael wasn't a fan of Jimmy Hill.

The games themselves were pretty one sided when it came to UK Versus… the facts were these, the sailors were professional service personal, trained every day and were fit, Michael and Co were not, Dad was well, 40 odd, also he drank and smoked, Steve was young (ish) but also Drank, and as for Michael, yes he as a teenager, but he never worked out, also beach football sapped your energy a lot quicker than regular footie. At one point an attempt was made to even the sides up, the less fit and able from the ships were given to team UK, despite this generous offer, they still didn't stand a chance, but a good time was had by all, and so the final was predictable OZ V NZ, it went down to penalties which NZ just edged. Then the real entertainment began. Whilst the BBQ was been set up, which the Aussies insisted on doing of course, Dad and Michael sat on the beach and watched the sunset, dad with a beer Michael a coke, 'You know you can ask me anything son' Dad's statement took Michael a little by surprise, 'Er yeah I know' dad wasn't finished, 'I mean, you know, well girl's and stuff' oh god, thought Michael, he's not going to have *the* talk, here, on the beach, oh god he is isn't he!, Michael felt he needed to respond, even if it was a grunt, 'Ok Dad, thanks' then there was the pause, they both took a swig of their drinks and stared at the setting sun. 'It's just you've been seeing that girl, Helen is it?' oh god he is going to have that talk, before Michael could respond or stop his dad from carrying on, Dad gently punched him on the shoulder, knocking his son a little sideways, 'It's just I got talking to Terry, and if you two are..' Michael didn't want to hear the rest, this was just too embarrassing, 'Dad I think I know where you're going with this' Michael lied, 'Trust me were just friends, nothing happened' although it wasn't for the lack of trying. Dad seemed to take his time digesting this, his eventually reply was of a typical parent, 'Good, I mean I'm glad you're seeing that girl, it's just I don't won't you to make the same mistakes I made when I was your age' this made Michael smile, for when his dad was young, he had drank, smoked, had loads of girlfriends and was a bit of a geezer, but like all parents, no matter what their back ground, he just wanted his kids to have a better life then he had, and for Michael not to have sex until aged 16, and his daughter, will not to have sex ever.

With the sun now set, it was time to go home.

Saturday 4th June – Home/villa.
'did not go to work, went to club, played snooker, Saw *For your eyes only*'

Because of the antics the night before, everyone was having a lie in. Around 10am Michael rose from his pit and went downstairs, on his way to the kitchen he found Steve and Dad, sitting on the couch together, both in real pain, they had made it this far, and no further. Dad couldn't walk another step, but now he needed the loo, this meant going back upstairs, he tried crawling on his knees but could only get a third of the way and had to give up, somehow Steve was worse, despite being in his late 20's Steve was a wreck. Michael just shook his head and had some breakfast.

The plan for the day was simple, go to the club, for a change, and catch the new movie, a bond no less. Thankfully for one or two of the villa's occupants, Michael and co wouldn't be going till later, giving Dad and Steve time to recover. Around noon dad had changed his mind, and didn't want to go, he was still in a lot of pain, but Michael really wanted to see the film, so he reminded dad the club had a great pain killer, alcohol. A couple of hours later dad crawled to the car and they set off.

Once in the Club dad made straight for a chair in the cinema room, Michael was tasked with getting him a drink, at first the bar staff weren't too sure if they should serve him or not, however once Michael explained where dad was and why he wasn't getting the drink himself, well Dad heard the laughter, even though there was a wall separating the two rooms.

The film itself was business as usual; it was a bond after all. This time 007 was assigned to hunt for a lost British encryption device, and prevent it from falling into enemy hands. For the next 127 minutes, Roger Moore travelled the Globe, surrounded by fast cars, cool gadgets and beautiful woman, what wasn't to like? Desmond Llewellyn was on fine form as Q, and the beauty in question was France actress Carole Bouquet, the film itself was full of excitement and action. What else would you expect from a bond? Even dad seemed to enjoy it, mainly because he could sit down for two hours without having to move. The end credits stated Bond would return in Octopussy, the title got a few of the regulars talking.

There was a quick drink then home to bed, the old farts needed their rest.

Sunday 5th June – Work/Villa.
'Went to Work, did not go out, wrote to friends'

'How can the pain be fucking worse than yesterday!' exclaimed dad, waking his son up from deep slumber, Michael opened up one eye to see Dad hobbling out the bedroom, swearing under his breath as he went. Michael turned to look at his watch, 7.30 am, *bloody* 7.30 am on a Sunday! No teenager should be awake at this time on the weekend. Michael thought about going back to sleep, but the villa was coming alive, also Dad was still swearing in the distance, 'Sod it' said Michael and got up. Mercifully Dad started to feel a little better within an hour of getting up, and Steve was also his old self, so the trip to work was filled with less expletives then last night's drive back from the club. The journey to work was pretty uneventful, until they arrived at the hospital, in the car park a crowd had gathered around a small white car, as they approached the vehicle Michael recognised it straight away, it was the same car from a couple of days back, the one that caused all the chaos in the city. The windscreen was wasted, it had a big hole in the middle of it, there was also a big dent in the bonnet. After speaking to some of the group, Michael learnt the car was being used by a Dutch electrician called Arjan, he had only been in the country a matter of days when he hit a bike, 'a bike' enquired Michael, 'What a motorbike or push bike?' 'Push bike' was the reply. Michael couldn't understand how a ten year olds bike could do that sort of damage to a car, A push bike could only do 10 maybe 15 mph max, apparently the kid walked away unhurt, yet the driver needed medical attention.

The rest of the day was a bore, and dragged, thankfully being a Sunday they left early, not that there was much to do at the villa, so after grabbing a sandwich and a coke, Michael sat down in the villa's lounge to read his Beano's for the tenth time, after reading the further adventures of Minnie the minx, (the female version of Denis the menace) Michael thought sod it, I need to write to my friends, but what to put?, The weather? The beach, the club, work, Helen? It was all fun and interesting to him, but he didn't want to write a War and peace style manual that would bore his friends. Michael as usual was really over thinking the problem, so after he stopped worrying about what to write, he sat at his bedroom desk, and produced ten identical letters, each one page long, that went on about the weather and where he worked, It was not the work off Oscar Wilde, but he couldn't be bothered to write anything else, it was hot and he hated writing so they would have to do. The rest of the day was spent listening to his Walkman, god he was bored, Sunday's sucked.

Tuesday 7th June – Work/Club.
'went to work, went up hill, went to club,
Saw *Blazing Magnum'*

Work was now becoming a chore, in fact in Michael's mind it was a glorified babysitting service. He was 14, and should have been knocking around with friends at the beach, or, or anywhere else other than the stores port-a cabin, ok he *didn't actually* have any friends his age he could go to the beach with, but that really wasn't the point. Dad had very few options to play with on the matter, he really couldn't leave his son on his own at the villa for more than a day, especially after the air gun fiasco, and god forbid he let Michael roam loose in the real world, it was far too dangerous, so Matthew was appointed to basically look after the boy. At first Michael didn't need any other kids around him, he was to busy getting used to work, the villa, and a whole new country, also Dad and steve were cool, and the lads at the club were great, they bought him drinks and didn't mind a game or two of snooker, but Michael was now starting to miss other teens, and the problem was he never went anyway other kids might be knocking around. Of course there was Helen, oh god Helen, but she wasn't really a friend was she, she was something else, plus he had no idea when he would see her again, if ever? Feeling sorry for himself, Michael went to lunch early.

Dad joined him around noon, and sensed straight away something was up, for Michael had a face like a slapped arse. Dad didn't really want to ask what the problem was, in case it something only a mother could help with, but his boy was down, and mum was a couple of hours away, so would be no help this time. So in true dad style he probed in sensitive and caring manner, 'What's up son, you've got a face like a smacked arse?' dad had a way with words, and called it like it saw it. Michael sighed, 'I don't know, I'm just bored I guess' dad couldn't believe his ears, 'Bored? Bored! Look where you are, in a another country, there's great weather, and you're living in a villa' Dad had a point, 'I know, it's just, maybe I want to see a bit more of the country then this' Michael looked around the canteen, Dad stared at his son, then smiled 'I'll be right back'.

Soon they were leaving the city, heading out into the country side, Michael, still in a funk, stared out of the passenger side window, his brain barely registering the stunning scenery on offer. Half an hour later were at the foot of a small mountain, 'come on' said dad 'Let's have a butchers'. The mountain was really nothing more than a big hill, but it still took half an hour to climb, once at the top you could look down on Karachi, It was a clear day with very few clouds, you could see for miles, 'So what do you think' Dad seemed quite pleased with himself, 'Yeah its nice' shrugged Michael, 'Nice!' Said dad 'nice, look around you, there's nothing for miles and what a view' 'Michael was impressed, both by the view and dad, he really was trying to help, but this wasn't what Michael had meant, yes they were doing something together which didn't involve the club or work, but Michael wanted to see the *real* Pakistan, the people the smells the colours, ok maybe not the smells but the whole deal, yet he would take this, this first step, it was a start. 'Thanks for bringing me dad, its, it's nice' Michael smiled, which seemed to signal to dad he was having a good time, thinking his job was done, they went home to get something to eat and shower, before heading to the club, for a change.

Once at the club, Michael learnt about that nights film, the 1976 classic, Blazing Magnum, also known as *Shadows in an Empty Room,* it starred Stuart Whitman and John Saxon, a euro trash film with American actors, who were only in it to lend the film some weight for the international audiences. Brief description, an Ottawa police captain searches for the person who poisoned his sister, who was attending Montreal University. So desperate is he for revenge that he began to use his own brutal methods to find the killer, and yes it was an 18. Michael saw about half the film, got bored, and hit the snooker table; he just wasn't in the mood for that type of film.

Wednesday 8th June – Club.
'Did not go to work, went to and played snooker'

Still bored and unhappy with his lot in life, Michael stayed at home and not so much sulked, as slouched in his bed, then the lounge and finally the balcony, he was in no mood to tackle life that day. He did go to the club later, and played snooker, for a change, would it hurt them to get a ping pong table?

Friday 10th June – Villa/Club.
'Day off, went to Intercontinental, went home, then to the club'

It was Friday, so day off. The gang decided to treat themselves and headed for the Intercontinental hotel, the scene of the Helen closet fumble, Michael half hoped to bump into Helen again, but Dad said Terry and family were out of the country at the moment, so maybe not. Anyway the day was not about woman, it was about lazing next to the pool, getting a tan, drinking coke and eating ice cream. And that's what happened.

3pm, bored and a little burnt they headed for the club.

Saturday 11th June – Home/Club.
'Did not go to work today (ill) went to club saw *Escape to victory*'

Around 7am Michael started to stir, from a very weird dream indeed, he had been walking in the desert, the sun beating down on him, searching for something, but couldn't quite put his finger on what it was he was searching for. Michael opened a blurry right eye, as he focused on his surroundings he caught sight of something odd, was that shredded skin? He jumped out of bed in panic, waking dad in the process 'What the fuck are you doing son? Did you wet the bed again?' having gone from sleepy to awake in a matter of seconds, Michael now wasn't too sure what had really just happened, 'No I thought I saw, it was, there's skin in my bed' Dad wasn't quite sure he had heard right, 'skin?' Michael held several layers of his own skin up to show Dad, 'Yeah I saw it, and thought a snake was in my bed and had shred its skin' Dad sat up and lit a cigarette, he took a good look at his son then smiled, 'You're going nowhere today are you' Michael looked at Dad, unsure why he would say this, all dad could do was laugh. Michael searched desperately for a mirror, finding one in the bathroom 'Oh crap' he muttered, he was red, red all over, 'I think you may have over done it yesterday son' shouted dad from the bedroom, dad was as ever very helpful in these types of situations. Thankfully Steve the sun god had been through it many times before, 'the trick to sunbathing is to keep turning and use a good sun tan lotion, now hold still' Steve was plastering some after sun cream/lotion onto Michael's body, normally Michael would feel a little awkward having another man massaging him with exotic oils, whilst wearing nothing expect swimming trunks, but Steve was a professional and Michael was in a lot of discomfort. Soon Dad and Steve were gone and Michael was left to slip and slide into the Kitchen to try and make some breakfast, holding cutlery was not easy.

By the time Dad arrived back from work, Michael was feeling a little better; yes he was still glowing like one off the kids from the ready brek TV adverts, but the lotion had been adsorbed and done its job, so at least Michael could now wear a t-shirt and shorts, just. To cheer his son up, dad took him to the Club.

The main reason Dad wanted to go the club was that nights film, a celluloid treat sure to get the troops going, and the red white and blue blood of every Englishman pumping harder, the film was Escape to victory. The 1981 classic that had it all, namely Football, it was us versus the Nazi's, and showing their skills with the ball included such stars as Pele, Michael Caine and Sly Stallone. The plot was pretty easy to follow, but still enjoyable, basically some allied prisoners of war, hatched a plan to use an upcoming propaganda football match against a Nazi team in occupied Paris, as a means of escape, hence the title of the film. oh and it had one bobby Moore in it as well, Ex West ham captain and the man who lead England to world cup glory in 1966, again against the Germans. Dad being a *huge* west ham fan loved it. By the end everyone was clapping and cheering, and within an hour a football match had broken out in the clubs car park.

Monday 13ᵗʰ June – Villa/restaurant.
'The start of Ramadan, did not go to work, you finish at 1pm for a month'

It was the start of something called *Ramadon? Ramajam?* Something like that. It was the first time Michael had heard of the festival, 'So is it a deal then?' Enquired a curious Michael, dad walked over to the coffee table in the lounge and grabbed a book 'To the locals it is, to us it means stopping work at 1pm every day for the next month' Michael beamed with delight' Wait, we only work half days for the next month?' Dad resisted stating the obvious, that his son only did half days as it was, according to Matthew his boss anyway, dad knew all about his son's sleepy afternoons, however being the grown up of the two, he didn't say a word on that subject and continued with the current conversation 'It's not bloody cool, this means I have to get twice the amount of work out a work force who do fuck all as it is' Dad was not happy, he was also running late, so left to catch Steve up.

Now on his own, Michael started to read the first couple of pages of the book Dad gave him.

Ramadan *(Arabic: Rama??n,) is the ninth month of the ;* Islamic calendar *worldwide observe this as a month of* fasting. *This annual observance is regarded as one of the* Five Pillars of Islam, *The month lasts 29–30 days based on the visual sightings of the crescent moon.* While fasting from dawn until sunset Muslims refrain from consuming food, drinking liquids, smoking and sexual relations; and in some interpretations from swearing.

According to Islam, the *swab*(rewards) of fasting are many, but in this month they are believed to be multiplied. Fasting for Muslims during Ramadan typically includes the increased offering of *salat* (prayers) and recitation of the Quran.

Michael put the book down and walked over to the window, he looked out onto the front lawn, taking in what the book and his dad and said about the upcoming festival, slowly the smile on his face grew, half days for a month, how cool was that! He didn't care what dad had said, this was going to be a blast.

To honour the start of Ramadan, dad decided to take Michael out, just the two of them, and this in no way was down to the fact Ali had the night off, leaving Dad to either make dinner, or take the boy to the club and have some crisps. Dad was to tired to make beans on toast, late alone a proper meal, so what the hell the boys were going out. Dad was taking Michael to an out of the way restaurant, for a curry, where everything seemed to sizzle and meats would arrive on very pointy sticks. The smells were amazing, luckily the place was only a third full, so they got seated quite quickly and didn't have to wait long for their food. Dad had a beer and insisted Michael had one too, 'It's tradition' dad stated, 'You go for a curry you have a beer' Michael not wanting to upset his dad had a beer, which he sipped throughout the night. It wasn't that Michael didn't like the taste of beer, it was the fact he had seen what alcohol could do to a person, time and time again, be it Dad, Steve or most of the adults he had come across since been in Pakistan.

The first course was some big tough crisp like dish, which came with a choice of dips, Dad called it a papadum, or something like that. The crisp was followed by a creamy prawn curry with yellow rice, Michael loved prawns, and *loved* prawn cocktails, with its sickly Marie rose sauce. Dad stuck with the chicken, he wasn't really into that seafood bottom feeding crap, for afters Michael had a hard ice cream type dish, with nuts in it, he didn't know what it was called, but really enjoyed it, dad had another beer, and a few more after that. By 7pm they had finished their meal, so after one more beer, for dad, Michael was full, they left. As they approached the Toyota dad dropped the car keys, it took him a whole minute to pick them back up, During this minute Michael noticed Dad was swaying with the breeze, but wasn't worried, nope, for Dad was a better driver drunk, then sober, also they were in the middle of nowhere, so there was nothing around to hit for miles.

Eventually they started the short journey home, at first it was just dirt tracks and unlit roads, then after ten minutes they hit some light traffic, which for some reason set dad off, he was moaning about bloody local divers not knowing what they were doing, and they were getting in his way, Michael thought this was a bit rich coming from a man without a driver's license, and was a guest in their country. Then they hit trouble, an army road block. Although Michael had had only one beer, he suddenly felt ill, dad though remained calm, perhaps it was the sheer amount of alcohol he had consumed, or dad just been dad, whatever it was he didn't seemed fazed one bit. Two of the three soldiers walked over to the now stationary car, they were wearing the typical army uniform, black boots, cream trousers dark blue shirt with braces, and armed with a lee Enfield rifle, the type British soldiers had in 1950's India, and looking at them they probably were the same guns. A solider asked in broken English for dad to switch the engine off, which he did, the solider then asked dad to get out the car, Michael was now very worried. Dad wobbled as he got out, he could barely stand, which was proven correct when he suddenly lurched to one side, this caught out the solider standing next to the truck, who quickly lifted his gun up from his side, and was now pointing it at dad, who thankfully had managed to right himself. The solider who could English, just, was now worried things could spin out of control, and marched over to Dad demanding his papers and driving licence, Michael know there was no way dad would be able to walk back to the car, and had to think on his feet, well bum, and remembered there was some documents from the Hospital in the glove compartment, some had dad's name on it, Michael got them and waved the papers at the solider. The moment the Soldier saw dad was working at the hospital, the *Aga khan's* hospital, the situation changed, He *apologised* to dad? Shook his hand? Waved to Michael and let them get on their way. God it was Matthew all over again thought Michael, what was it about white people and the locals, just because dad was working *at* the Hospital, and not for the Khan's himself, he was let of a drink driving offence. Dad confirmed this, whilst slurring. 'All you have to do is show them something with the Kahn's seal, or name, and they will let you do anything' the rest of the journey was uneventful.

Wednesday 15th June – Club.
'Did not go to work, did go to club,
Saw *Return of the golden cobra*'

It had been two days since dad's DUI, and neither father nor son had spoken about it, nor had they been to the club. Dad wasn't embarrassed, as such, but something had registered in his mind that maybe drinking every day wasn't such a great idea after all. There was also a lot to do at the Hospital, with the work force finishing at 1 o'clock every day, so dad was going in earlier to play catch up. The opposite was true of Michael's days, now Ramadan was in full flow, most of the stores workers were busy praying or talking about the festival, Matthew being a Christian wasn't as interested as his workers, but respected the fact they believed in a god and let them get on with it, Michael though saw no reason to go in, so stayed at home. Around 2pm Dad and Steve arrived back at the Villa, Steve was not in a good mood, even before they walked through the door Michael could hear Steve, 'I'm just saying they shouldn't be fuckin working there' Dad for once almost sounded the voice of reason, they walked straight past Michael and into the kitchen, 'Look Steve, mate, without them we wouldn't have a work force, we would be miles behind' for Dad knew the truth, that despite all the shouting and cursing he had done over the past few months, they (the European overloads) still needed the locals, otherwise the job would never get done, but Steve had had enough, it was bad enough they were lazy and undisciplined, but this stopping at 1pm was the top hat. Steve was though listening and went upstairs to have a shower, Dad turned towards Michael, 'He's in a right one isn't he, must be his time of month' not fully understanding Michael still found himself laughing.

Due to Steve's foul mood, dad decided they would go to club that night, and after a beer and some crisps, Steve seemed to calm down. Dad latter found out he was just homesick and lashed out at the workers for no real reason. The film that night was *Return of the cobra*, an instantly forgettable pile of trash. The next film was called 'A young Doe in love' this was no Disney film; nudge nudge, wink wink, and Michael had to leave the cinema room. So he played Snooker whilst the grownups had they're *me time*. By 10pm it was time to go home.

Chapter Seven.

Helen – Part 3.

Friday 17th June – Karachi/Club.
'Day off, went to WSS, then went to club'

'I'm going to school! That wasn't part of our deal?' Michael
was in shock. Dad had been pondering for a couple of weeks
the possibility of getting his son a play date, yes he was now
14, nearly a man, and could hold his own with all the lads, who
had really taken to him, but he still needed to knock around
with kids his own age. 'It's only for an hour or two then it's off
to the club' soothed Dad, Michael wasn't happy, the deal was
simple, he would not have to go to school, as long as he got a
job, which he did, admittedly he didn't go much, but he still
had a job, he also had to do his homework, which he did, again
sometimes. Dad explained on the way it was just a chance for
Michael to see other kids his own age, whilst he sorted out
some pluming problem at a villa nearby, where one of the
engineers he knew was staying. 'Fine I'll go, but they better not
expect me to do any work' Michael was serious, Dad couldn't
help but laugh, spoiled little shit he thought. Around 10am
they arrived at the WSS (World schooling services) building
and parked up, The WSS had been set up to offer foreign kids
living in the city, somewhere to continue their schooling, the
kids that attended ranged from 3 to 17, it was pure bedlam;
they had arrived at break time. The moment Michael walked
into the school he felt out of place, in part this was down to
the kindergarten scene that greeted him, but weirdly it was also
the teachers, he hadn't seen any in weeks, so it was a shock to
be in the presence of one again. It had been nearly two months
since he was last at school, and it had been Bliss, two months
of not running late for class, no bullies, no canteen food, in
short he had been his own boss, and he had loved it. But now
he was in the loins den, what would they do with him, *oh god
not lines*, he hated writing out lines, of course within five

minutes he had forgotten all this worry, and was made more than welcome by everyone, including the teachers, who were really over qualified babysitters, yes they tried to teach, but with the ages and nationalities they had to deal with, well they tried their best. Michael was then struck by an odd feeling, a sensation he hadn't really had before, and was very unexpected, he was home sick, no not home sick, but *school sick*? Again that wasn't it, but it was closest to what he felt at that moment in time. It was the chairs, the way the seats were arranged reminded him of his registration class back home, and the two girls who sat him front of him, Susan and Charlotte, both were nice enough in their own way, but whereas Charlotte kept to herself and was quiet, Susan was an out and out flirt, well in Michaels mind she was, but he had limited experience with the opposite sex, and much of his early knowledge about girls and what they liked and disliked came from over hearing their conversations. Michael's train of thought was interrupted by a familiar sight, Helen.

Michael then felt a new emotion wash over him, he could feel his cheeks burning red, he also felt slightly sick, *Oh god she's coming this way*! Michael couldn't decide if he should play it cool, which may have been a little difficult considering he looked as if he was wearing blusher, or to play it.. well it didn't matter how he was going to play it, Helen walked passed without even looking at him, he was stunned, she must of seen him he thought, there was no way she could of missed the glowing teenager slouched against the wall. This was Michael's first lesson in dealing with Girls, and he didn't like it. For the rest of his visit Michael sat chatting to some 12 year old boys from Italy, by 2pm Dad arrived.

On the way home Dad kept asking how it went, and did Michael have a chance to talk and knock around with other kids, Michael said yes, and lied that he had had a good time, this seemed to please dad, who after all just wanted his son to be happy, just like any other father. Yet Michael was far from happy, and was quiet for the rest of the day. He couldn't stop asking himself questions, why did she blank him?, was it something he did, something he said, something he didn't say or do? By the end of the evening he concluded it was all Helen's fault, and she had used him, this conclusion may not of been the truth, but it did at least help him get to sleep.

Saturday 18ᵗʰ June – Work/Club.
'Went to work then went to club,
Saw *The Dark crystal twice!*,
beat dad and guy called Trev at snooker'

Michael woke up feeling strangely ok, no better than ok, he felt *great*. Yesterday he had gone through a break up of some kind, and today was the start of the rest of his life. No more wondering if he would see Helen again, no more worrying about what to say or do next time they met, nope Michael was young free and single, he was even looking forward to work. It was Steve who first noticed the extra bounce in Michael's step when he appeared for breakfast, 'Christ what you feeding this lad, look at him, his chomping at the bit' Dad was just as surprised as Steve, he didn't have a clue why his son would be so happy 'Don't know Steve, but he can cut out being this perky in the morning' Joked dad in reply, Michael ignored both of them and grabbed some fruit, nothing was going to spoil today. Even the trip to work was pleasant, it was still early enough for the air to fresh and crisp, and for the sun to be but a weak ball of fire in the sky. Due to light traffic they made good time, so Michael was early enough to see dad's latest pipe run, where he was running several 3 inch water pipes from a basement pump floor to the first floor toilets. Around 9am Michael went to the stores, he was just in time to witness Matthew chewing out one of the workers, this was an unusual sight, normally Matthew was a calm soul who mostly got on with his workers, but with the workforce finishing at 1pm every day, work was starting to pile up, and this was getting to the stores supervisor, on seeing Michael Matthew smiled, he was again a happy man, he could count on the boy to clear the back log.

It was noon, and Michael was bored, he had entered all the weeks data on to computer, so with little else to do went to lunch, he was having soup, then a salad with an ice cream treat to finish, Dad arrived ten minutes later. As always he was having a light lunch, a sandwich, and that was it, no wonder he never put any weight on thought Michael, although the amount of calories he must have consumed through alcohol probably made up for the lack of real food dad wasn't having. Michael Senior didn't say a word as he sat down, not even a *hi* or *how's your day been*, Michaels first thoughts were the workforce have done it again, maybe this time they had made a hole so big half the hospital had collapsed, although there was not enough rubble on dad's shoulders for that to have happened, then Michael clocked the smirk on his father's face, he could see it clearly now, dad was up to something. They eat in silence, the odd look exchanged, finally Michael couldn't take it anymore and broke the silence, he needed to know what was going on, 'So dad how was your morning' asked Michael in a Causal just asking sort of way, dad replied just as causal 'Oh you know, so so, not to bad' *Ok* thought Michael, I'll play your game, and probed deeper, 'So did you get that pipe work finished?' 'We're about half done' mumbled dad whilst eating his sandwich, then followed a brief pause, during this time Michael finished his ice cream. With his treat eaten Michael carried on the game of chess, 'Oh I thought you would have got that done today?' Michael hoped this would force dad to play his hand, he couldn't take anymore, 'Well we would off finished, but I was called to the office, there was a letter for me, I thought it was from Mum, but it turns out they had the wrong Michael' Dad took the letter from his shirt pocket and slide it across the table towards his son, without touching it Michael could tell it was from Helen, he had that funny feeling again in his stomach, like the one at the WSS school, the feeling he had when Helen walked towards him, just before she blanked him. 'Not going to open it' enquired a more then curious dad, Michael was frozen in fear, but tried not to show it, what the hell did she want?. Eventually he managed to reply 'I'll open it later, I'm sure it's just junk' *Junk my arse* thought dad, he know it was from a girl, he could tell this from the perfume on the envelope, Michael had to think fast, and without thinking stood up 'Crap, sorry dad I left my sunglasses in the stores, I'll be back in a second' as Michael rushed of Dad couldn't help but laugh, he then thought to himself was I every that stupid and green at that age.

Michael left the canteen, then happy he was out of sight of dad, run to the toilets. He made a beeline for the middle stall, closed the door and sat down, completely gripped by fear of the letters contents, but Michael didn't have the luxury of time to be afraid, he had told dad he wouldn't be long, so had two choices, wait till he got home, or read it now, well waiting wasn't an option, it would tear him apart waiting until later, so high on adrenaline he ripped through the envelope and started to read the letter. After reading the two page letter for the third time, all he said was 'Oh' Michael then got up walked back to dad, it was around 1pm so they left site, Michael still hadn't said a word to dad since returning from "the stores", he was totally confused, dad sensed something was up and left his son to it. Dad got this from the look on his sons face, and the fact he never came back with any sun glasses.

By the time they got back to the Villa, Michael had processed the information in the letter. Helen had started by apologising for blanking Michael at the school; he had taken her by surprise that day. She then went on to explain why she didn't talk to him, even after getting over the shock of seeing him; it was simple, people talk. If she had said anything, even a simple 'Hi', word would have gotten back to her dad Terry, rumours would have started about a strange boy Helen knew, who didn't go to the school, and Terry would have stopped her attending, and she loved going to the school, her girlfriends would also have teased her endlessness about him. She then went on to beg him for forgiveness, and stated several times how much she missed him, and hoped they would see each other again, soon. Now back in his bedroom, Michael sat at his desk and re read the letter, afterwards he felt the freedom and independence he had gained yesterday, slowly disappear, back came the feeling of being lost and confused, yet there was a positive, a glimmer of hope, for out there was someone who loved and missed him, and for once it wasn't just his mum. He then did the only thing left in his power, he wrote a letter back, forgiving her.

Around 6pm the group headed for the Club, feeling a bit better about life, Michael chatted with Dad and Steve about everything and nothing, all was fine until Dad asked the bar man what that nights film was, 'the dark what? That's the one with bloody puppets in it!' dad was not happy; for the evening's entertainment was to be "The Dark Crystal". The 1982 Jim Henson classic, yes it was a Muppets film, without the Muppets, but it had a charm to it for all ages. Set on a distant planet, it was a sort of lord of the rings type film, where a young hero was on a quest to find a shard of magical crystal, which would save his world. Despite Dad, and others having reservations about the film, it was a hit with the crowd, in fact for the first time ever the film was shown again, no other film had been shown twice in one evening. This was of course after a quick beer and fag break.

Sunday 19th June – Work/beach/club.
'went to work, had a haircut, then went to the beach,
Then went to club, saw *The burning*'

It was going to be another busy day for the gang, so with that in mind everyone had a quick breakfast, then headed for the hospital. It no longer felt strange going to work on a Sunday, in fact Michael found it a nice change of pace from the norm, He and the rest of the villa would work till 1 pm, then hit a hotel or the beach, and have some fun, today it was the beach, well to be 100% correct, it was work, *haircut* then beach. Michael was becoming a hippy, Dad had declared a few days before 'It's not the 70's anymore, get a haircut you lazy sod' dad even threatened he was going to get Ali to cut it if he didn't get it sorted. It wasn't that Michael liked long hair, it was just down do, well yes he was just lazy, but with the possible threat of meeting Helen again, or waking up one morning to find Ali standing over him with a pair of scissors, Michael decided today would be the day, and luckily there was a hairdresser on site, so he wouldn't have to go into town.

Michael arrived at work around 9am, Told Matthew he was getting a haircut, and made his way over to Admin block "B" where a young man called Paul worked his Magic, Paul was a nice enough guy, but god he loved to chat. The "salon" itself was a small broom closest about 15 feet long and 10 feet wide, it had one window and a dodgy looking ceiling fan. There was someone in front of Michael when he arrived, so he plonked himself on the wooden bench near the entrance, and waited. Five minutes later the creation was complete, another triumph, and Gary the plumber was on his way with a much skinned head indeed. Then it was Michaels turn, he made his way to the wonky old wooden chair, sat down, and explained he just wanted the same as he had already, but shorter, thinking his part in the haircut was over, Michael settled in for what surely would be a quick snip and cut, alias this wouldn't be the case, instead it was a haircut and the Ballard of Paul the barber. Paul had decided he wanted to travel the world; this decision was made shortly after his break up with Gary. Gary had been the love of Paul's life, but after he had caught Steve with that Bitch!, (The bitch was never given a name or sex) Paul left his swanky high paying position with some Knightsbridge salon, and was now having the time of his life in Pakistan, he was also living with a local man, and Paul *loved* the fact their love was forbidden, 'it feels so dangerous, it makes it feel so much, so much more *real*, you know?' was he telling Michael this or asking him a question?, Michael was a 14 year old, who up until a month ago had very little life experience to call on to answer such a question, and couldn't think of a thing to say. There was now a silence, Paul had also stopped cutting, *Oh god* thought Michael he does want me to say something, thinking fast Michael tried to steer the conversation towards a more neutral subject, the weather, Paul adored the fact he could tan himself every day, sometimes naked, also he could sit on his balcony and drink tea in the afternoons, again sometimes naked, Michael now wished he had just answered the original bloody question. One short(ish) cut later Michael was ready for the beach, Paul said 'good bye sugar' to which Michael had no idea how to respond to, so politely smiled and left.

The rest of the afternoon was spent at the beach; it had been a while since they had gone the seaside, the last time being the BBQ and Navy football tournament, the sand felt nice underfoot. After a nice long sizzle and swim in the sea, the gang decided there were no girls to show off to, so went to the club, all looking forward to that nights new film, the burning.

Like a lot of horror flicks in the early 80's, the film was set around a summer camp, and involved teenagers been killed off in new and disgusting ways by a killer who could not be stopped. After watching the film Michael was of the opinion, No child should see the burning, ever!!

Monday 20th June – Villa/club.
'Did not go to work, did go to club,
Saw '*10 to midnight*'

With work at the stores a bit slack, Matthew had given his star worker (Matthews words not Michaels) a couple of days off, The stores boss was also worried he was working Michael too hard, yes Pakistani boys and girls worked ten hour days by the age of 14, but Michael was different, white children went to school and learnt English and maths, then got jobs in offices, well that was Matthews view anyway, so while things were quiet, Matthew gave his young charge a much needed break. It was 10am before Michael awoke, the Villa long since deserted. He slouched his way down to the kitchen, the marble feeling nice and cool on his feet, as he sleepwalked down the steps his mind drifted, he wondered what his school friends would be doing first thing on a Monday morning back in Essex, double English maybe?, now in the kitchen he grabbed some fruit and sat down, for some reason the chairs didn't feel very comfortable, so Michael decided to finish his mango and oranges breakfast in the Lounge. The day was really starting to warm up, so he got up and switched the two big celling fans on, which although noisy did the job, then sat back down, looking forward to reading his comics. Halfway through a beano, which he had read twice before, Michael noticed something move out of the corner of his eye, now he had seen many a creature since arriving in Pakistan, but he had never seen a praying mantis, it looked alien, a weird odd green alien, with its odd head and large body, Michael couldn't take his eyes off of it, he wondered if it might want a piece of fruit, maybe mango, however just as Michael was about to see if it fancied something to eat, it jumped, or maybe flew? Michael wasn't sure if they could fly or were just really good jumpers, either way it can't of had very good eye sight, because at 6 and a half feet it was sliced in two by a blade from the ceiling fan. With the animal show now over, Michael went for a walk around the compound.

Around lunch time Ali briefly broke up Michael's day, the house boy had been fishing and now returned home with the catch of the day, a *huge* long fish, Ali slammed it down on the Kitchen counter and started to de scale the monster. Michael had never seen a fish de scaled before and looked at the ease and speed the old man displayed working on the beast, within ten minutes the job was done, the fish was stored in the fridge, and Ali left to do some shopping, leaving Michael once more alone. After trying to do some homework, and then giving up, deciding it was too damned hot to be doing any sort of thinking, Michael had a mid-afternoon nap. Around 5pm dad was home, and after a wonderful fresh fish curry it was on to the club, with yet another new film.

Michael felt like Barry Norman with the amount of films he

had seen recently, not that he was complaining, they certainly helped with the boredom. By the time they arrived a queue was already forming outside the cinema room, word on the street was the film was an action flick, and a pirate, 'So it's a pirate action film?' asked a slightly confused Michael, dad didn't know whether to laugh or cry, was his kid this green or just dumb, in the end he put it down to youth and innocence 'No son, pirate means someone went into a cinema where the film was playing, and made a copy on a video camera' 'Isn't that illegal?' replied Michael a little too loudly, several members of the queue looked in their direction. Now dad wanted his son to have morals, but also see the bigger *picture*, as far as he was concerned life had a habit of screwing with him, so if he got to see a dodgy copy of a movie before it was official released, so what, he paid his taxes and worked hard, yet he did have an obligation to raise the boy right. 'You may be right son, but we're thousands of miles away from home, and I miss you're mum, so let's just enjoy the film' Michael processed this, to him it made sense, dad had made a good point, also sometimes he did over think situations.

The film is question was 10 to midnight, a great Charles Bronson flick; - Charlie played a LAPD detective, who is on the trail of a very handsome young man who had been seducing and slashing young women. It really was a top notch thriller, and Bronson just owned the screen. It was leaps and bounds beyond the burning, the pervious nights film; it had everything including the wonderful actor Wilford Brimley.

After the film, it was a quick game of snooker then home.

Wednesday 22ⁿᵈ June – Work.
'Did go to work'

Today I'm going to work on my wood, thought Michael, it had been a while since he had last worked on the pieces of crates, and something that morning had stirred in Michaels mind, yes it was always going to be a table, but it would now have a

draw, how cool would that look. Michael was also now over
the disappointment his creation would never leave the hospital,
due to its size, and had decided the table would make a great
thank you gift for Matthew, who would be staying on for a bit
after the hospital had opened. Apparently someone needed to
stay on and account for everything that had been bought used
and lost during the construction of the complex, so the table
would have some use after Michael had left for England. By
11am Michael had attached two of the four legs to the base of
the table, and in the process only used fourteen nails, instead
of the usual fifty, so he was definitely getting better, with half
the job done he went for a well-deserved break and headed for
the canteen. Michael then dropped by the stores, to show
Matthew he was still alive and in one piece, then it was off to
find dad and home for a shower, but **not** to the club
afterwards, for tonight they would be babysitting.

The Toyota was the only source of light on the dark country
roads currently been used by father and son. Dad was
explaining who they would be babysitting for, apparently a
couple of researchers were over from England, to help set up
the labs at the hospital, and for some reason had brought their
young children with them? They were the type of people who
would rather stay at home and read or talk to each other, then
go out for the evening, Michael thought this behaviour to be
odd, but that was just the type of people they were. Tonight
though they had to go out, having been invited to a party held
by some big wig at the hospital, but what to do with the kids?
Then they met dad, who was only too happy to help out, 'And
they're ok about us doing this?' questioned Michael, dad
laughed 'They can hardly call a babysitting service can they?
You take what you can get over here, plus your dads charm
helped' it was true; dad had charm by the bucket loads. Dad
went on, 'I remember when we lived in Walthamstow, we got
neighbours, uncles, even passer-by's to look after you when
you were young' Dad laughed again, Michael remembering this
was in fact true, didn't, dad was right, back then him and mum
let any bugger look after him.

Dad parked the Toyota in the villa's large car park, had a quick cigarette, then walked towards the house, as he and Michael reached the front door, the researchers appeared, all dressed up and ready to go. Sarah and Nicklaus were nice enough, both were thirty something, universality educated, and were very glad Michael and co had turned up. Apparently the kids, 3 year old twins Jessica and Ben, were already asleep, so really they were there just in case the twins woke up, the couple explained they would be back by 11pm, at the latest, so dad and Michael should make themselves at home and relax. Within five minutes of the pair arriving the researchers had gone, now alone dad and Michael started to look around the pad. Apart from Terry's place this was the first house Michael had been in since arriving in Pakistan, and it was a house, not a villa with five bedrooms that had ten foot walls surrounding it, or a 60 something house boy who slept in the garden with a big bloody knife, no it was just a house, a very normal house.

'Ah' said Dad 'There it is' Michael went to find dad who was in the lounge, wondering what he had found, it was the researchers television set. Michael hadn't really missed TV, as he saw a film most nights at the club, but dad loved his Television, and had been looking forward to this moment all day. Happy he had found the source of the nights entertainment, dad then helped himself to some snacks and beer, he then sat on the couples rather expensive sofa, and fumbled for the remote, Michael getting into the spirit of the evening, grabbed a coke and sat with dad, ready for a night of TV.

Despite mostly being in Arabic, dad still enjoyed the shows on that night, the majority seemed to be chat shows, although not the European type the lads were used to, there was also a lot of singing programs, or programs that had singing in them and any rate. An hour later they hit pay dirt, sport, it was cricket and not football, but who cared, sport was sport. The Game on that night was the world cup semi-final between the home boys Pakistan, versus the mighty West indies, it all made sense now to Michael, a lot of workers at the hospital over the past week seemed very excited about something, but Michael couldn't make out what. The match was being played at the Oval, which of course was in London England, this to Michael was just bizarre, here they were watching Pakistan playing in London, when they were in Pakistan, mind blowing stuff, well it was to a teenager.

Although they couldn't understand the commentators, dad and Michael could still follow what was happening on the pitch, and it was going to be close, but there had to be one winner, and it wasn't going to Pakistan's night. The west Indies won by 8 wickets (with 68 balls remaining) 188 runs to 184. Pakistan had lost, and this was despite a fine innings by their opener Mohsin Khan, who hit a 70, but the West Indies hit back, with Richards finishing 80 not out. The West Indies were in great form, and through to the final, but India would go on to beat them 3 days later, which further dampened the mood in Pakistan, because not only were they out of the world cup, their bitter rivals India bloody won it. With the game over dad then asked an odd question, 'Do you like horror films?' Michael thought this was odd because of some of the films he had seen with dad over the past month or so, including the burning, 'They're not my favourite, but some are ok' dad taking this as a yes disappeared outside to the car, then re appeared several minutes later with a VHS tape, 'Some guy at work said this was the best horror he had ever seen' as dad slotted the tape in the machine, Michael could only wonder what summer holiday camp this one would be set in, but this movie wasn't set in any type of camp, no it was set in a mall (shopping centre) as the tape started to roll the title popped up, it read **Dawn of the dead**. Michael spent most of the film with his eyes closed, Zombies were some scary shit, you just couldn't kill them, and if you did three would take its place, and then there was the flesh eating sound effects. Two hours later the films job was done, Michael had hated it, yet at the same time *loved* it, but it had scared the bejesus out of him. Still

getting over the film Sarah and Nicklaus walked in nearly
giving the poor lad a heart attack. He would not sleep well that
night, or indeed for a few nights to come.

Thursday 23rd June – Work.
'Did go to work, then a walkabout'

Michael was glad to see daylight as he woke, the film from the
night before, which he both loved and hated in equal measure,
was still fresh in his mind, every creak or bang brought images
of the un dead walking through the villa straight into Michaels
mind and dreams, bloody dad he thought, after a quick check
for zombies under the bed, Michael got up and headed for the
bathroom. Teeth and face brushed, Michael walked back into
the bedroom and past the window next to his desk, as he
walked past something outside caught his attention, he stopped
and looked out, there was Rabies the guard dog, Michael really
did feel sorry for the mongrel, it wasn't her fault she was
diseased, he wondered if a bite from the old girl could start a
zombie style outbreak, people running around afraid of
puddles of water and licking their crouches, god he needed to
watch another film, anything, even Disney! anything to get that
bloody film out of his head.

Work was a bust, there was nothing to do, so Michael just sat
at his desk for much of the day, listening to the workers moan
about their cricket team losing to the West Indies the night
before, the whole place was a downer. Thankfully it was still
half days and Michael had a walk about to look forward to, he
had no idea what one was, but as long as it didn't involve
Cricket or zombies he was game.

Now Michael had of course heard of the Aboriginal
walkabout, the whole world had, but that was in Australia, he
had not heard of one involving Pakistan. So after work he and
dad drove to the meeting point with Ali, dad explained this was
a big deal, 'he (Ali) doesn't just do this with everyone you

know, he seems to have taken a real shine to you' this was all well and good thought Michael, but it still didn't explain what a walkabout was? they left the main road and headed down a small track, eventually they found a make shift car park, next to a large lake.

There was nothing around for miles expect sun drenched trees and birds, lots of birds, all crowing and calling, god it was noisy, waiting for them next to the lake was a smiling Ali, who was putting a small wooden boat into the water. As the pair walked towards Ali, he pointed at Michael then the boat, Michael then spotted some fishing rods, he stopped and turned to dad, 'we're not going fishing in that are we?' Michael pointed at the water craft that on further examination looked as if it would spring a leak just being near water. 'of course not' replied dad, Michael sighed with relief, 'I wouldn't fit in that, it's just you two going fishing' although Ali couldn't speak much English, he had now got the gist of the conversation and smiled, it was such a big smile that Michael could count the three good teeth left in the house boys month, 'but, but I can't go out in that' protested Michael, 'You can swim can't you' countered dad, Michael couldn't come up with a quick enough reply and before he knew it, both he and Ali were in the boat and on their way to the middle of the lake, hang on thought Michael, and turned to ask Ali a question, but this would have been futile so called to dad instead, who was on his way back to the Toyota, 'dad, DAD!' Michael senior turned around, 'WHAT?' 'I thought you said this was a walkabout? this is more like a row about?' dad seemed to find this assuming and chuckled as he replied, 'Oh don't worry, this is just the start, the walkabout comes later' god Michael hated dad sometimes, *later he* thought, what the hell does that mean? normally Michael would now go into sulk mode, until he got his own way, but he was in a boat with a pensioner he couldn't talk to, so sulking would get him nowhere, there was only one option left, get the whole thing out of the way, then everyone could get on with the rest of their lives.

Ali sensing the boy was ready, gave him a rod, now Michael hadn't done much Fishing before today, but he knew a bamboo stick with a piece of string on it anywhere, after a minute of staring at each other, Ali guested to Michael, who knew what was required of him, but was feeling rebellious again so sat motionless, he was stuck on a boat with a man who didn't speak much English, had no hat and a boiling sun above them, he hoped Ali would sense his displeasure with the situation and row them to shore. Ali however had other ideas, in one shift movement he raised his right hand and held three fingers up, he then picked up his rod with his left hand and signalled this as one, the house boy then held a 2nd finger up, and grabbed a worm from an old plastic bucket, he stuck the wiggling beast onto the Rods hook, then cast the line into the river, a little late and a bit obvious, Ali held the third and final finger up, he then pointed at Michael, expecting him to do the same. Michael was already holding his rod, so was a third of the way there, and after a quick fight with one of the worms, he too was soon casting off, then the waiting began, not that Michael had much time to get bored, his mind was alive with questions, why didn't dad tell him where they were going? Why didn't dad give him a hat? If Michael had been given a head ups about the trip he could have brought his Walkman, no Michael was not a happy bunny, he stared at Ali, the man had a look of utter peace, he didn't care about the world's problems at that time, or any time for that matter, he was just enjoying the scenery. Michael was beginning to roast and wiped his brow for sweat, sensing the boy was hot, Ali took off his floppy wicker hat and gave it to Michael, then in his own language seemed to give the boy a mild telling off, for not telling him sooner he was hot, Ali then rowed the boat closer to the shore to gain some relief using the overhanging trees. Slowly Michael started to enjoy himself, changing location also helped with the fishing, within moments Ali had caught something, something big, without warning Ali thrust his rod into Michael's hands and grabbed a net from out of nowhere, Ali franticly motioned to Michael to pull the line out of the water, as he did so Ali put the net into the lake, and after a brief battle, it was over, they had won, somehow between them they had landed Jaws, or at least a two foot scaly monster, Ali happy with the catch dispatched the fish with a large rock to the head, then rowed the boat to shore, fishing was brutal.

Once on shore Ali put the Fish in a plastic carrier bag, then hide the rods in some bushes, Michael sensed the old guy only every fished in these waters so had no need to carry home more than he needed to. Ali did however leave the bucket of worms for the next fisherman, nice gesture thought Michael. Once they had secured the boat the walkabout began, really the walkabout was just a ramble through the bushes, it was about five miles to the Villa and with Ali leading the way it wouldn't take that long, it did however cross Michael's mind that if you *didn't* know the way, a walk like this could go wrong fast and end up as a very long hike, but that wasn't going to happen today. They past many a family, most living in tents, huts, old shacks, all seemed to know Ali, and were very friendly towards Michael, offering him food and drinks, even though they could barely afford to feed themselves, talk about community spirit. By 3pm they were back home, Michael thanked Ali for the day, and then went to find Dad, to have words, after having a quick shower of course.

Friday 24th June – Beach/club.
'Day off, went to beach, went to club,
Saw '*operation Crossbow*'

Michael had been in the country for about 10 weeks now, and was glad he was too young to drink, if he had been a year or two older he would have been a full blown alcoholic by this point, and looking to go into rehab on return to the UK. Of course Coke, Pepsi, 7 up, or whatever he was having at the club, wasn't exactly health drinks, god knows what all that fizzy stuff was doing to his insides, he remembered at school his chemistry teacher had cleaned a dirty 2 pence piece with some coke, Michael didn't have a fizzy drink for a week. He could only guess at the amount of Alcohol dad, Steve, and the rest had consumed since he had been at the villa, and what it doing to them, Christ they were even brewing the stuff in the spare upstairs bedroom! for a Muslim country it was bloody easy to get a beer, yet Michael had to drink something, and so did dad, and his argument was simple, the local water was rancid and the bottle water was either to expensive or difficult to find, so beer it was. Michael now bored with the usual fizzy drinks rubbish hit upon a cunning plan, mix the two, dad had said he could drink a small amount of beer, so he would add a drop or two to lemonade and make a Shandy type drink, Simple yet refreshing. Now armed with his new refreshment, Michael along with Dad and Steve hit the beach.

Steve being the young buck, frolicked in the sea, trying to get the attention of some western nurses dipping their toes further up the beach. Dad was hung over, so was sun bathing next to Michael. After thirty minutes of sizzling like a couple of sausages, Michael decided to have a cold drink, and rummaged in the cool bag, 'You're not having a beer are you?' Michael Jumped, he thought Dad was a sleep. 'What, no I was getting a' dad laughed, 'Don't worry, you know I'm kidding, I said you could have one or two' Michael grabbed a bottle and walked over to dad, 'yeah I remember, you just surprised me that's all, thought you were asleep, did you want a drink?' Dad looked at his watch, 'yeah why not, it's after twelve somewhere in the world' dad laughed to himself, Michael just stared at him, 'Tell you what dad, try this' Michael handed him a bottle of homemade Shandy, Dad took a swig, then another and several more after that, until he had finished the bottle, 'That was bloody great, what was that?' Michael now needing another bottle, walked back to the cool bag 'Its beer and lemonade' replied Michael 'Ah Shandy, nice isn't it' dad called over to Steve, who was striking out with the nurses, 'STEVE, try this' dad held his empty bottle up. Within the hour all five bottles that had contained Shandy were now empty, *bloody adults* thought Michael, who in the end only had one to himself, but he wasn't really bitter, well maybe a tiny amount, but his drink was a triumph and at least on this trip dad had given his liver a little rest bite, so Michael was happy about that.

Later they went to the club, dad even ordered a Shandy, well one, then he hit the harder stuff, but every little helps. The evenings film was operation Crossbow, it followed allied agents attempting to infiltrate some Nazis secret research site. It starred George Peppard, Tom Courtenay, John Mills, and Sophia Loren. The blurb on the film read something like this "In the annals of Allied history this true (ish) story was one of the most secret and certainly most desperate covert attempts to destroy the Nazi's ultimate weapons" whatever it was about, a good evening was had by all.

Saturday 25th June - Villa/Club.
'Did not go to work, went to club,
Beat dad at snooker then got
Beat by dad'

Michael spent the day at the Villa, he had no go in him, the same was true at the club, he *just* about beat dad at snooker, before losing the rematch.

Monday 27th June – Work/Club.
'Went to work, went to club,
Saw *Holocaust 2000*'

Monday saw the start of a new week, which gave Michael a renewed sense of purpose; he completed the previous week's data input by 10am, and even resisted the normal temptation to play around on the computer, looking for games to play like pong or chess, nope it was all business today. With the data input complete, Michael strode off to work on his table, it was really coming along now, even passer-by's could tell what is going to be when finished, normally people would hurray past or just laugh at his creation, but now, now it was taking shape. By 11am it was lunch, Michael put his hammer down and wiped some non-existent sweat from his brow, then stood back, and like his name sake before him, Michelangelo, stared at the pieces of nailed wood in front of him, 'Yeah not bad, not bad at all' he then went to meet dad. by 1pm the day was over and it was back to the villa, but Michael was still on a mission, and even did some homework, there really was no stopping him. Later it was off to the club, and Instead of Snooker, Michael played Darts, and found yet another game he could beat dad and the rest at, yes Michael was on a roll, he then went into the clubs film room to settle down for that nights *blockbuster*.

The film was a X rated piece of late 70's pulp, "An executive in charge of a Middle Eastern nuclear plant discovers that his son is the Anti-Christ and sets out to stop him from using the nuclear power at his fingertips to wipe out mankind" Was the write up. In every respect it reminded Michael of The Omen, which was made a year before Holocaust 2000. Yes of course there were differences, but really it was the same story, and not even Kirk Douglas could save it.

With the film over there was just enough time for Michael to find one more *victim*, after two quick games of darts it was home time.

Tuesday 28th June – Market.
'Did not go to work, but went to
The market at night'

Two weeks! That's all he had left in the country, two short weeks, the same amount of time the average family spent holidaying in the south of France. Michael had been in Pakistan since April but really hadn't *seen* the country, yes he had been to the beach, the hospital and even went on a walkabout, but really you could have crammed all that in a long weekend. Michael needed to do more, panic was starting to set in, he also needed to get his friends and family presents.

Michael of course could pick up any number of T-Shirts or baseball style caps up at the airport on his departure, or get something for everyone at the hospital's gift shop, which for some reason was open already, despite the hospital being months away from opening its doors to the public, but he wanted to get authentic gifts, something that said, *Pakistan*. Michael also had homework to do, so took the day off and hit the books, by lunch time he was bored and hungry, so hit the Kitchen. With sandwich in hand he flopped onto the lounges wicker sofa and switched on the radio, as always the news was light and happy, a Bridge section in America, along the I-95 in Greenwich Connecticut had collapsed, killing 3 people, oh and NASA had also launched Galaxy A, a communications Satellite, so not all bad news then. Around 1pm dad was home, with a surprise.

'I got paid again?' Michael couldn't believe it had been a month since last pay day, dad handed over the envelope and this time it was all Michaels, he owed dad nothing, but what to do with it, he couldn't take it home, he was pretty sure the local newsagents wouldn't take it, even though it was run be an Indian family, and he probably wouldn't get much if he exchanged it back into sterling, then dad offered his son a chance to spend his money, and get some presents for everyone, a trip to the market, at night. 'Will it be safe?' Michael didn't want to sound scared but felt it was an important question to ask, dad was busy getting ready and didn't seem to pay the question much attention 'It's about as safe as anything else you do in this crap hole of a country' dads reply really didn't answer his son's question, but they were going and that was that. The villa had an early dinner, then around 5.00pm dad, Steve and Michael were on their way, apparently they would be meeting Ali at the market. Dad was driving and appeared to be on a mission to hit every ditch and pot hole there was, after the tenth *thud* he tried to blame the fact it was dark, but Michael and Steve were having none of it, and gently poked fun at the old mans driving skills, who for once took the abuse on the chin. Slightly battered and bruised they arrived around 6pm, having found a parking space, a piece of desert on the edge of town, they got out, rubbed they heads, then headed towards the market.

To call it a market was to do it an injustice, it was the size of a small town, in fact it might have been a town, a town completely made out of stalls and awnings. The smells were the first to hit, they smacked you in the face the moment you got out the car, the stench of amazing spices and foods, all been carried along a hot nights breeze. To complete the attack on your senses was the incredibly wave of sounds, thousands of people walking talking haggling, and playing music, either for live or via huge tape players, it certainly beat the Sunday morning flea pit of a market in Basildon. By the time they reached the first stall they were all hungry, despite having dinner an hour or so before, the smells in the air had done they're work. After attacking some "meat" on a stick, it was down to business, what to get his friends thought Michael, in all he would have to buy 15 items, so there was no time to waste. They had several hours but with no map of the market to hand, it could take days to find individual gifts, so Michael soon decided one stall would do it all, dad too had plans for his hard earned wages, he would be going home with Michael so needed something for mum and Sarah, Steve was just there to look for girls and any new tapes for his Walkman. At first Steve had laughed at Michael when he got his, then borrowed it one day when the cars radio cassette broke, after that there was no stopping him, soon Steve had his own and was wired for sound. 'Do you think Sarah would like this?' dad held up a many coloured traditional head scarf, 'She would stand out a bit don't you think' replied Michael who was picturing his 7 year old sister walking along a cold grey morning in Essex, wearing the brightly coloured scarf, dad seemed to ignore his son's comments and bought it anyway, as a "backup present" he also got mum one, again just in case he couldn't find anything else. Dad really was crap at buying gifts. Michael on the other hand, well was just as bad, he really didn't have a clue what to get anyone. Dad looked at his watch 'come on its

8, we need to meet Ali' it had been agreed that they would meet their house boy at his cousins stall, near the middle of the market. Around 10 past they arrived at the stall, Ali was in full converse with his cousin, they seemed to be having a heated debate over an item, before approaching, the group waited for a deal to be struck, transaction complete, Ali and cousin shook hands and everyone was friends again. Happy with his purchase, Ali then took dad and co on a tour of the market, although Ali couldn't speak much English he knew the guys, and what they liked and didn't like. also where to buy your food and where to avoid.

The first stall Ali took them to, was cheap, cheerful, but really just full of crap, the 2nd was no better, although stocked with amazing rugs and carpets, they couldn't use them in the Villa, not on marble floors, and there was no way they could take them home, so it was on to the 3rd this at least held some hope, the stall was full of general odds and sods, local trinkets and objects, but again nothing useful. The 4th was a food stall, dad was really getting into meat on a stick, and Ali was pretty well connived the meat wasn't cat or dog, but couldn't be *100%* sure. By 9pm they arrived at the 5th Stall, this one was clothing as well as carpets and rugs, by now Michael was tired, not even a free coke helped, he just wanted the experience to be done, over the evening he had decided most of the things he could buy or afford would be to heavy to pack, or just to plain tacky, so had made a decision, t-shirts it was, they were cheap, light weight and easy to pack. At first he was afraid of what his friends might say, *you went all the way to Pakistan and all you got me was a lousy t-shirt*, then he thought screw them, it's a free bloody gift. So at the 5th and final stall he bought 5 small, 5 medium, and 5 large T-shirts, some black, some blue, all with the same design, big letters stating "Pakistan 83" on the chest with a big eagle underneath. Job done he showed dad what he had bought, who thought his son was mad buying everyone a gift, but hey it was his money to waste. Shopping done they headed home. After one more stick of meat for dad.

Wednesday June 29th - Work/Club.
'Went to work, went to club,
Saw *'The Beastmaster'*

Feeling a lot happier with life, after the previous night's buying expedition at the market, the results of which were now safely packed in his suitcase ready for England, Michael got ready for work. With ten days left in the Country there was still plenty to do, and with that in mind Michael needed to crack on the moment he got to the site.

Once at work he said later to Dad, then headed over to the stores. Today would be one of the last times he would go to work, not the last, but one of the last, despite this fact Matthew was already showing signs of tears and hugs, luckily Michael had a plan to avoid any embarrassing scenes, he would get the mornings paperwork out of the way, then when no one was looking, hit the wood, for today he would finish his creation. Bang on 11am the stores workers went for tea, and with everyone briefly distracted, Michael seized the moment and slipped out to the area where his table was located. He had been building the damn thing for weeks now, and really it was still just some pieces of wood with a lot of nails in it, however to his constant amazement no one had touched it, back in England it would have been binned or turned into fire wood after a couple of days, but here people seemed to have respected what he was up to, and had left it alone.

Hammer in hand Michael stared at the table, the right side was done, the legs were hammered on with a thousand nails (yet despite the amount of iron pumped into it, this piece of furniture was only to look at and not to touch!!) so all that remained was for the left legs to be attached. Michael approached the table, stopping just short, he wanted to inspect the half full paint can of nails on the floor, he counted how many were left, *'hmm I might not have enough'* he mumbled to himself. Twenty minutes and thirty nine nails later, the legs were on, and after finding a plaster for the bleeding finger on his left hand, which he had hit during a sneezing fit whilst striking nail twenty two in, Michael could now relax, the main part of the job was done, which was just as well as the midday sun was really beating down on him, he had a major sweat on, thankfully all he had to do now was paint the…. 'Balls' he half shouted, 'Balls! Balls! Balls!' he had forgotten to sand down the table before putting on the legs. Michael couldn't believe what he had done, he had really wanted to do a proper job this time, *needing* for once to get something right first time, but that wasn't going to happen now, yes he could still sand down the rest of the table, but that wasn't the point, no, it was ruined now. After a quick sulk he decided to move on, just paint the thing and get on with his life, get the farce over with, but what colour to paint it? The choices were yellow or blue, the corridors in the hospital were a lovely egg shell yellow, and the waiting rooms blue, but neither colour worked for Michael on their own, so in a move that would have pleased his year two art teacher Mr Jones, Michael mixed the two, the result should have been green, but this wasn't green, well it was, but a very *light* green, the colour reminded Michael of the time he had had his bowel problems, god it really did. Maybe it will dry a better colour lied Michael to himself, yes of course it will, and so convinced a miracle would happen in the very near future, he started to paint the table. By noon it was done, all that was left was for the paint to dry, and then give it to Matthew in a couple of days. Sweaty and achy Michael went to find dad.

When Michael found dad, he was in the middle of telling his workers to fuck off for the day, apparently they had made such a big hole for a water pipe, that even Jeff the bricklayer couldn't help; and it was going to take three people a whole day to fix, so dad called it quits and took Michael home.

After dinner it was off to the club, however after his morning exploits, Michael still wasn't happy how Matthews table had turned out, he was in no mood to play darts or snooker, so it was a quick shandy, then off to the cinema room, ready for the evenings viewing. Tonight it was the 1982 fantasy classic "The Beastmaster" starring Marc Singer and Rip Torn, the story was a sword-and-sorcery fantasy, about a young man's search for revenge, armed with a big sword and supernatural powers. The handsome hero, (Singer) and his animal allies, waged war against marauding forces. Michael loved it, he was the right age for the film, it had it all, including sword fights and lots of awful dialogue, the rest of the audience however were not so taken with the film as Michael, most felt inadequate, as our hero had bigger muscles then them and spent most of the film in nothing but a thong and a skimpy open chested top, but it wasn't all bad news, there was a pretty girl for the lads to look at (Tanya Roberts) who didn't wear much more than Singer, god bless fantasy films, so everyone got something out of the viewing experience.

Thursday 30th June – Club.
'Did not go to work, went to club,
Beat Bill, lost to Dan'

The day was as follows, woke up late, scratched arse, late breakfast, listened to Walkman, Lunch, dad home, club, snooker, home and bed.

Friday 1st July – Karachi/Club.
'Day off, just went for a drive around Karachi
Went to club, saw *Omen II.*'

Today marked the end of Ramadan, and dad could not have been happier, in fact he was so full of joy he had gone into early, waking Michael up in the process, dad had shouted something to Steve, and Michael could have been Paraphrasing, but he swore he heard dad shout 'Right its time those part time lazy fuckers to do a decent days work' despite what he had said to Steve, dad in fact liked his workforce, well most of them, but the month long festival had put his team well behind, however all that half days nonsense was now behind them, and it was time for some hard graft, god help them thought Michael, for dad was on a mission. With the noisy boys gone, Michael could finally get some more Sleep, finally drifting of around 8.

Michael picked up his watch, it was 10.06, the day was truly awake, unlike him, with both eyes now open he could see the beams of sunlight pouring into the bedroom, but it wasn't the time or sun that had woken him up, no it was something more biological, and there was no escaping it, try as he might, he was bursting for a wee! so it was get up, or find a bottle, and with no empty bottle to hand, he reluctantly headed for the loo. Bladder now empty, he put on some shorts and left the bedroom, the place was quiet, Michael was all alone in the cold empty marble villa, and for once it was cold, so returned to the bedroom and put on some socks, toes now cosy, he headed for the ground floor.

All was well until he reached the third step of the stairs, then an animal outside barked really loud and close, startling Michael, thinking a stray dog had maybe got into the compound, he went to run down the steps to investigate, it was at this point he found marble and cotton **do not** mix, slipping on the fourth and fifth steps he grabbed on to the banister like a drowning man would hang on to a life raft, in doing so he stopped himself falling down the staircase, Michael sighed with relief, but there was no time to think about what had just happened, as the creature barked again, it was really close now. Two minutes later, after inching down the steps, completely forgetting he could have taken his socks of at any point, Michael was on the ground floor, and could now finally investigate where the barking was coming from. Michael was worried Rabies had got in; maybe she had dug a hole? he careful jogged towards the lounge, it had the best view out onto the lawn, however instead of turning from the corridor into the room. he skidded straight past, and would have carried on forever but luckily a wall stopped him five feet later, he was now on his bum, after checking for any broken bones or cuts, Michael carefully stood up, as he did he heard the animal bark again, he could tell it was further away now, it must have been right next to the gate when it first barked he thought. Still thanks to whatever made the noise, Michael had found a new game.

Five minutes later the game area was set up and ready to use, the red cushion on the floor marked the starting point, you would run up to it, then start sliding, when you stopped, mark this point with another cushion, then keep going until you get your best score. For 1 - ? players, aged 14 or under, mental age that is. His first attempt was ten feet, a poor try really, Michael put this down as a *test run*, the second slide was a lot better, nearly hitting the 20 foot mark, the third was around 25 foot. 'Getting better' he quipped to himself. After a sip of coke and a quick brush up of the playing field, Michael lined up for his fourth run, this time he would start with his arms behind his back, then throw them forward as he past the red start cushion, he practised for a second, then after psyching himself up, went for it. After stopping, Michael was extremely happy no one else was around to see that attempt, not only was it the same distance as the last run, 25 foot, but when he throw his arms out to get more length, well he looked like a right tit. He paced the floor again, he could, in theory, get around 40 foot, if he really went for it, hell for leather and so on, but was he prepared to risk injury just for a longer slide, of course he was, so after a quick calculation and some minor changes, minor been a change of socks, his current pair were a bit sweaty, he was ready. This was it, the fifth run, and five was his lucky number, so it all looked good, no it *felt* good, like a sprinter out of the blocks, he lurched forward hitting full pelt as he was level with the red cushion, then the slide started, before he knew it he was past the ten foot marker, then 20, before hurtling past the 25 foot point, he was now in uncharted territory, and unsure how long could he keep going, the end wall helped him answer that, a gentle thud marked the end of the run. After getting up and dusting himself down, Michael walked the distance, 43 foot, a new record, one that could never be beaten, not because he was scared to try again, no it was because he couldn't physical go any further, well not without removing a wall first. Pleased with his mornings work, he went for a nap.

Around 3pm dad got home, and although Ramadan was now over, he was home early, he mumbled something about he had had enough of his workforce for the day, and needed a drive to calm down, so he had come back to the villa to pick his lazy arse son up, and get him some fresh air, Michaels schedule was wide open, so off they went. The drive itself was really a tour of the local area, then back to the hospital to pick Steve up. Along the way dad stopped to buy some cigarettes, he had run out of duty free ones he bought over with him, so now he had to buy local, which he detested, as they both smelt and tasted like camel dung, this may have been the prime reason Michael never took up smoking, why would you want to inhale something that smelt like camel droppings? yet dad still bought them, mumbling along the lines he had to smoke something, as they kept him calm? Calm! tell that to his workers. About three roads before the building site entrance, they noticed a small crowd had gathered; dad carefully squeezed by, as they did Michael caught a glimpse of a dead body on the floor, it was a horse, fly's covered its head, dad said it had been there for a couple of days now, Michael was amazed how matter of fact dad sounded as he said it, like it was an everyday thing, then it struck Michael, it was.

Soon Steve was collected, and the group were on their way back to the villa, but seeing that horse, all covered in fly's, for some reason was still with Michael, even as they arrived at the villa, Michaels mind was still turning, he had seen dead horses before, but why was there a crowd around it? What was going on? Even on the way to the club Michael couldn't stop thinking about it, maybe that night's film would help distract his train of fault.

The film was Omen 2, Damien was now 13 years old, so around Michael's age, the film was fine, nice acting and such, Michael liked the military academy parts, and the death rate was decent, eleven in all. But it wasn't really the type of him he enjoyed; still it killed a couple of hours.

Saturday 2nd July – Villa.
'Did not go to work, stayed in
Listened to tapes'

Michael was dreaming, normally it was about scoring the last minute winner in some cup final for Liverpool, or visiting America, he always wanted to see what all the fuss was about, In all the movies he had seen which were shot in the US, the people in them all seemed to be these bigger than life characters, with big cars and wide open landscapes to roam in. But his favourite dream was a mix of all the sci-fi films he had seen, the dream was always the same, he was the hero, saving some princess, and at some point of the story he would throw his life on the line, to save the day, then at the last minute escape from the jaws of death. All good teenage fun, normally, but tonight something wasn't right, in this dream he was on the floor, or maybe he was really short? Or the people were tall? Either way he was surrounded by a group of people looking down on him, they weren't laughing of shouting at him, just staring and pointing, he was of course the dead mare he had seen the day before, it had really got to him, why were all those people gathered around a dead horse, why? the country was starting to get to him, there had been the family living in the bushes across from him, the kids who's bones were broken so they would get more money when begging, and so much more. As he woke, Michael decided he couldn't face the outside world that day, no today he would listen to tapes for as long as the batteries lasted.

Sunday 3ʳᵈ July – Karachi.
'Did not go to work, or the club,
But went around town, got a cassette,
Abba'

It had been a few days since his son had last been to work,
however dad hadn't given up trying to get him to go in, ok
they were flying back in a week, and the stores weren't that
busy, a lot of the engineering jobs were now done at the
Hospital, so Matthew and the guys weren't that pushed with
equipment requests, and yes even dad wasn't that busy, but
that wasn't the point, the lad had to learn a work ethic, and
today dad was going to take the boy to work, even if he didn't
want to. Yet all that changed when dad looked out the
window, the day was stunning, hot, yet with a nice breeze and
a few clouds to keep the sun off you from time to time, So dad
made a managerial decision and took a rare day off. Steve had
already left for work, so it was just dad and Michael, and It had
been a while since they had gone into the heart of Karachi, so
today they would have a wander around and see what last
minute gifts they could buy.

The drive in was like every other trip Michael could remember
in this blasted sand bowel of a country, hot and dusty, the
journey also started the same as every other, pull out of villa,
turn right, then for the next couple of miles nothing but sand,
the vista would be populated every once in a while by men
walking with either a camel, horse, or donkey, sometimes all
three, and that was the first hour of the car ride. Then without
warning things would turn green, with tree's bushes and grass
signalling you were getting closer to somewhere that sustained
life, twenty minutes later you hit the city. The streets were
busy, busy with people trying to sell, people rushing, people
haggling, people *everywhere*. Once out of the car, the noise's
and smells hit you, you couldn't escape the sensory over load
that was the city, for once though it was a nice smell. Being
lunch time everyone was making something, they passed a

number of venders making Chapattis (an unleavened flatbread) from scratch, Michael loved the speed and skill involved, dad though was after meat on a stick, he just couldn't get enough of them, eventually his efforts paid off and soon dad was happy and Michael was eating a meat filled Chapatti. After an hour they had looked around all the shops dad wanted to visit, so then it was Michael's turn, 'So where now' asked dad, Michael wasn't sure what he wanted, it wasn't like home where he knew where all the shops were and what they had to offer, no instead he had an entire city to choose from.

Eventually he made his choice, music, but this in turn caused a problem, for there were no HMV's or our price stores in Karachi, which was a great shame, because Michael enjoyed going to these stores, with all the sights and sounds they offered, and he *loved* going into Woolworths in Billericay on a Saturday, with all the vinyl records and tapes it had on offer, Michael could spend a whole morning in there, looking at the new releases, checking the bargain bin for any records he missed first time around, and what he enjoyed above all else was looking at the art work on the 12inch singles and albums, from U2'S War to THE THE'S Soul Mining, truly amazing work. But he wasn't home, no he was here, there was however some good news, because no matter what the main selling item of any store was, be it carpets, clothes, food, they all had a tape section, all were boot legged of course, but they were still tapes with music on them, and that was all that mattered. Sometimes you got a surprise, he bought a Queen tape a few weeks before, and at the end of side two someone had added half an Mike Oldfield album, bizarre.

By 3 pm dad was bored, 'last shop son', Michael agreed, he was a little tired to, 'ok, let's look in here' Michael had spotted a large shop, it looked like a supermarket, he couldn't read the posters on the shop windows, but most of them featured food. The shop turned out to be half a supermarket, half a tailors, this was a stroke of luck for dad, so whilst Michael went looking for tapes, he went over to ask how much it would cost for a silk shirt to be repaired, the stitching in the shoulder region on one of his favourite shirts had come apart, dad could sew but wanted the job doing right. Sure enough Michael found a tape section, between the bags of rice and bags of flour, there was a rack of about thirty cassettes. *Got, got got, don't want*, he either had most of them or didn't like the bands, he really wasn't a culture club or wham fan, and he really didn't like Paul Young, so in the end it was down to two, Queen or Abba, which didn't really help as he had loads of tapes of both bands, but he didn't have super trouper, so Abba won the day, although in reality there could have been anything on the tape, just cause it said Abba didn't mean a thing, it could have been Johnny cash for all Michael knew. With the tape bought they Left, although dad would come back later with his silk shirt.

Chapter Eight.

GOODBYE MICAEL.

Monday 4ᵗʰ July – Wednesday 6ᵗʰ July
Work/Villa/Club.

The first part of the week was a bust, with Tuesday being the only real highlight, and that was a film! Yet this wouldn't be just any film, no it would be the last film Michael would see in Pakistan. Thankfully it wasn't a dud; instead it was a classic, Airplane II. There was no doubt it was silly, very silly, but that didn't stop it going down a scream, everyone loved it, even Captain Kirk was in it. Michael hadn't seen William Shatner in anything other than star trek, so it was a revelation to see him doing something different, it was like seeing your mum outside the house doing anything other than shopping or going to the hairdressers.

Wednesday also brought another last, Michael's last day at work. The morning was an odd affair, Michael would see people talking normally, yet when he looked at them they would go quiet or walk into another room, very odd indeed, Matthew of course was in tears the moment Michael had in the walked in the stores, he had grown to love the lad like he was part of his own family, and in turn Michael had grown to see Matthew as some sort of uncle, or distant relative. Around noon, eyes now wiped, Matthew walked up to Michael's desk, 'Michael sir, can you please input the figures for the week' Matthew then put some files on the desk, now this was odd, very odd thought Michael, with him not being in the Friday before, someone else should have inputted all the weeks data, still a job was a job and he liked using the computer, so with a 'ok' he was on his way. Michael decided to take his time; it was his last day after all, so went the long way round, past the research department, through the canteen, past Steve who was chatting to a rather attractive and rather married nurse, Michael did think about saying hi, but Steve didn't look like he was in the mood, his chat up lines were not as yet working, but fair play to the lad, he wasn't going to give up without a fight, a few minutes later Michael was in the admin office, ready to input the data, he found the comfy chair and got settled. It became clear very quickly to Michael that someone had already inputted the data from the week before, he wasn't impressed 'god damn it' sighed Michael, why would Matthew give him a job that had already been done, he picked up the files and walked back to the stores, it must have been some employee leaving prank thought Michael, he didn't think Matthew was that type of guy, so good for him, he did have a sense of humour, this put a smile on Michaels face.

As Michael arrived back at the stores, it soon became clear the whole data input job was indeed a ruse, his first clue was the huge handmade banner that now hung from the ceiling, the message read "GOOD BY MICAEL", ok the spelling wasn't quite there, but the sentiment was more than clear, the second clue was Matthew rushing out of his office, with a big wide smile on his face and a good bye card in his right hand, he shook Michael's hand, rather vigorously, then handed him the card, 'we will miss you Michael sir, you have been my number one worker' Michael knew this was a Lie as he had slept at his desk for most of the shifts he had bothered to turn in for. Michael looked around at the other employees, they also knew the truth, but what else was Matthew meant to say? Thank god you're leaving you lazy little shit! Matthew however was not finished, 'We also have this to give you' like a bolt of lightning Michael suddenly remembered the table, 'Stay right here' he said to Matthew 'I'll be right back', he then run out of the cabin, only to reappear 5 seconds later 'I need two volunteers' he shouted, confused and caught up in the moment Matthew pointed at two workers and told them to follow the young lad, it was at this point Michaels cake was brought out, a huge sponge cake that Matthews wife had spent the last two days working on.

Five minutes later Michael arrived back, he was out of breath
'Matthew follow me please' Michael noticed the cake, which
had been put on his desk 'that looks nice' Michael then
vanished, feeling that his wife's hard work had be validated,
Matthew followed.

Matthew was stunned, stunned into complete silence for a
whole minute, then without looking at Michael he spoke, 'and
this is for me?' 'Yes' replied a very smiley Michael, there was a
brief pause, then Matthew finally looked at the boy, still not
fully understanding what was happening 'You made this for
me?' Michael walked over to the table and patted it, very
lightly, 'To be honest not at first, but when I realised I couldn't
take it home with me, I thought now Matthew, there's a guy
who deserves a present, for putting up with me all there's
months' that was all Matthew had to hear, tears soon sprinkled
out of his eyes, he spoke, well more blubbed, before hugging
Michael, Jesus thought Michael, I'm glad I didn't get him a real
present now, god knows what he would have done then! but
Matthew could not have been more touched if Michael had
bought him all the store produced gifts in the city, no that
would just take money, this *meant* something, this took sweat,
Matthew was so happy; this would be his new office table,
something he would proudly show off to visitors. After
another hug they went in for cake and tea.

Thursday 7th July- Villa/Party.
'Did not go to work, went to a party
at Mikes House, stayed till 1am'

After the emotional roller-coaster that was yesterday, Michael
had a lie in, not that there was any reason to get up early
anymore, as he was flying home on the weekend, so with work
now done with, he was killing time at the villa till his flight.
Once up it was the same routine as most other days, a fruit
breakfast followed by a wander around the villa, hoping to find
some exotic creature that had found its way in somehow, but

nothing too big, Michael wasn't looking for loins or badgers, just something new, something to break up the norm, however as usual all he found was an empty marble building.

He checked the home brew room, which was now bare, the only evidence left the night of a thousand exploding beer bottles ever happened were the strange marks on the celling. Michael went out into the garden, it was still empty, which is what he felt like at that moment in time, yes he was a *free man*, but at what cost? the walls to protect him made him feel like he was a prisoner in a one man prison, of course this was complete bull, what prison allowed its inmates to have free access to the kitchen, and day release to go to work or the pub at night, no Michael was just bored, he was just feeling a little melodramatic, and with that he went to the living room, and put the radio on.

After flicking through various radio stations Michael found a news report that interested him, it was about an 11 year old American girl called Samantha Smith, which sounded like a made up name to Michael. Apparently the girl had written a letter to the newly appointed soviet premier, Yuri Andropov, and received a personal reply back which included an invitation to visit the Soviet Union, which she accepted, the news report went on to say she was flying from the US to the Soviet union that day. Samantha had written the letter because she was worried about the possibility of war between the two countries, and had written to Andropov to convey her worries. Christ she was 11? thought Michael, he was three years older, and yet the only letter he had written of any note was to a pen pal. He had done this via school, a year or so back, the school was taking part in a scheme to encourage links between school pupils from all around Europe, he had written to some guy in France, and despite taking time to write a letter, Michael never got a reply, *typical Frenchy* Michael had thought, *lazy buggers*, although looking back Michael's France was not the best in the world and perhaps, just perhaps, the boy hadn't understood a single word in the letter. By two Michael was asleep.

Around four he was woken by dad and Steve coming through the front door, 'look at this Steve' quipped dad, 'What a lazy sod', Steve joined in, 'The problem is you're not feeding him enough, he's got no energy to stay awake', they both laughed at this, it was well known there was no feeding up the lad with hollow legs. Steve walked off still laughing, dad turned off the radio that was still quietly playing in the background; 'come on its time to get ready' half asleep Michael wasn't with it, 'Ready? Ready for what?' dad shook his head and walked off.

They drove along yet another bumpy back road, Michael stared out of the passenger side window, he was watching the sun set on the desert; it was a truly wondrous sight. Dad explained they were off to some party held by a guy called mike, now Mike was middle management so he and dad wouldn't normally mix in the same circles, let alone attend the same parties, but dad's crack team were now ahead of schedule, and this had impressed the top brass, so as a thank you to dad and co, they were invited to tonight's shindig. As they pulled into the car park, Michael could tell these people had money; the place was HUGE, with BMW's and mercs surrounding the white piece of trash that was the Toyota. The complex really did put Michael and dads villa to shame, although to be fair most places did, it was amazing, when Michael first arrived he thought they were staying in a four star marble mansion, now it looked more like a council semi built in the 60's compared to what was really out there.

Once inside they were met by the host Mike, he was well groomed, mid 40's and just *smelt* like typical middle management, he had slim brown rimmed glasses, receding black hair and currently wore a smile that said "welcome, but don't touch anything" he was an ok guy, but you wouldn't want to spend too much time with him, as he was all business. Thankfully for Michael he was soon called away to meet some people just arriving to the party, unfortunately for dad his ordeal was far from over, 'If you excuse young Michael, I just need to borrow you father for a moment, I have some people I would like him to meet' with that Mike politely dragged dad to another part of the room, Steve smiled, 'Don't worry son, he'll be fine, there's plenty of booze at this do' Michael laughed, Steve was right, dad would be fine, his old man was one of those people who could just get on with anyone, and if there was beer involved so much the better, and what's more people *liked* him, he was like Del boy from only fools and horses, a wide boy from the east end who everyone liked. Michael though was the complete opposite, shy and awkward, and kept himself to himself, and with dad otherwise engaged Michael started to feel self-conscious, so he went to find a corner to lean on, as he walked through the party he noticed where the music was coming from, they only had a real life bloody DJ! With his own lighting rig! And a load of Vinyl! This party had it all, coke, Pepsi, even Tab, and loads of those little sausages on cocktail sticks! An hour later dad returned, with perhaps the biggest Cocktail Michael had ever seen in his life, and Michael could tell it wasn't dad's first of the night; 'You know what son' dad was doing a good job of not slurring, but had to start again as he forgot what he was going to say 'You know what son you're a good kid, bit quiet but still a good kid, I could of done a lot worse than having you' Michael was taken back a little by this, because this speech right here was one of the nicest and longest dad had every given to him, Michael of course knew dad loved him, but this, this was nice. 'Thanks dad, crisp?' It was all Michael could think to do or say, he offered dad a crisp from his plate of food, dad smiled 'You're always eating, good on ya, but you wait, when your older your belly will blow up like a balloon' dad patted his stomach and laughed, he then rubbed Michaels hair and lurched off to mingle, leaving Michael to thank god Steve was the one doing the driving later. Steve wasn't drinking of late, he said he found it easier to chat woman up sober, then blind stinking drunk for some reason, but where was Steve? Thought Michael, he scanned the room, Steve was missing, theory must have worked out for him assumed Michael. Around midnight the music got quicker, and louder, Disco replaced the middle of the road stuff they had been playing, out came Yazoo, Human league, Imagination, and all was going well until Kool and the gang's hit "Get down on it" was put on, this was too much for Michael, he was sober, and way too young to join in with the old farts dancing and singing in the room, so slipped out into the garden, the cool air felt nice, he hadn't noticed just how sweaty it was in the house. As the last notes of Shalamar's "a night time remember" faded away, that was it, the night was over. It was around 1am by the time Michael found Steve, who had long given up or said good night to whatever lady he had had his eye on, Steve had already put dad in the back of the car, so they started back home. Thirty minutes later they arrived at the villa, dad wasn't so much asleep as in a coma, so was dragged into the house and dumped on the sofa, Steve then said Goodnight and it was bed.

Friday 8ᵗʰ July – Villa/shop/Marine base.
'Did not go to work, went to shops,
Then went to marine base'

Michael awoke around 11 am, still tired from the night before; he wanted to get more sleep but *really* needed a wee. Now up and a bit more awake he thought best to check on dad, who was last seen comatose on the sofa downstairs, so Michael washed his hands and jogged downstairs, to his amazement dad wasn't on or near the sofa, no he had in fact gone to work, the guy was more machine then man? Still dad had always said that if drink every got in the way of him going into work, he would pack in the booze, so to never give up he would always go in, no matter how bad he felt. Michael was always impressed by dad's work ethic, rain or shine he always went in, and was always early! So Michael should have felt a little embarrassed about not going in with him, after all he was younger and hadn't touched a drop of alcohol the previous night, then he thought screw it, he had stuff to do today, like pack for home. It was a weird feeling that in less than 48 hours he would be on a plane heading back to England, back to Mum, sis, his friends, all the people in his street, and the life he had left behind, but where to start? Well packing was as good place as any. Like all travellers Michael was taking back more than what he had brought with him, namely the t-shirts he had got as gifts for friends and family, luckily been a teenager he hadn't packed a lot to start with, also he was now thankful dad had insisted he had left behind his beloved green body warner, Michael could laugh at that whole episode now, just. By 1 the packing was complete, only toiletries were left out, they could be thrown in at the last minute, or even left if need be, thinking ahead Michael also left out two days' worth of cloths, plus some warmer items for the flight home, yes he might be hot and a bit sweaty on the way to the airport, but at least he wouldn't be cold when they hit London. Feeling good about his day's work he went and got a Coke, but not from the kitchen, no from the shop at the top of the road!

At the end of the month Michael would be 15 years old, a long way down the road to becoming a man, and if a man wanted a soda, he would go to the shops to buy one, he also wanted to say good bye and thank the man who had given him a free plaster after the whole *doggate* incident a few weeks back. Michael careful opened the Villa's big brown gates, looked both ways, checking for Rabies and any other dangers, then made the two minute walk to the shops. After a quick look at the cans of pop on offer, Michael chose his drink, then strode with purpose to the till, showed the man the can of pop, and the sign language and pointing began, because neither had bothered to learn the opposites language. Eventually Michael held out his hand, which had various coins in it, the shop owner then took some and the transaction was complete, or was it, Michael then pointed at his finger, expecting the man to remember that he had given Michael a free plaster, Michael then give him some more coins, thanked the man in English and left. This May of bemused most shop keepers, but this man had seen it all, so without any emotion put the money in the till and carried on stocking shelves. Proud of what he had just done, Michael walked back to the villa, completely forgetting to look as he crossed the road, thankfully the car that was about to hit him honked its horn, the driver didn't turn or slow down, just honked, Michael jumped back, just missing the car. After composing himself he looked both ways, twice, then hurried back to the villa, still happy with how the day with progressing.

Around 5pm dad came home, 'Come on we're going out', and with that he went upstairs to change, *Out again?* Thought Michael, we only went out last night, he hurried to find dad, but he was already in the shower, Michael heard Steve come in so asked him what was happening. 'We're going to a marine club?' questioned a confused Michael 'That's right' said Steve, 'a *marine* club?' repeated Michael, 'What with soldiers and stuff?' Steve laughed 'Marine is sailors, but yeah military is a theme' before Michael could ask any more questions dad reappeared, 'Come on you two, we need to be there by six'.

On the way to the Marine base Michael felt put out, it wasn't the fact dad hadn't told him what was happening in advance that got Michael, no, it was the fact he hadn't planned for anymore parties, so his careful packing had gone to waste, because he had put all his going out clothes at the bottom of the suitcase, still he was more than a little curious as to what the night had to offer. As expected the bases entrance was manned by armed guards, however it was a more low key then Michael had expected, once through it was a short drive to clubs car park. Inside Michael recognised a few of the Marines from the previous nights do, this was where dad had met them, and worked his charm on getting an invite, apparently to keep up moral the US government held parties like this for foreigners working in the country, mainly yanks, but a few Europeans made it in as well. The club house was nice enough; it was one large room which could hold around 60, with a few table and chairs scatted for effect, and at the end of the room was a door which took you out on to the balcony, which had a nice view of a small lake. The military personnel were in smart dress, with the guests likewise, and again like most of the parties Michael had been to, the mood was geared more to adults then teenagers, then again why wouldn't it be? Playing from some hidden record playing was Middle of the road music, adding to the noise of the room were the sounds of people talking and laughing, Michael would have hated this type of event a few months ago, but he was getting used to this type of gathering now, plus it was nice to get out of the Villa and go someone new, also dad could of quite easily just left him at home, whilst he went and had a good time, so Michael was grateful for the fact he hadn't, but dad wasn't like that, he liked having his son around. Dad also had an agenda tonight, he wanted to get the boy out more and get used to socialising, as Michael spent far too much time in UK in his room, so maybe this was the spark the boy needed, and when he returned home he *might* want to get out more, well dad could always hope.

Around forty people in all attended the do that night, and as the evening progressed more and more alcohol was consumed, which meant the conversations got louder and so did the music, most of the songs been played wouldn't have been Michaels first choices, but it was an American base so the music was mainly from that part of the world. By10pm Michael was bored, dad and Steve would check in with him every twenty minutes or so, as would some of the wives of the serviceman, partly out of pity, partly because they missed their own kids who were state side, and used Michael as a sort of surrogate son, to appease their guilt of leaving their own so very far away, however despite all this attention he was still bored, these people were nice enough, and they didn't have to make the effort, but facts were facts, he missed kids his own age. Thankfully around 10.30 his prayers were answered, a couple of kids arrived with their dad's, Michael recognised them straight away, they were Kevin and Matthew, Michael had met them at the WSS School a couple of weeks before. They were nice enough kids, but if Michael was 100% honest they were also a *little* boring, but as the saying goes, beggars can't be choosers. Both were a year or so younger than Michael and it showed, their conversations were all about ET, the film, the toys, the bloody games, now Michael of course loved sci-fi movies, but ET was a step to far, in his mind it was a kids and chick's Sci-fi film, but like most people on the Planet he had seen it, so he could at least join in the Conversation 's Kevin and Matthew were having, however there was only so many times you could talk about or hear about 'Remember when Elliot did that?' or 'Wasn't it sad when ET and Elliot both got sick at the same time?' Michael politely nodded, but could feel his brain seeping out through his eyes. Slowly he started to switch off, Matthew continued 'Ah that Gertie, she's so sweet, I would love to, oh look there's Helen, yes I would love that Gertie to be my sister' Kevin nodded in agreement, Michael woke from his trance. 'Huh what did you say?' 'Oh, I was just talking about how much I would love Gertie..' Michael stopped him mid-sentence, 'No not that part, the part about Helen, what did you say?' Matthew pointed towards a far wall 'Oh Helen, she's over there' Michael nearly gave himself whip lash as he scanned the room, there near the door leading to kitchen stood Helen, Michael know he wanted to go up and talk to her, to be near her, maybe kiss her, but his legs didn't seem to be working, then doubt started to creep in, what if she blanked him again?. What if she was with another boy? There were so many what ifs, then finally some common sense kicked in, if he didn't go and talk to her he right now he would regret it, maybe not today, maybe not tomorrow, but some day he would, so he summoned what courage he had and got up 'Would either of you two like a drink' Coke please' smiled Kevin, 'Same' said Matthew, Michael left the two lads to their childish conversation and walked over to Helen, they would have to wait for their drinks.

As he approached Her his sweat rate upped from moist to damp, and it didn't help the room was already boiling, everyone was either dancing, talking, or moving around, the heat was rising, as was the music, the party was in full flow, but the sight of Helen in a low strap floral dress was adding to the temperature, 'Didn't expect to see you here' he said over the music, Helen tried to smile but something was bothering her. 'I know, I didn't want to come but dad insisted' 'Oh, where is he?' Michael looked for Terry, 'disappeared with some client or other' Sneered Helen, 'Mum wouldn't let him come on his own, in case he got drunk and made a fool of himself, again' Michael remembered when he and Helen met at the Holiday Inn and Terry got a little worse for wear, 'Sorry' Michael couldn't think of anything else to say. Helen put her drink down 'look do you want to get out of here' Michael wanted to, but dad or Steve would see them, plus Terry might come back any minute, Michael had to say something, anything, but his brain wasn't working, she had that effect on him, finally he replied, 'I could do with some air' he really could things were getting hot!, then came the unmistakeable sound of breaking glass, they both turned to the find where the sound was coming from just in time to see the first punch, from what Michael could gather a contractor had walked into the wife of a local businessman, a row broke out, the businessman perhaps having had one cocktail to many blamed the contractor for deliberately walking into his wife, a punch was thrown, then all hell broke loose, the military personnel wisely decided to stay out of it, letting the men tire themselves out, everyone else was cheering the pair on, Helen took her chance and grabbed Michael, who like everyone else was in a trance watching the two drunk old farts pushing each other and shouting things like 'Come on then I'll fucking smash your face in', the last thing Michael saw was the contractor picking up a chair and three people wading in to take it off him,

Michael and Helen were now outside, standing on the balcony that looked out onto the small lake, Even though Michael had very little experience with the opposite sex, he could tell Helen just wanted to talk, no funny business. So they sat on an old wooden bench and looked out on to the water, Helen took his hand and held it, she then rested her head on his shoulders, god she smelt nice he thought. Slowly the sounds of the fight faded and the music was put back on, two more records and the party was over, Helen lifted her head up and kissed him on the cheek, despite not been on the lips there was still passion to it, she then whispered into his ear '*Thank you*'. They decided to go back into the party, Helen first, then a minute later Michael, so no one would know they had been outside alone, when Michael walked into the room Helen was already gone, gone from his life again. The contractor and the businessman were now best friends and dad, well dad knew, he had seen Helen come back first, followed shortly after be a rather sheepish son, dad smiled. Michael smirked back. Steve walked out of the toilets; 'Ah there you are, come on time to go home' yes it was thought Michael, yes it was.

Saturday 9th July – Villa/Karachi.
'Did not go to work, went around town with Paul'

It was Michaels last full day in Pakistan, so he was certainly not going to spend any of it at work, there were things to do, for starters pack, or rather re pack, dad had reassured him there were no more parties on the horizon, so he pack with some confidence. Michael again left his travel clothes on top of his suitcase, however this time instead of carefully packing the rest of his clothes, he just stuffed everything else in the case, he would sort the damn thing out back in England. Then there was a brief panic, where he thought he had lost his passport, now located this too was thrown into the suitcase. Seeing his passport suddenly made Michael miss home more than ever, the big black rigid document just screamed British, pride swelled in him every time he used it, and tomorrow he would be feeling the emotion again.

Once packed Michael went down stairs for breakfast, dad and Steve were just finishing their fruit. 'morning sleepy head' commented dad, Michael laughed 'Funny dad, real funny' 'all packed for tomorrow?' asked Steve, 'You must be looking forward to seeing all your mates again' Michael had a spoon in his mouth so just nodded in agreement, Steve looked at his wrist watch; 'oh shit, come on you two we'll be late if we don't leave soon' Steve rushed off to get ready, 'get ready for what?' asked Michael, 'Paul's back today' replied Dad, 'oh, is that today?' Michael had forgotten Paul was coming back, Steve hadn't, and was over the moon about his return, yes Steve liked dad and Michael, and didn't mind going to parties and the club with them, but Paul was around Steve's age, he was single and good looking, so was the perfect wing man, and Steve couldn't wait to hit the town with him.

The trip to the airport was used as a dry run for the next day, to get an idea of how long it would take, because dad was *not* going to miss that flight, and was going to be on it one way or another, he was pining for mum and British beer. The day itself was sunny yet cool, the sky was blue and Michael was in full Holiday mode, which was of course odd considering he was going home and not on holiday, but that's what it felt like, he had been in Pakistan for so long it had really started to feel like this was his home now. In all the journey took an hour, the flight the next day was at 5.45pm, so they would leave around 2pm, giving them plenty of time to book in and make their flight. Paul's flight was delayed, and with nothing to do in the airport they waited, dad hated waiting, waiting for a bus, a train, people, he hated been idle and not moving, so even though the plane was only 30 minutes late, dad was more than ready leave when Paul finally showed his face. After the hello's and how was England pleasantries, they left for town.

Supplies at the villa were running low, no one had bothered to go shopping, either too busy with work, or going out, and with Ali only been one man, well, they needed to do a supply run, toilet rolls, canned goods, etc. So the afternoon was spent wandering around town, Paul was updating the group on what had been happening in the UK over the past couple of months, however dad and Steve weren't interested in the latest fashion's or the music scene, nor Margaret Thatcher winning a second term in a landslide victory the month before, no all the pair wanted to hear about was the boozers he had been in, and Lester Pigott the jockey, who had won the Epsom derby for the ninth time on a horse called Teenoso. 'I knew I should have put a bet on' whined Dad, although being in a largely

Muslim country that would have been difficult, not impossible, just tricky. In fact it was one of the few pluses mum could see in her husband being in Pakistan, yes he could spend money on drinking, but he couldn't *piss* the rest away on gambling, her words not Michael's. By 4pm they were on their way home, once inside the compound they started to un load the car, Paul got out the Toyota and stared at the Villa, 'Ah home sweet home' he then noticed Michael struggling with his suitcase, 'Here let me help, and I want to hear everything you and your old fella have been up to while I was neck deep in woman' Michael smiled, but wasn't sure if that was a joke or not.

By 6pm Paul was asleep, despite his youth, the trip still took its toll, and with no one else being bothered about going out, it was a quiet night in for all. Michael spent his last night on the balcony, staring out onto the neighbourhood.

Chapter Nine.

Up up, and away.

Sunday 10th July – Villa/Airport.
'Left Karachi for London, flight time 5.45 pm,
Will stop over at Dubai and Oman'

Today was the big day, and everyone was up early getting any last minute jobs or packing out the way, well *almost* everyone was up. It was now 9am, and Michael was still fast asleep, and funny enough dad was in no mood for his son's lazy antics today. Dad was in the kitchen having breakfast with Paul and Steve when he noticed the time 'look at the at?' he said '9 a bloody clock! lazy sod' dad got up and went upstairs to wake his son, within a minute he was back down in the kitchen, 'already up?' asked Steve, who was currently head deep in a two day old Times newspaper, 'No' replied dad, who was filling up a small glass with water, 'but he will be in a minute' dad had a grin on his face, no it was more of a smirk, it was the type of facial expression that said this person is up to something and someone else is going to get it! The someone was of course Michael, and the *get it* was a wet bed.

Dad slowly made his way back upstairs, careful not to spill any fluid from the glass. 30 seconds later there was the scream, followed by a laugh. Dad reappeared in the kitchen and sat back down, followed a moment later by a wet haired Michael, dead panned Paul spoke to the dripping teenager, 'Are you wearing your hair different today? is it a fashion thing?' Michael was not happy. '*No'* he moved some damp hair out of his eyes before carrying on, 'it's, oh look my dad's a four year old again look!' Paul couldn't help but burst out laughing, finally dad spoke, 'Sorry son, but I couldn't find a lobster' It took Michael a second to work it out, then it hit him, dad had seen a chance for revenge for the whole lobster in the bed incident that happened what seemed a life time ago, and took it. Dad wouldn't risk such a move at home, mum would kill him, so it was today or never. Well played thought Michael, well played. Paul was feeling slightly left out 'Lobster?'

The rest of the Morning was spent double checking bags and travel documents, oh and saying goodbye to people. Michael would say his goodbyes to Steve and Paul at the Airport, the guys at the club, well they were just guys at some seedy club, so no problems there, Matthew and co were already taken care off, as was the guy who run the corner shop, Helen, hmm, well that was a little difficult, so really it was just Ali left to do.

Ali was a tough one for Michael, in part because of the language barrier, but also the emotional factor, he had seen Ali as an uncle, a crazy uncle with a big sword! But still family. Ali of course was used to saying goodbye to workers, after all many had come through the villa's doors over the years, to stay for a few months, then move on to another job or country, but Michael was the youngest he had every looked after, so was special. In the end it was decided by mutual consent, if they couldn't talk to each other there was only one thing left to do, hug, with the sappy part out the way there was just enough time for a quick lunch, then they *had* to leave.

Dad threw their bags into the boot of the beaten up, falling apart, rust bucket of a car, god Michael was going to miss the Toyota, he was also going to miss the Villa, he took one last look at it, by comparison, the house in Essex, despite being split over four floors and boasting three large bedrooms, would feel small and cramped, here there was freedom and space, England carpet and sisters. Still home was home.

The feeling of sadness Michael was now experiencing for leaving the country would soon be replaced by the thrill of flying; he loved airplanes, traveling from one country to another, he felt so middle class. The 80's promised fun and excitement after the brown days of the 70's, god the 70's sucked, with all its camping and dirty Chalet rooms at holiday camps around the coast line that looked more like concentration camps from old war films, but the 70's were over, long live the 80's, and Michael was part of revolution. An hour later they arrived at the airport, 'See ya kid' Smiled Paul, then it was Steve's turn to say bye 'You know for a teenager you weren't such a pain in the arse to be around' they laughed, 'Well most of the time' the guys then said bye to dad, and with that they were gone. Now all alone and with nothing better to do, father and son picked up their bags and went in search of the check in desk, dad of course knew the way, having booked in several times before, and it wasn't long before they were settled in the departure lounge, awaiting their flight.

The departure lounge was busy, with people from all around the world sitting in two's and three's, all chatting away, reading newspapers or trying to nap before their respective Journey's. This waiting around had allowed Michael time to form an important question, 'How many more trips are you going to have to make before the hospital is finished?' asked Michael, dad looked up from Thursday's Sun newspaper, courtesy of Paul, Michael caught a glimpse of the Page 3 model, I really should read more papers he thought, dad had a quick think before replying, 'One more son, the place is nearly finished' Michael seemed happy with this, 'Good, I like having you around' dad smiled. 'don't worry son, I'm not going back for at least a month' and with that dad went back to his paper, and Michael turned on his Walkman.

Michael could see dad's lips moving but couldn't hear him? then he remembered he had his walkman on, so took off his head phones, as he did this dad caught the last chorus of Waterloo, 'Come on our flights ready' Michael had somehow lost an hour, then again listening to Abba could do that. As they approached the exit doors which lead to their aircraft, Michael half hoped/expected Helen to appear from nowhere, to run up to him, and kiss him goodbye, but this of course was real life and not the ending to some cheesy Bogart film, still it would have been nice. He took one last look at Pakistan from the top of the steps which lead to the plane, and with that he was on board and ready to leave. Ten minutes later the engines started up, and they began to taxi along the runway, there was a pause, then the captain started to throttle forward, now Michael could feel the raw power of the plane's engines, and with that they were in the air, destination, well not the UK, not even close, no first stop was Dubai.

They were flying gulf air again, so at least Michael could enjoy the view, so to speak. The stewardesses were as always polite and friendly, and Michael didn't mind them fussing around him, asking "did he need an extra blanket" or "would he like a coke" in fact he welcomed the interaction. By 9 pm they were in Dubai, so they had to disembark, find their luggage, and book in for another flight, which wouldn't be leaving for another four hours. 'Four hours?' squealed Michael, 'Four hours? What are we going to do for four hours?' dad wasn't happy either but there was nothing else they could do, this was the way of things, 'Window shop?' replied dad. Michael hated shopping at the best of times, but airport shopping was the worst, it was full of stuff you would never want to buy or receive in a million years, but of course they were trapped, they couldn't leave the airport, so with little other options available they started to wander around. Being 9pm the shops were closed, so they could only look through windows at the items on sale, *Perfect* thought Michael, just great, not that they could of afforded anything anyway, the first store had gold watches with jewels stuck on them, fur coats costing hundreds of pounds, and other expensive tat, they went to next shop, which had more fur coats, this made no sense to Michael, and for once it wasn't the price, he just couldn't understand who would need one in a desert climate? It was just plain odd? By Midnight they were bored, then hungry, then tired, thankfully by 1am they could board their next plane, this would also make a stop, in Oman, but they wouldn't have to get off so both went to sleep.

Monday 11th – Plane/Home.
'Still flying, 6 am got to Paris, then onto London'

Around 4am Michael was woken from his slumber by a strange
voice, it was the planes intercom system, currently the voice
was informing passengers they were either approaching or on
their way to Paris, Michael couldn't speak French, but the
disembodied voice definitely said the word Paris, so he just
assumed the rest. They were close; not that you could tell by
looking out the window though, it was still dark, but Michael
could tell they were getting close by the people around him,
some were waking up, others checking their passports, the rest
getting their overhead bags ready. They would first stop at
Paris, to refuel and let passengers disembark, then London and
Home. Dad had been up for ages, the man was a machine,
barely needing any sleep, he had already eaten his breakfast of
fruit and croissants, and had grabbed a tray for his son. 'There
you go, sorry it's not a fry up, I did ask' by dad's smile you
could tell he was only joking, however Michael wouldn't have
put it past him to have asked, the man loved his sausage and
eggs. After eating what he could, after all it was only 4 in the
bloody morning, Michael too checked his passport and his
carry-on bag, around 5.30am the sun broke through the clouds,
what a fantastic sight, shortly after they landed in Paris, not
that he could see any of it, on this trip Michael had landed in
many countries, but all he had seen of them was tarmac and
grey buildings. After refuelling they were in the air, again,
thankfully though this journey would be their last by plane, and
was just a short hop over the English channel. The day was
now fully awake, along with most of the passengers, all were
excited, looking forward to carrying on their day in London,
and beyond, soon the channel gave way to land, England, with
its fields and towns, it should have been a stirring sight for any
Brit, but all Michael could think of was the long haul ahead,
first by Tube, then train, and finally taxi. Minutes later they
landed at Heathrow, one step closer to home.

After clearing customs, it was time to fight their way to the

Tube station. Whilst waiting for the train to Liverpool street, a thought popped into Michaels head, he was no longer in the third world, no longer a working man, he was a spotty teenager in one of the busiest cities in the world, and it was bloody noisy. The tube carriage was appealing, it was smelly, cramped, and as for the noise! christ, every corner was torture; the sound of metal on metal put your teeth on *edge*. Liverpool street station was as always busy; there were people everywhere, you couldn't stand still for a second without someone walking at you! men and woman all suited and booted, all pushing and shoving their way to whatever 9 to 5 job they would do until they died. Thankfully for dad and Michael they were traveling the opposite direction to everyone else, which meant whilst the average commuter was getting off a train ready to start another boring Monday at the rat races, dad and Michael could jump on a near empty train, put their feet up and enjoy the view. The heavily populated towns of Stratford and Romford soon gave way to fields and cows, twenty minutes later the train pulled into Billericay station, they dragged their cases up the stairs to the ticket office, and went in search of a taxi, luckily they didn't have to wait long, and soon they were heading home in a big black cab. The cabbie couldn't believe where they had come from, 'Bloody Pakistan! why did you bloody go there for your hols?' it was nice to be home, and to hear a Essex accent, but Michael had forgotten the casual racism and swearing you got from a some of the locals. Dad went on to explain he had been working out there, 'Yeah mate, you wouldn't catch me going out there with all those *Indians*, wouldn't take my kids either, god knows what they would catch' dad and Michael were too tired to argue, or agree, so they sat back and watched the world go by. Soon they were on Salesbury Drive, all the cabbie had to do now was the follow the long winding road for about half a mile, then turn left into their cul-de-sac, and the thousand mile journey would be complete. A few minutes later they arrived, the street seemed quiet? Michael guessed everyone was either at school or work, dad paid the taxi driver, leaving him free to be on his way, so to spread more joy and happiness in the world. As they approached the house, mum come rushing out, she didn't know who to hug first! she was just so happy to see them both alive again. In the end she hugged both of them at the same time, and after some tears and kisses the three of them went inside, dad quickly found his Daughter and hugged her tight, Sarah then turned to Michael, who said 'hi'. After putting down their bags and drinking a cup of "English" tea, dad announced he wanted some *quiet time* with Mum, so Michael was tasked with walking Sarah to school 'it's nice to have you back Michael, mum hated you being away' Michael was touched by this, 'Thanks squirt, missed you to' after safely delivering Sarah to her class, Michael walked the short Journey home and collapsed in bed, leaving mum and dad up to their catching up.

Chapter Ten.

Home sweet home, again.

Tuesday 12th July – Home.
'Saw my friends, gave out presents'

After sleeping most of the previous day, Michael was raring to go, ready to get out there and see his friends, he wanted to show off his tan, oh and to give out the presents he had so carefully chosen for everyone. Alias the school's in the area hadn't broken up yet, so Michael would have to wait until later for his friends to get home. As for Michael, well he wasn't due to go back to school until the following week, so was kind of at a loose end, and with few options available, he decided to get to know television again, along with his beloved Atari game system. His two favourite games were Pac man, and something called "space shuttle" which he both hated and loved playing! in this game you had to launch a NASA shuttle, fly it in space, and then land it. Now the taking off part was easy, Michael got this right every time, then you would have to fly in space for a bit, again piece of cake, but when it came to the landing, it was cruel, to say the least. You had to get the angle just right, and the yoke just so, it was *damn close* to maths and that didn't appeal to Michael one bit. It was probably easier to land the real bloody thing, so several crashes later Michael gave up, and went to grab some lunch.

Gone were the healthy choices from the Villa, no fish, and no fruit, in their place was white bread, various jams, and potted meats, in other words the good stuff, Michael had missed them all. After two Jam sandwiches Michael was full, he could feel the fillings in his teeth tingle as the sugar settled on them, god he loved Jam. Around 4pm his friends started to arrive back from school, by quarter past they were out playing in the street, excitedly Michael put his Dunlop green flash trainers on and grabbed the bag of T-Shirts, now ready to impress his friends with gifts and his tan he went outside. Sadly he would wow his friends with nether, firstly the weather had been nice for the past month, really hot, so everyone had a bloody tan, yes his looked slightly darker, but really it didn't stand out as much as he had hoped, then there was the gifts, 'A T-Shirt!' Exclaimed Sean, 'And what's that on the front of it, a bloody pigeon?' Sean was not happy, not happy at all, '*No!*' replied Michael, slightly taken a back, 'it's an eagle, and it has Pakistan on the front' Sean took the present; after all it was a gift, but he wasn't totally impressed, and he wasn't the only one, within the hour Michael had given out all the T-Shirts, with all the recipients taking them and thanking him for the gift, but no one was exactly thrilled by them, last time I buy anyone a bloody gift thought Michael.

By 6pm, everyone including Michael had forgotten about the T-shirts, and it was back to playing football in the street, hitting and punching each other, and telling silly slightly dirty jokes, god Michael had missed this. 'No Phil, you're thinking of another country' Michael hoped that would put an end to questions about Pakistani woman, Phil wasn't giving up though, he was reaching *that* age. 'But there were woman?' 'Yes Phil, but they were mostly covered up' 'oh' Replied a disappointed Phil, 'so there was no naked woman at all?'.

As the sun started to go down the group sat on the high garden wall at the end of the street, 'So you didn't shag anyone then?' Ross as always was to the point. 'Well there was a girl called Helen' Michael could feel himself starting to glow as he told the group the story about him and Helen, 'so in short no then' replied Ross. 'Yeah but he got more action then you this summer' laughed Dolph, this started some playful pushing and shoving between Ross and Dolph, ending in a less then friendly shove and a 'Fuck off you twat you nearly had me over the wall' from Ross. One by one the group were called in, after all it was a school night, soon Michael was on his own, so went home to see what the family was up to.

A Patten for the rest of the week slowly developed. Sleep in late, breakfast, Atari, then instead of playing snooker at the club, he played in the living room, on the 6 by 3, it wasn't full size but it would do, film night was now film afternoon, dad had recently bought a VCR, a top loader no less, so Michael would watch any films laying around. Just like Pakistan, he was falling into a routine, with the only relief coming around 4 o'clock, when his friends were home, but they couldn't always play out because of homework, or other silly excuses, Michael of course had homework of his own to do, but he was leaving that treat till the weekend.

Friday wasn't the same though, oh no, he had been looking forward to Friday since he got back to the UK.

Friday 15ᵗʰ July – Basildon.
'Went to Basildon, went swimming,
Then to the pictures, saw *Return of the Jedi, 10/10*'

Today was going to be a great day, Michael had been looking forward to this day for some time, because he and the rest of the clan were going to Basildon. Basildon was a new town located a couple of miles from Billericay, just down the A129. Now compared to Billericay it was a bit of a dump, however it had produced several hit bands including Depeche Mode, and Alison Moyet, It also had a huge town centre, along with a big swimming pool and a cinema, and Michael was going to both.

First stop was the swimming pool, his current school Mayflower had a great indoor pool, he loved using it, and it sure beat his old Jnr school pool, which basically was a glorified blow up kiddies pool, in which you could swim about ten feet in any direction, and that was it, not that you wanted to stay in it any longer than necessary, because for some sadistic reason it was nether indoors or heated, meaning you could only use it a couple of times a year, thank god.

The rest of the time the kids had to travel to another pool, so once a week a bus would leave Billericay and head for Basildon. It was a joyous occasion, because it got you out of school, and you had the bumpy bus ride to look forward to. The bus was always a double decker, and would take the county lane back roads route every time, at speed! It was all fun for the first mile or two, it was like a theme park ride, then they would come to the *tree,* the one tree that was taller than the rest, and its branches over hanged more than any of the others. Every time the top front of the bus would *crash* into it, and by some miracle never brake any of the windows, the kids loved it of course and couldn't wait, everyone would sit silently, waiting for the **thud**, then the scream would go UP, the scream of terror and fun. Today however Michael and family took a single decker into town, and avoided any drama.

Once at the pool Michael had a splash around with Sarah, whilst mum and dad grabbed a coffee in the cafe. it wasn't the swimming pool at the holiday inn Karachi, but Michael still enjoyed himself, then it was off to the Cinema. The film they were going to see had been out since June, but was still playing to packed audiences, the film in question was "Return of the Jedi", and in two hours' time Michael's life was going to be complete. Since 1977 there was only one film series for Michael, Star wars, he had all the figures, toys, games, guns, he even dressed up once as Han Solo for a school fate, Sean went as Darth Vader, he should have gone as Chewie, but his mum couldn't find enough fur for the costume. Episode IV, a new hope, was a classic according Michael, and could not have been bettered, Empire was ok, but he didn't like the ending, Han getting frozen had upset him, but now the trilogy was coming to an end, and he was going to see it on the big screen, with the whole of his family, which was an event in itself, as dad was normally away, usually it would just be mum and the kids, or if dad was back he would take them, leaving mum at home to *rest*, but today all four were going.

As the red curtains pulled back and the star wars fanfare began,

Michael shushed mum and started to read the prologue, as it slowing ascended from the bottom of the screen, before long there was a sea of words, promising the next couple of hours would be fun and exciting. Two odd hours later it was over, Michael had enjoyed it, of course he did, it was a Star wars film, however he did have one or two *quibbles* with it, firstly what the hell was with all the care bears? by the end of the film Michael couldn't have cared less if they had lived or died, also Yoda pegged it, because he was old? He was a Jedi master! Who had managed to live 800 years, then what he just got tired? it didn't make sense, there was other parts that were not great, but overall a nice film, he would rank it 10/10, because Han Solo was in it. And he got to kiss Carrie Fisher again, what a babe.

Sunday 17th July – Home/Park.
'Played Snooker, then football at the park,
Got ready for school'

Michael woke to a glorious morning, Mum was making breakfast, bacon and egg, and he had a full day ahead of him, the only black patch on the horizon was school, Michael was due back the next day, and he still had homework to complete, but that was all later, much later, now was about getting another twenty minutes sleep.

After breakfast Michael played some Snooker with dad, then it was off to the park with friends. The park in question was Lake Meadows, it was up town and a good hours walk, but Michael had been away for three months so enjoyed the journey, seeing places he had missed or had forgotten about. Lake meadows had it all, a nine hole golf course, tennis courts, football pitches, and a cafe, also a swimming pool was coming soon. The match lasted about an hour, then with everyone bored, and the score irrelevant, Michael made his way home, there was work to do, homework. The school had giving him the homework over three months ago, and there were so many times he literally had nothing better to do with his time, but still chose not to do any, so now it was down to the wire.

Once home it was straight upstairs and to the books, he had an hour, two tops, then a break for the most important part of the evening, then maybe another hour till bed time. He had maths English and history left. English was easy enough, do a 500 word essay on your favourite author, Michael didn't really have one, so looked at the one book he owned, Star wars. Michael didn't so much talk about the author, but rather the film, adding all the parts he loved, and of course Han Solo. His teacher wouldn't mind this type of report, the fact he had done the homework and it was about a book would please her, being remedial English she wasn't used to pupils handing in any homework, so another A+ was on its way. Michael was also in remedial Maths, so again quite straight forward, some adding and taking away was involved, That was about it, that been said it still took him over an hour to complete the work, this left just History to tackle, but there was no time for that now, it was dinner time.

Michael loved Sunday evenings, first he would have a bath, he would play with his plastic submarine and his solider with the parachute, then it was bathrobe and dinner, normally a roast, he lived for them, Michael preferred Lamb but chicken would do just as well. This would also be the point the whole family would sit down and watch TV, or a pirated film. After dinner it was up to the Atari, for a few games of Pac Man, it really was a full day. Around 7 he would go down for a snack, this would be sandwiches and cakes, and maybe some pop, and this Sunday was no different, expect after Pac man, he had History homework to finish. Michael loved the idea of history and what had happened over the years, all those battles, journeys, explorers, he just hated having to remember all the dates and facts. By 9pm he was done, it really was the bare minimum but it would have to do, so with an hour till his bedtime, he decided to play tiddlywink football, Michael turned off the bedroom lights, and switched on the electric fire, the fire omitted a strange orange glow, it threw odd shapes out into the room through its grills and vents. He felt safe in his room, playing with the little plastic players by the orange light, it was England v Germany, and England would win, they always did.

Monday 18th July – School.
'Went to school, saw a lot of people, it rained for a while'

'Michael! out of bed now! you'll be late' for once the human alarm clock trying to get Michael out of bed wasn't Dad, it was mum, and she took no prisoners, 'it's quarter to eight, the bus is in Thirty minutes' mum wasn't letting up, she then opened his white womble curtains with a flourish, and left her teenage son to drag himself out of his pit. 7.55 am he was up, now maybe he was still half a sleep, or maybe it was the fact he hadn't needed to button many shirts over the past couple of months, whatever it was. it took Michael three attempts to button his fresh white school shirt. After a brief panic looking for his school tie, he stuffed the homework books into his black Addis school bag, and headed for the kitchen, being late he would only have time for one bowel of rice krispies, with extra sugar of course. Fully awake and high on a sugar rush he ran for the bus, now there were two ways he could go, the short way, or long way, both had their good and bad points, like the short way was closer, but the bus would call here first. Yet without thinking and on instinct alone he went for the short way, he had a good feeling about the day, but already running late Michael missed the buss by a clear five minutes, or would have if it hadn't been running late itself. Just as he arrived the bus pulled at the stop, breathlessly he paid the 25p and tried to find a seat, to no avail.

Normally the journey was long and boring, yes he had Trevor to talk to, his friend who sometimes got the bus and lived next to the stop Michael had just run to, hence the choice he made that morning, they would discuss the finer points of the day, Girls, and how to talk to them, computers, Trevor had a ZX spectrum, so could write code, Michael was a little jealous of this, but today he was on his own, Trevor must have caught an earlier bus, so this gave Michael time to look out the window, and take in the sights and sounds of a town he hadn't seen in three months. The bus   made its way down Hillway, then along to Outwood common, the bus stop was next to the huge playing field Michael and his friends would sometimes knock around on, and where the 1977 silver jubilee celebrations were held, then it was past his old Jnr school and on to Hillside, then town, there he would pass his beloved Woolworths, the post office, and the start of the many, many pubs in the town, the white hart, the red lion, the railway, the list went on, apparently the town was a great place to have a pub crawl, not that Michael knew about such things. Soon they were on Stock Road, taking them past St Johns, a private school where the kids wore shorts? And were the hatred rivals to Michael's school, not that he got involved in any of the fights, he really wouldn't have been any use, soon they would be pulling into the school gates, and one by one the contents of the bus would pour out ready for another day at the grind stone.

From the moment Michael stepped of the bus the questions and comments started, even from people he didn't know, they ranged from 'What was *India* like?' 'where you been?' 'I heard you killed a kid?' to 'Oh, I thought you had left, shame' A bemused Michael headed to class. Susan and Charlotte were already there, chatting about some boy band or other, Michael sat at his desk, not expecting a standing ovation from the class, but hoped for some type of response, *nothing*, the bemused school boy was now a little deflated, eventually Susan acknowledged his existence. 'Oh so your back are you' she smiled, Michael was used to being teased by her, 'Missed me have you' he replied, 'not a lot, forgot you were gone really' 'Thanks Susan, you're not the only one, I've been getting some odd looks and comments this morning' Susan pushed back her long red hair and decided to fill him in, it seemed Michael hadn't told enough people where he was going, so when he simply didn't come in one day, people thought he was ill, then after a couple of weeks the rumours started, which ranged from Michael moving schools, to him having a terminal illness, also there was one about him stabbing a guy? Susan had tried to tell people where Michael was, but this sounded as far-fetched as the other stories, and when some pupils heard Michael was giving time of from school to go abroad, a few saw him as a hero, but the rest were resentful and jealous. After hearing this all Michael could say was 'Oh makes sense I guess'

The rest of the morning was spent explaining to people where he had been, and he hadn't done 3 months inside for murder, thankfully it was then lunch time, which gave him a chance to get away from all the silly questions he had been asked, and he could meet up with his mates on the playing field, all were in attendance, including Nat. Nat was a hippy, he was funny and a nice guy, but still a hippy, he had long brown hair and bell bottom trousers, the *gang* would hold him down sometimes to measure the cuffs on his trousers, to see if they were getting any bigger, the record was 12 inches! In the afternoon Michael handed in his homework, the sheer amount staggered him, yes he may of only done the bare minimum, but by his standards the final haul was still impressive, alias it wouldn't take a teacher long to read, well normally, but with his handwriting it would take someone the rest of the week to try and decipher the scrawl in front of them, and with school breaking at the end of the week, will if there were any issues with the work he had done, that was Septembers problem. Just after 3pm it was all over, one day closer to the summer holidays. So it was back on the bus and home. A quick change then out with his friends. it was like he hadn't been a way at all.

The rest of the week was fun, a wind down for Friday, and end of term, Michael was now clear of handing in any more homework till at least September, having handing in so much on Monday, so could enjoy himself. Soon he was in another routine, life was full of them, bed, School, lunch, avoiding the bullies in the afternoon, bus, home, change, out, play, dinner,

TV, bed, up, school, repeat. A small break in the monotony came in the form of a letter from the Middle East, it was from Gulf air, a young falcons newsletter, although it was just a newsletter, aimed at the younger kids, Michael couldn't help but think back to Pakistan, Ali, the villa, *Helen*, they were fast becoming distant memories, nothing more.

Friday 22nd July – Home/School.
'Went to school, for last time this term, played out, got asked out'

Michael was late, really late, too late for bus late, mum had tried to wake him, but to no avail, it was now 8.15, so he had only one choice, the woods. By half past he was dressed, 8.35 out the door, sandwich in mouth, mum always said breakfast was the most important meal of the day, and had made him a jam sandwich, god bless her. Michael ran as fast and as far as he could, until he hit Outwood common road, but he still had a good two miles to go, mostly uphill, before he even got to Norsey woods. He hit the woods in a pool of sweat, he really was going to be late, but he couldn't run or walk fast anymore, so he had to travel at normal pace, and just come to peace with the fact a late mark would be entered in the roll call, all he could hope for now was to be on time for his first class. Normally Michael loved walking through the woods, but today he was late, late and alone, halfway in he hit some mist, seeing the mist made his mind race back two nights pervious, when the family had watched the Howling, every time a twig snapped he thought he saw a shadow or some movement, and his mind raced to one conclusion, werewolf! that film had really screwed him up, luckily from somewhere he found new energy and jogged along the woods paths, checking around him for any signs of the devil creatures. By 9am he was out of the woods, he could see the schools perimeter fence.

Michael arrived at the school gates around 10 past 9, seriously out of breath. Once his heart stopped trying to escape his chest, he tried to book himself in, being the last day no one cared, he could have bunked off and got away with it, but this was Michael, he never bunked of, he was too afraid of being caught. After being processed by the receptionist, he ran to his first class, English, being completely honest Michael did very little in remedial English, and today was not exception, 'ok pupils settle down' Miss tried to quieten the masses, 'I know it's a big day, but we do have some work to do today' the teacher was 40 something, plump, and smiled a lot, she had low expectations of the group, and as a result never really tried to push them. 'Today I want a 100 word story on what you plan to do over the summer holidays, a 100 words thought Michael, no problems, this was the type of class work he loved, it required no facts, figures, or dates, it allowed him to ramble on about anything he wanted. However as he picked up his pen to start, it accrued to Michael, just what was he planning to do over the six week break?, he had nothing planned, After English it was PE, and what a surprise they played football, it was like no other sport existed, yes Michael liked playing Footie, but he wanted to try other sports too, Tennis, rugby, cricket they had the facilities, it was just they used them once a year?. With PE done it was on to Humanities, where they had to write *another* story about what they would be doing this summer, Christ thought Michael, just how much training does a teacher really need? all they do is read out of text books, show videos, or maybe a slide show, then ask you to write the same story over and over, and if you talk in class they shout at you. Michael surmised a long weekend, a week tops was the training period, finally came the bell, and lunch, the last he would have as a third year, with his options picked Michael would be moving classes and meeting new people, yes he would still see his mates at lunch, but things would definitely change come September.

After lunch it was back to registration, where Michael would spend the rest of the afternoon. His form room was at the top of a five storey building, which meant after the exploits of the morning, running through the woods and playing football,

Michael needed a break about the third floor, god he was unfit, these stairs would be the death of him, it was at this point something strange happened, no not strange, just plane bizarre, a girl asked him out, straight out, no beating around the bush, just 'Will you go out with me' the girl in question was Jackie, she was the same age as him, dark long hair and slim build. She appeared almost out of nowhere, before Michael could say *hi* or *oh didn't see you there*, Michael just freaked, no this wasn't happening, she was joking right? she asked again, Michael ran, he just panicked, she was put up to it, she must have been, no girl asked him out, ever!, Jackie gave chase, asking him again, although most boys dreams may involve a girl chasing them and asking, no *begging* to go out with them, Michael was having none of it, like a gazelle running from a lion, he was off, after another flight of stairs he was clear, Safe. As he walked into the classroom he allowed a strange thought to fester, could she have been telling the truth, could she have meant it? He soon shook the silly notion out of his head, no she was put up to it, this was his final thought on the matter.

The rest of the afternoon was spent quietly chattering and playing board games, with the odd quiz, around 2.45 pm everyone was clock watching, hoping they would be allowed out early. A few minutes later the bell went, term was over, Freedom. Michael said 'See ya' to Susan and Charlotte, then joined the scrum trying to get down the stairs, and out the building. A lot of people were signing each other's shirts, Michael wasn't in to that, Mum would kill him, so it was on the bus and home, home for six weeks with nothing but lie ins and TV to look forward to. Sweet.

Saturday 23rd July – Home
'Start of the holidays, it rained for a bit, but stopped, Went town shopping, then played football, then watched TV'

Being a Saturday Michael would have been of school anyway, but there was still that sense of, *YES*, no more school feeling in the air, well until September, but that was ages away. Normally Michael would laze in bed on the weekend till 10am at least, but today he was energised, there was a lot to do, for starters shopping, he and Trev headed for town, Trevor was a bit of a style guru, the 80's suited him, and he wanted to look at the clothes shops. Michael on the other hand wanted to look at the latest vinyl releases in Woolworths, Luckily Trevor loved music as well, so they first the hit the record section of Woolies. The police had a new one out called "wrapped around your finger", Michael wasn't really a police fan, there was something about Sting that put him off the band, Sting, what a silly name? Shakin Stevens also had a new one out, God Michael hated him even more then Sting, at least Sting could sing. In the end Michael bought the new Thompson twins single called "Watching" then it was off to get some cloths. Michael needed some new Dunlop green flash trainers, while Trevor wanted a Nike jumper. With the shopping done they headed home.

Having said bye to Trevor, Michael called around his other friends, he had four groups of friends, neither really knew each other, which was nice, because if you fell out with one lot, you could always knock around with another lot till things cooled down, plus each group were different, Trev was Tech, music and Snooker, another group were into Football and adventures, such as going to the woods and climbing trees, then there was the *real music lot*, who listened to Talking heads, early Ultravox, THE THE, and Bauhaus. The fourth bunch were his religious friends, and although they were *into* god, they didn't go on about, also they were really nice people, he would spend most Saturday nights around one of the mums houses, Ann would run a coffee evening of sorts for all the kids who went to her church, it was a place for young people to hang out, Ann was nice like that, so depending on his mood, Michael would pick a group to annoy.

That afternoon Michael picked the adventure and football group to hang with, Sean, Ross mark, Rob Etc. they played till

3pm, when it started to rain, Ross and mark said 'Fuck this' and went to Mark's to listen to the Clash, which left Michael to go home and have some dinner, later he watched TV with the family, overall not a bad start to the holidays.

Sunday 24th July – home/park.
'Went to park, it rained, come back home, Met Chris and went camping'

Today Michael was going fishing, Ross and co were already up Lake meadows, unlike Michael they could get up in the morning, Ross always said the best fishing was done in the early hours, Michael though was quite prepared to sit there all day and not catch a damn thing, as long as it meant he got his ten hours sleep. It was approaching 10 am by the time Michael arrived, it was one of those summer mornings where the day hadn't woken up yet, it was chilly and misty, but you could tell it would brighten up later, so despite been cold, Michael wore shorts and a t-shirt, he was betting it would be nice later. As Michael approached the gang, Ross was just casting off, the guys were well prepared; they had seats, rod rests, a tent type thing to sit under, and a flask for hot chocolate, Michael sat down next to Mark, who was trying to put a worm on a hook, the worm seemed to be winning, then it rained, there was something very relaxing looking out over the lake as the rain gentle filled it up, the ducks and swans made for the small islands that littered the vast lake, it also cleared the few walkers and picnickers who were also enjoying the park, soon the only people left were the fishermen, quiet descended. Despite mastering the art of fishing with Ali in Pakistan, Michael decided not to fish, he still couldn't stand touching those damn worms. So Michael just watched Ross, who was on a lucky streak, by lunch time he had caught three fish, which he kept in a partially submerged net, he wasn't going to kill them, and would release them at the end of the day. By 1pm the sun arrived, the day started to warm up, so they moved the seats outside, and caught some rays. Around 2pm Ross announced he was bored, so they packed up and headed home.

On the way home he met Chris, Michael hadn't seen him since returning to the UK so they caught up, Chris was, well, a sensitive soul, who's mum didn't like the local kids much, and worried about him playing out with them. She really believed her family was better than everyone else's, but she couldn't stop Chris from going out, not really. Chris was Michaels age and his Mum was getting annoyed by him always been under foot, so despite her reservations regarding the area and people, she didn't mind *too much*, her son playing out with Michael, she thought he was a nice boy who didn't play rough games, she obviously didn't know about the games of stick or rock, in which Michael and others would stand still and throw only what was on the floor around them, it wasn't really a game, just another way of killing time and hurting your friends.

Both Chris and Michael were at a loose end so decided to do something together, but what? After some thought Michael had an idea, 'how about camping' Chris wasn't sure 'I'm not sure my mum would allow me to go camping, she says camp sites are filthy and diseased ridden' Michael laughed 'no you spaz, in my back garden, I do it all the time' Chris looked a lot happier 'Oh, oh right, yeah my mum should be ok with that, I'll go and ask' Chris skipped off to find his mum, who although was a little concerned at first, that her only son would be out of the house all night, still agreed, Chris grabbed his sleeping bag and they headed to Michael's. After a quick chat with his mum, Michael headed to the larder and started to stock up the nights supplies, grabbing bags of Crisps, some biscuits, and bottles of fizzy drinks, 'Are we ok taking all this pop?' asked Chris, Michael grabbed the last bottle of the cherryade 'Yeah its fine, the pop man will be coming tomorrow, we can get some more then'. The pop man was great, he would call door to door and ask how many bottles of coloured pop you wanted, within minutes a crate would appear, and that would do you for the week, it was cheap and convenient; and it saved you carrying heavy glass bottles home from the corner shop. Michael grabbed a torch and they were in business, stocked up they headed for the back garden. That night's accommodation was an old Dutch army tent, made out of heavy canvas, it was water proof, of course, you didn't want troops getting wet now, but being made out of a heavy material it got hot, real hot, and leaving the flaps open and sitting near the entrance wasn't going to help on a summers afternoon, so like the explorers before them, they went looking for a cool watering hole, namely Michaels living room, here they could play Atari, have a game of snooker, and eat sandwiches. Around 7pm the evening was cool enough to head back to the tent. As they lay down, heads sticking out of the tent looking at the stars, they shone their torches at the sky, then into the tress next to the tent, all was quiet, the only noise being the wind gentle pushing through the branches above them. 'Do you think' started Chris, 'Do you think I could ever play for England?' Michael was a little confused, 'what Subbuteo or tiddlywinks?' Michael laughed at this, but Chris looked serious, 'No, I mean football' Michael paused before replying 'well for starters you need to be playing for a top side like Liverpool' 'well of course I would have to, but I can pass and shoot really well' replied Chris, 'Hmm' started Michael 'I still feel your best chance to represent you country would be tiddlywinks' Chris stared at him, they both burst out laughing. within the hour they were both asleep.

Monday 25th July – Park.
'Went to the park and helped out,
Come home, played out'

Camping was the one time Michael would wake up early, really early, by 7am he was up and having a quick pee at the end of the garden, he and Chris then went into the house and ate corn flakes, with a dense sugar crust. After walking Chris home, Michael was unsure what to do with himself, he could go back to bed, but the sugar rush he was experiencing wouldn't have allowed that, he had a lot of energy, but nowhere to go and expel it. Mum tried to help, 'You could go to the park and help out' apparently there was to be a jumble sale at the end of the week, and the organizes were looking for volunteers, 'Yeah right mum, I'm on holiday remember'. Within the hour he was on his way to the park, if it was up to Michael he would spend his time at home, split between watching TV and playing snooker, but dad had made it quite clear, his lazy arse son wouldn't be spending every minute at home and needed to get out more. So of to the community centre it was.

When Michael arrived, the only people in the centre's car park were a couple of middle aged woman, with no one else around, Michael approached them and asked who was in charge 'What, you're here to help out!' exclaimed the dark haired woman, Michael didn't know what she was smoking, but it stank, the other lady, a slim blonde woman, who dressed in clothing about ten years too young for her, joined in 'Wow that's great love, we need more kids helping out, you wouldn't get mine coming down' 'Nor mine' added the dark haired one, Blondie carried on 'You're a credit to your parents, they raised you right' the community centre's door's then opened, the dark haired woman gentle grabbed Michael's arm, 'Come on love, stay with us, we'll look after you' at this point more middle aged woman turned up, there were some younger girls, but they were still a clear 7 or 8 years older than him, then it suddenly hit Michael, he was sent by mum to make *her* look good, no other kids his age would turn up, and word would soon get around what a great mother/parent she was, well played mum, thought Michael, well played.

The *job* was simple really, there would be a fair later that week, in aid of some charity or other, and part of the fair was a jumble sale, so today he would be sorting cloths into one pile, and toys into another, it wouldn't take long, but Michael could think of a million better ways to spend a Monday morning, unfortunately none of them were available at that moment in time. The one good thing about helping out was the snacks, being the youngest the woman would bring him pop and

183

biscuits every ten minutes or so, and by 11 he was full of jammy dodgers and tab, tab being some diet cola crap the woman seemed to love. With the job done he was a free man, or so he thought, as he walked out of the hall the dark hair lady collared him, 'thanks again for today young man' she took a drag from her cigarette then exhaled, to be fair she blew it in away from Michael, but being near the door the wind brought it back into his face, he coughed, she continued, 'We were so impressed with you today, we were wondering if you could come and help out on Thursday?' oh crap he thought!, he didn't want to help out, he had done his bit, ok yes he wanted to come back on Thursday, but only to have fun and spend some money, that was it. The problem was he *couldn't* say no, he had been brought up to respect people, and have manners. Whilst waiting the lady took another drag, then exhaled, just as Michael replied, making him splutter his answer 'I would love to' mum would pay for this.

The remainder of the day was like the rest of the week, knocking around with friends, watching TV, or playing Pac man.

Thursday 28th July – Park.
'Helped out at the Jumble sale/fair,
then played out'

The big day arrived, he had been a little sore at mum at first, about tricking him into volunteering, but it was for a good cause and it wouldn't last all day. As he opened the curtains, the morning sun shone through the single glazed windows, Michael noticed the crack in the top right small window, he really should have told dad about it when it first happened, but that was six months ago, and it would have meant Michael admitting he got into a silly gang war, where both parties were using black widow catapults, thankfully those days were behind him now, and it didn't let a lot cold air in during the winter, so no one needed to know, or get in trouble over it. The only down side about helping out was having to get up early, 8am! The same time as getting up for school, *outrageous*, still he could have a lie in tomorrow as a reward for all his hard work. Around 8.30am he headed for the fair.

When Michael arrived, the common was already a buzz, the men were doing the heavy lifting, erecting tents, un-stacking the table and chairs, whilst the woman, who were more than happy to let the men do the grunt work, were arranging the tables, also organizing who went where, and what merchandise would be put out first, they did all this whilst looking after the little ones (Their kids) who were high on sugar and were on the lookout for more. Soon the bunting was up, the sponge cakes were ready for sale, and the bouncy castle was inflated, all that was left was for Michael to be placed, he hoped for a fun placement, but nothing to front line, nothing with too much pressure, the Bouncy castle was perhaps a step to far for his first posting, but he wanted something with an edge. In the end he was given the second hand stall, it was full of crap that no one wanted, this was the stuff people couldn't sell, so gave *away* for *free!*, these people thought, *I know let's give our broken rubbish to a charity event,* that way both sides win, the giver frees up space, and the recipient can make money without paying for the stock, well that was the theory, in reality who would buy an action man with one leg? or a my little pony with its Mane cut off? still this was the stall he was given, so he would make the best he could of it. Trade was slow at first, mainly young kids who had 5p to spend, and wanted a toy they could hit their brother of sister with, or to put in their mouths and suck, god kids were dumb thought Michael. Then there were the grandparents, who had a vague idea of what little Timmy or Jane liked, and didn't mind paying ?1 on the off chance Timmy didn't mind a one legged action man, but they were few and far between. Some of the grandparents would ask Michael for his advice, a man in his 60's, flat cap and braces asked 'Oi sunshine, you know what kids like, being one, do you think my grand kid would like this' he was holding an England football team 500 piece jigsaw puzzle, with 25 pieces missing, the picture was of Trevor brooking scoring a goal, the man continued 'He's into football and all that, so what do you think?' yeah thought Michael, every football mad kid wants to sit for an hour piecing together a jigsaw only to find half of it missing, instead of playing out with a ball, but Michael didn't say this, he needed sales, 'Yeah of course he would love it, I was thinking about getting it myself' on hearing this the man paid the 25p asking price, and walked away smiling in confidence his grandson would like, *no* love the gift he had bought, Michael of course knew better, but there would be no refunds that day. By 11 the Common was **Full**, Michael had taken over ?4.50, and decided it was time to have a break, Dawn on the next stall offered to cover, she was on cakes, and with most gone, had time to spare. This gave Michael a chance to look around.

Temperatures were hitting the high 20's, even the most manic of child was starting to flag, their parents long since collapsed under whatever shade they could find. So it wasn't a huge surprise the best performing stalls were the ice cream ones, oh and dunk an adult, this involved getting someone over the age of sixteen to sit on a plank of wood, below this was a small kiddies paddling pool, people would then throw wet sponges trying to dunk the person, thus getting them wet, and if possible humiliate them a little in the process. Normally you would have to hunt high and low for volunteers, but with the chance of getting dunked in cold water on such a hot day, well you didn't have to look far for willing participants, however the fact it was such a nice day meant the throwers were getting more water on themselves, then the intended target, not that anyone cared, people were more than happy to pay 20p for three throws, they got to cool down a little, and the fair raised more money, also the person on the plank could *accidentally* fall into the pool, so everyone won. Michael of course was used to this type of weather, being a veteran of the middle east, but even he was developing a sweat, so went and bought a funny feet ice cream to cool down, after another five minutes of wandering he headed back to his stall, but his services were no longer required, Dawn explained, 'It's alright Love, you carry on enjoying yourself, I sold all that tat in five minutes' *it may have been tat*, thought Michael, *but it was my tat!*. Dawn however had played a master stroke, she had combined both stalls, her cakes were already selling fast, so she quickly whipped up a sign, BUY A CAKE, AND ADD 50P TO GET A TOY, ok it wasn't a snappy, but it worked, for an extra 50p you could pick any toy, large or small. Michael, no longer needed, headed in search of another funny feet, then home.

After dinner Michael went out to play with his mates, the usual suspects were there, Sean from next door, his younger brother Steve, Phillip from the top of the road, and Dave, who lived about ten minutes away, next to Michaels old Jnr School, Dave was alright, but was more of a friend of Sean's then Michael's. As Michael walked up to the group, Dave had his Walkman on, he was dancing to some pop song, he also had on the biggest pair of yellow headphones Michael had ever seen, they looked ridiculous, totally out of place, Michael spotted something else that was out of place, Dave had his right arm in plaster, 'What the hell happened to you?' asked Michael, 'WHAT' replied Dave, Michael motioned to Dave to take his headphones off, instead Dave pressed stop on the cassette player, 'I said what happened to you?' repeated Michael, Dave stared blankly back, Michael pointed at his arm, 'oh that' replied Dave, 'did that weeks ago, fell over a wall' Michael couldn't help but laugh, it wasn't *that* funny, and Dave must of gone through some pain at the time, but it was just the matter of fact way Dave had said it, that had tickled Michael, Dave stared back, unimpressed, he then pressed play on his Walkman and went back to his 80's pop. By 9pm people started to go back home, mums could be heard calling for their offspring, as Michael walked back to his house his mind drifted, it was only three more sleeps to go, before the big day, he would soon be 15. Nearly a man.

Chapter Eleven.

Rumbelows, Woolworths, and a bag of Chips.

Saturday 30ᵗʰ July – Town.
'Went up town, bought presents for me, got some Discounted tapes'

Michael was asleep, well half a sleep, he was enjoying yet another dream about him playing for Liverpool, yet something wasn't right, there were voices, he recognised them, but couldn't quite place them, 'Maybe we should let him sleep' said a female voice, 'it's after bloody 9' commented a man, 'we'll come back later' continued the female, after a short pause the male replied 'Tell you what, I'll get a lobster, that should wake him up' with that Michael sat straight up, 'I'm awake, no lobsters' Michael had sat up more on instinct then actually being awake, it took him a further second or two to make out the two figures standing at the foot of his bed, 'Mum, Dad, what are you doing in my room?' Mum sat next to him, 'Well it's your birthday tomorrow, but we wanted to give you your birthday money today, so you could spend it, because the shops are closed tomorrow' Michael took a moment to take this in, and still wasn't completely awake when he replied, 'thanks Mum' Mum got up and walked to the door, 'now come down stairs, I'm doing breakfast' Dad had an evil grin on his face as he spoke. 'We're cooking lobster' Michael was about to reply, but decided against swearing at dad. That was the funny thing about dad, he would let you smoke, a little, and have a drink, sometimes, but god help you if you swore in front of him, his kids didn't do that, well, that he know of at any rate. Now awake there was no going back to sleep, and breakfast did smell nice, so it was a quick scratch of the arse, followed by a yawn, then down stairs for a couple of egg and bacon sandwiches, then it was off to find someone to go up town with. 'Sorry Sean's had to go out love' said Sean's mum, so on to the next house. Ross's parents lived on the way to town, *I'll try there* thought Michael, Ross's dad answered the door, 'Sorry Michael he's out, not sure where, I think it was fishing' Ross's dad was a nice man, and had recently bought a brand new diesel car, Christ the *noise*, you could hear it from half a mile away, it sounded like a tank!, He also had the coolest job in the world, he drove tankers full of chocolate! he went to and from various factories delivering the stuff, then at the end of his shift, he would open the barrel up, and using a chisel, knock out large slabs of chocolate that had gone hard and stuck to the sides, he would sometimes bring them home, and if you timed it right, Ross's dad would hand you A3 sized blocks. that man was probably responsible for five of Michael's seven fillings, not that Michael cared, he loved the stuff. With no friends found, Michael headed for town, alone.

Town was busy, *really* busy, but it was a nice sunny morning, so it was no surprise that so many families were out in force, shopping and having fun. Michael's first stop, as always, was Woolworths, Billericay really needed another record shop thought Michael, as he skipped through the same old albums and cassettes, 'got, got, don't want, Jazz sucks arse, got, got' eventually he bought an album, and some cheap blank tapes. Then it was off to the library, a place Michael loved, but not for the many fine and important books it must have had on its shelves, no he was there for its music lending dept, ok the records were a few months old, Michael had surmised the staff either didn't have a clue or the money to get the new releases in, but in the main it was still good stuff, and it was free, you could take a couple of LP's home, copy them, hence the blank tapes he had bought, then take the LP back, and no one was the wiser. After a quick flick through the racks, he chose the Human league album Dare. Next stop was Rumbelows, dad had spoken about getting a new TV, so Michael wanted to check the latest models they had in store, by new dad meant a new rental TV, but it would still be new to Michael. Really they all looked the same, big boxy things with a couple of knobs and switches on the front, the only good thing about getting a new TV was this one wouldn't have a box on its side for 50p's, there was nothing worse than watching a film or program, for the TV to then suddenly switch off, you would then have to fumble around looking for a coin and hope you hadn't missed to much of what you were watching. Dad had heard about a way you could get around the whole 50p problem, you put a magnet on the meter, but the only one he could find big enough to do the job, was so *big* it interfered with the Picture itself, so that was a no go. With notes in hand for dad Michael left, he was hungry, so to the chip shop.

The chip shop Michael loved going to was opposite Clinton cards, they had started to use cones instead of trays, which was great, because all the salt and vinegar would pool at the point of the cone, this in turn would soak into the burnt crispy bits, which were also at the bottom of the cone, giving them an unrivalled flavour, until they went cold, then they were disgusting. There was a bit of a queue when Michael arrived, so he read the back of the Human League Album, trying to work out if it would fit on a C60 tape, if not he would need to break into a C90. A few minutes later it was his turn, and a familiar voice took his order, 'What can I get you love?' Michael was more than a little taken a back when he looked in the voice's direction, 'Jackie?' there in front of him was a young girl, dark haired, freckles and a wide smile, her name was indeed Jackie, she was 15, and last Year she and Michael dated for a few months (This was a different Jackie to the one who had asked him out on the last day of school, Jackie's just seemed to be into him) Michael really couldn't think of anything sensible to say, so defaulted to the obvious, 'How long have you worked here?' not how are you? or nice to see you, what a wally he was. Jackie sensed she had spooked him, so didn't feel too hurt when he didn't ask how she was doing, 'Oh about a month' she replied, Michael really wasn't one for words, especially when it came to girls, and couldn't think of anything else to say, so Jackie carried on the conversation, 'been shopping I see, got anything nice?' she looked at his Woolworths bag, this seemed to relax Michael; this was something he could talk about, 'Yeah, it's my birthday tomorrow, so got some tapes' god that sounded sad thought Michael, even if it was true. Jackie leaned over the counter and lowered her voice 'Well if it's your birthday, these are on me' she handed him an over flowing cone of chips, she then gave him a quick kiss on the cheek, Michael blushed, 'Ok, er thanks Jacks, I'll er see you around' with that he smiled and left the shop. At first he had felt completely blindsided by the meeting, but as he walked home, in deep thought, a smile grew, when he and Jackie had spilt up it wasn't on the greatest of terms, there was no shouting or fighting, but Michael felt he could of handled it better, but it was his first proper relationship, so it was also his first break up, yet the moment back then in the shop, and that kiss, well it laid a few ghosts to rest, he felt it a nice way to say goodbye as a boyfriend and hello as a friend.

Michael checked the mat as he walked in the house, the mat was bare, my birthday cards must be coming Monday thought Michael, '*bloody lazy postman*' he said under his breath, mum heard her son come in and shouted from the kitchen, 'If you're looking for the post it's in your room' a dejected Michael perked up, 'Thanks Mum', he almost leapt in one bound the three flights of stairs that lead to his room. At first he couldn't see any cards, then he spotted them, they were seven envelopes on his bed, not a bad haul he thought. Michael sat on his bed and started to open them; a couple had no stamps on them, so must have been hand Delivered, one was from Sean, It had a simple message, Happy birthday Git face, Sean was no poet, but he had a way with words, next was a card from Heidi and Pip, (Philippa) they were the daughters of Ann, who ran the Saturday night coffee club, there was also one from Ross, which was along the same lines as Sean's, the next one had an overseas post mark, India! he didn't know anyone from India? the moment he opened it he knew who it was from, it was from her, her perfume was all over the paper, Helen had written a letter, and sent a card, apparently her family was in India for some conference Terry was attending, although it was only for a few days and they were staying in a nice hotel, she was homesick, how bizarre was that she said, homesick for

Pakistan, homesick for a country she barely knew, feeling down she had thought of pleasant memories from her recent past, and Michael was one of these moments.

She had remembered it was his birthday so sent a letter and card, she knew by the time he received the letter she would be back in Pakistan, but it would help her at that moment in time, Helen said she missed Michael and wished him a happy Birthday, and hopefully they would meet up again one day, although they both knew this wouldn't happen. Michael lay down on his bed, this day had bought him two women, both from his past, both ex-girlfriends, one he would never see again, and one who would give him free chips, Michael smiled, he was a lady killer. He couldn't wait for the next victim.

Sunday 31st July – Home.
'My birthday, went round Sean's,
saw Rollerball, Battlestar Galactica, mad max II'

It was the big day, Michael was Fifteen, *Fifteen*, where had all those years gone? Not that the lump in bed knew it, it didn't know what day it was, let alone it was its birthday today. when dad entered the bedroom his son was sound asleep, 'come on lazy bollocks, up you get' Michael opened one eye, dad was standing there with the downstairs TV, the BIG TV, Michael had forgotten whenever it was his birthday, or when he was ill, he got the Living room TV set, yes he had one already in his room, but it was only 18 inches, this was 30 odd inches! you hadn't seen or heard Pac Man until you had played it on a BIG TV, 'Well come on then son, make some space' dad was in good spirits, but the object in his arms wasn't getting any lighter. Michael jumped up and moved the smaller TV that was next to his Atari games console, dad put the big TV down, then as he was leaving Mum walked in with her sons breakfast, a fry up, with extra toast! 'Morning son, happy birthday' she gave him a kiss then left, Michael called her back, 'Mum' she walked back in, 'Yes son' 'You forgot the red sauce'.

After finishing his breakfast it was time for computer games, but what one to play first? Tank command decided Michael, after a few quick games it was then onto Pac Man, followed by one more crack at the space shuttle simulator, Michael thought maybe a bigger TV would help with the game, it did not, he crashed and burned, badly. Around 11 Sean from next door knocked and was sent up to Michaels room, 'happy birthday mate' Sean was already fifteen, back in April, but his height made him look seventeen, 'alright' replied Michael, he motioned at the Atari, 'Quick game?' 'Nah' said Sean, 'we've got a new computer game system, come and have a look'. Michael quickly got dressed and followed Sean the thirty feet from his bedroom to his neighbours front door.

Sean's house was identical to Michaels, it had three bedrooms, the house was split over four floors, and each had a large back garden. Both homes also boasted a bottom or "sunken floor" where the living room could be found, the reason this level appeared sunken was simple, both houses were next to a slight hill, from the front door to the bottom of the back garden the drop must have been at least 10 feet. Although the houses were the same, Sean's Living room was completely at odds to Michael's, for a start there was less wood, and there wasn't a homemade bar with real optics in the corner of the room, with stuck on glass tiles. No Sean's living room was open and light, with neutral colours and fluffy sofas, basically a little boring. As they walked into the living room, Sean went over to the large TV and started to fiddle with some leads, Sean did indeed have a new games console, the "Intellivision" from Mattel electronics, it was an odd looking thing, it was still made with about the same amount of wood as Michaels Atari, but there were differences, for a start the games were pre-loaded into the console, how cool was that! no taking a cartridge out and then spending five minutes looking for the one you wanted to play, nope, just choose a game, and go, although this did have one minor draw back, you couldn't add new games, so you were stuck forever with the games the system came with, also the controllers weren't the joystick type Michael was used to, no these had 12 buttons on the top half and a wheel type disc on the bottom, all very odd, but this didn't put Sean and Michael off, no like most kids within ten minutes they had mastered the controls and busy playing pong. An hour later, and worried that her son's eyes might start to cross if he played any more, Sean's mum declared a lunch break, followed by films, yes it would mean staring at the TV again, but at least everyone could join in. After lunch Sean, Michael, and Sean's two younger Brothers sat down for the first film, this was "Rollerball" a *gentle* sports film set in a near future that had already passed, so it was hard to take seriously, the film was made in 1975, it was now 1983, and the future Michael was living in was far more advanced than the film predicted, so the kids just enjoyed it for the gory fun it was, next was another futuristic film, this time set in space, Battlestar Galactica, it was difficult for Michael to watch any space film without comparing it to Star wars, but Battlestar had just enough originality to keep his attention, he also loved the robot dog Muffit, with its orange fur and odd eyes, it was reassuring to know that even in space you could play fetch with man's best friend. The films plot was decent enough, the last survivors of some planet/Planets were running away from the Cylons, (Robots with a groovy voice) and looking for a new home, which funny enough was called Earth. After the film it was time to go home, Sean's mum had been more than polite, and didn't want to throw Michael out, but she had a home to run, and Michael wasn't part of her brood. 'Sean, shouldn't Michael see his own family today, I think you've played with him enough, it is his birthday?' basically, it was time to go. After saying his goodbyes Michael went home.

When Michael got back, all the family were in the kitchen, 'Ah here he is' declared dad, 'I told you he hadn't forgotten where he lived' Michael's sister hugged him, 'Happy birthday Michael' she smiled, a very wide smile indeed, Michael noticed she was missing a couple of baby teeth, she looked silly without them. Mum seemed to note her son was home, 'Oh so you do remember where we live' Mum always seemed to have a habit of not hearing what other people had just said, then saying the exact same thing a few moments later, but she normally had an excuse for this, basically she was always busy, and at this moment in time she was busy making dinner and a cake.

After dinner Michael and Sarah played with some Lego, Sarah was building some sort of house with fifteen windows, and Michael was constructing a plane with an awful lot of guns on it. An hour later it was Sarah's bed time, as Mum took a reluctant little girl upstairs, dad fumbled for a VHS cassette box, 'It's here somewhere?' he said. 'Ah got it!' a triumphant dad slotted a tape into the VCR, then sat next to Michael on the sofa, 'I think you'll like this' he seemed very confident Michael would, although dad knew someone who wouldn't, Mum, but it wasn't her birthday. Mum walked in as the titles appeared, *Mad Max 2*, 'oh great another silly film' Commented Mum, dad shushed her 'Shush yourself' she replied back. The film was of course a classic, one which both son and dad enjoyed, and maybe so would have mum, if she hadn't have fallen asleep, Michael enjoyed it for another reason, it was like being back in Pakistan, watching a film with the guys in the clubs cinema room. When the film finished it was getting on for 10pm, so Michael went up, after stopping in the kitchen for another generous slice of chocolate cake. Once in his room he switched on the big TV, and looked for something to watch, being a Sunday the choice of programs was pretty crap, so Michael turned down the volume and started to read some of his comics, every once in a while he would look at the Television screen to see if anything decent was on. After a couple more comic adventures Michael lay back on his Bed, the only light in the room now coming from the 30 odd inch television set, it was producing weird flickering shadows on the Bedroom walls and ceiling. Michael reached for another comic but this time grabbed a book, his book, "The case that had to be won" he stared at the title, then opened the A4 pad and started to read page 5, once he had read the page he put the pad on his chest, maybe, he thought to himself, m*aybe*, if I worked on this over the holidays I could finish it and get it published, after all I do have the whole summer! This thought made Michael smile, yes he would finish it, after all with a title like that who wouldn't want to publish it. As Michael started to drift off, his mind found its way back to Karachi and the villa he had lived in only a few short weeks ago, he was now sitting at his old bedrooms writing desk, looking out over the desert, where he first started his book all those months before. 'Look at him' said mum, 'Fifteen, can you believe it' dad leaned over Michaels bed and turned off the TV 'From all the food he eats and electric he goes through, yes I bloody can' dad said with a smile, they both stared at their son, than left him to his dreams. Whatever they were.

The End.